CONSEQUENCES

Sarah Libero

BELLA
BOOKS

2017

Bella Books, Inc.
P.O. Box 10543
Tallahassee, FL 32302

Printed in the United States of America on acid-free paper.

First Bella Books Edition 2017

Editor: Vicki Sly
Cover Designer: Judith Fellows

ISBN: 978-1-59493-536-7

About the Author

Sarah Libero was born and raised in Maine. She lived in Massachusetts for several years before returning to Maine where she currently works as a software developer. When not writing, she enjoys jogging with her Siberian Husky, kickboxing, and coaching the company softball team, which is steadily improving. She lives on a lake where she engages in kayaking and other water sports as she develops her characters into stories she hopes readers will find entertaining.

PART ONE

CHAPTER ONE

Snow crunched beneath her tires as Emily drove down the gravel road. She went slowly, searching for the camp along the dark roadside. She was confident that she was on the right road but she wasn't sure how far down the camp would be. She began to worry that the snow might have hidden the sign and she had missed it. Deciding to keep going a little further, she drove on, continuing to search for the camp's sign among the thick growth of pine trees lining the way.

Headlights appeared behind her as a truck approached and then passed her. It was the first vehicle she had seen in a while. She wished she could have asked the driver if they knew where the Miller's camp was. It had sounded pretty simple when she had gotten the directions from her boyfriend, Tom, earlier that day. Emily was home in Maine for a few weeks during Christmas break from college in Boston and she was excited about seeing Tom. They had been dating for a couple months. She wasn't ready for anything serious, but they always had a lot of fun together. He had driven up from Massachusetts the previous day, and she was planning to meet up with him and a few of his friends that night. They were going to head over to Sugarloaf Mountain to hit the ski trails in the morning. A storm had hit the day before, so there was plenty of fresh December snow. The ski conditions were supposed to be great. All the snow was making the back roads more slippery and treacherous than she had expected. There weren't many houses on the road and she hadn't seen one for a few miles.

As she drove around a corner, Emily saw that the truck that had passed her had pulled to the side of the road and was sitting there with its lights on. The driver had pulled alongside a mailbox and although she couldn't see what he was doing she thought he might be checking for mail. She decided to stop and ask for directions. There weren't many people living around here; he might know the Millers. She really wanted to find out how much farther it could be or if she had passed the driveway by mistake. She pulled over a short distance in front of the truck. She turned off the engine, leaving the keys in the ignition, and got out of her car to walk back toward the truck. As she did, she noticed that the man driving the truck was alone and had rolled down his window.

She called out, "Hi there, I was hoping you could tell me how far I am from the Miller's camp?"

The man was difficult to see in the dark with the truck's headlights shining in her eyes. Emily shielded her eyes with her hand as she walked toward the driver's side of the truck. She stopped near his door, becoming aware of how quiet it was and how very alone they were. She couldn't tell if there was a mailbox after all and she hadn't seen any driveways nearby, now that she thought about it. This was an odd place for someone to pull over.

"Sure," he answered, "their place is about a half a mile down on the left."

"Okay, thanks, have a good night," she said and turned back to her car. Suddenly, she heard the truck door open and footsteps pounding on the snow-covered gravel behind her. Time slowed down. Before she had a chance to turn around, something hard struck the back of her head, knocking her forward onto the side of the road behind her car. She struck her knee, ripping her pants, and collapsed. Her senses went into high alert while she lay motionless. She could feel blood trickling from her scalp but, strangely, felt no pain. Adrenaline coursed through her body. Emily fought back her panic and tried to lie still with her eyes closed.

The man nudged her with his boot. She felt another sharp blow to the back of her head, but still felt no pain. Then he lifted her feet and dragged her on her stomach back to the ditch next to his truck. The night was absolutely still. The only sound was the man's heavy panting as he stopped and dropped her feet. He flipped her over, unbuttoned her pants and pulled down the zipper. He slipped his hand into her pants and underwear. Emily fought to keep her eyes closed and breathe slowly so that he would think she was unconscious. He slipped his hand out of her pants and spoke in a low growl, "If you move, you are dead."

He stood as if waiting to see if she moved before walking back toward his truck. Emily knew that she had just this one chance to get away. While he was lifting something from his truck, she leapt to her feet and ran with blind terror toward her car.

Slipping, scrambling madly, she flung the door open. She felt a flash of relief when she saw the keys in the ignition. Slamming the door shut with one hand, she turned the engine over with the other. Her mind was blank with fear as she flung the car into drive. Her terror nearly overwhelmed her as she pinned the accelerator to the floor. The car fishtailed in the snow and almost slid into the ditch. Praying that she would get away, she looked into the rearview mirror and saw the man jump into his truck. Knowing he was going to come after her, she frantically tried to keep the car on the road and find a house. Too panicked to watch both the man and the road, she tried to concentrate on driving. She managed to go a short distance around a corner before sliding into a ditch. A few hundred yards ahead, she saw a driveway among the snow-covered trees.

She had no idea if the man was still coming after her or not. She floored the accelerator, but it only sank the car deeper into the snowy ditch. She was an open target if she stayed with the car. Emily flung the door open and ran wildly toward the driveway, bracing herself for the truck's approach.

She glanced over her shoulder, the dark forest night was all she could see. Emily ran as fast as her injured leg would allow, too panicked to notice any pain that could slow her down. She ran up the gravel driveway and saw a light shining from the windows of a rustic log home nestled in the woods ahead. Still hearing no signs of pursuit, she reached the front door and pounded with both hands. "Please, let me in!"

A porch light came on and the door opened.

CHAPTER TWO

Emily gasped with relief at the sight of the man and woman who opened the door and stared at her in surprise. "What happened, were you in an accident?" he asked.

Emily shook her head. Still terrified, she wasn't sure what to say.

"Please, come in," the man said, waving her in. "My name is John and this is my wife, Anne."

"I'm Emily." She stayed on the porch. Emily looked at the couple nervously, realizing that she didn't have much choice but to trust that they would help her. The man was neatly dressed in a plaid flannel shirt and jeans. He and his wife appeared to be in their thirties.

Anne, a petite brunette, was wearing glasses and a bathrobe. She reached toward Emily to try to guide her into the house, placing a comforting hand on her shoulder.

Emily shrank back and tried to explain what happened. "I'm okay, I just got away from someone who tried to attack me down the street when I stopped to ask for directions. My car went into the ditch near the bottom of your driveway."

"What?" Anne asked in a shocked voice. "This happened just now on the road? Someone tried to hurt you?"

John glanced at his wife. "Let's go in and sit on the couch where it's more comfortable."

Emily stepped into the house and John closed the door behind her. She followed Anne into the adjoining living room. A fire blazed in the woodstove. The room was warm and welcoming.

"Do you want to sit down?" John asked. "We need to call the state police."

"No. I don't want to call the police. I'm fine. I-I just need to get my car out of the ditch so I can leave." Emily briefly considered turning back toward the door, but realized she had no way to get anywhere.

The thought of explaining what happened filled her with fear and she tried to control her rising panic. Stopping and asking a stranger for directions at night on a deserted road had been a really stupid thing to do. She was ashamed that she had allowed this to happen. There was no way she was going to tell anyone about the man getting into her pants.

Emily saw Anne exchange a worried look with John and she knew they were both trying not to stare at her. Her clothes were torn and bloody and she was a mess. Blood had seeped down from her scalp through her shoulder-length blond hair and onto her jacket. She had buttoned her pants back up before she walked in and was hoping John and Anne hadn't noticed. Her pant legs were shredded, exposing deep gashes on her knees. The sleeves of her ski jacket were torn and dirty from the gravel road. Her hands were bleeding and shaking.

"We have two daughters sleeping upstairs," John said gently. "I wouldn't want anything like this to happen to them. If the police could help us find who did this to you, we can make sure he doesn't do it to anyone else."

Further ashamed that she had reacted so selfishly, Emily nodded and sank down into the chair. To her embarrassment, she continued to shake uncontrollably. Anne walked into the kitchen and brought back a glass of water. "Here take a drink and try to relax. You're safe now."

Anne and John went into the next room to call the state police while Emily sat silently waiting and wondering what she should do next. Tom had been expecting her by now and was probably worried. John and Anne came back into the living room and sat down on the couch across from her.

"I was supposed to be going to a camp on this road owned by the Millers, do you know them?" Emily asked.

"Yes, I know where that is," John said. "It's about two miles down on the right. It will take a little while for the police to get out here. They have a big area to cover so it could be an hour before they arrive. Do you want me to go to the Miller's place and find the people you were supposed to be meeting?"

"Yes, thank you," Emily answered quietly. "I'm supposed to be meeting my boyfriend. His name is Tom Stratton. I drove up tonight from Orleans."

"Okay, I'll go find him. I don't want to try to move your car until the police get a chance to look at it," John said.

Emily had an alarming thought. "Wait. What if the man comes here looking for me?"

"She's right John; you probably better stay here with us," Anne said.

Two state police cruisers pulled into the driveway an hour later, their headlights shining into the house. John went out to greet them while Anne and Emily stayed in the house. He came back inside a few minutes later, followed by a state trooper.

"I'm going to go check on your car with the officers," John said to Emily. "They want to take a look around and then we're going to get the car out of the ditch. This officer is going to stay with you and ask you some questions."

Emily nodded and John went back outside, leaving Emily and Anne in the living room with the trooper. Anne headed for the kitchen. "I'm going to make some coffee."

Emily sat back down and quietly described to the man sitting in the chair across from her what had happened. She answered his questions about the sequence of events, giving as many details as she could remember, leaving out only the part about how the attacker had touched her.

"I would recommend that you let us take you to the hospital in Farmington to get checked over. You sustained some pretty serious cuts and bruises and you may have a concussion."

"No, I don't want to go to the hospital," Emily said. "I'm fine, I just need to wash up."

"I have to ask you, did any sexual assault take place?" the trooper asked.

"No. I got away and I'm fine." She started to cry. The shame she was feeling about getting attacked was compounded by the fact that she was crying in front of strangers. Her self-confidence had deserted her and she wished she could disappear.

The trooper shrugged and stood up. "Well, we won't make you go, but I think it would be a good idea."

Emily shook her head and stared at the floor. She didn't want to talk or face any more questions. She just wanted this night to be over.

A knock sounded at the door and Emily looked up apprehensively. She watched from the living room as Anne walked to the door and looked through the window to see who was outside.

Anne opened the door. "Hello, officers. Please come in."

Emily felt some of her tension dissolve when Tom walked in, accompanied by two state troopers. He greeted Anne, "Hello, I'm Emily's boyfriend, Tom Stratton. Is she here? Is she all right?"

"She's in the living room," Anne said. "Go on in."

Tom rushed through the doorway and over to where Emily was sitting. His curly brown hair was disheveled and tears glistened in his eyes. "Emily, I am so sorry. I didn't know what happened. When you were late, I went to look for you and found your car with the state police inspecting it."

Emily stood up and Tom wrapped his arms around her, pulling her close. Relief flooded over her. Finally, someone she knew and trusted.

"Please, let's just go," she murmured to him.

CHAPTER THREE

Emily awoke with a splitting headache. The winter sun shone brightly through the window in the small bedroom of the cabin. She looked over at Tom sleeping soundly next to her. She wondered if she would ever sleep soundly again. Every time she closed her eyes, all she could hear was the sound of footsteps in the snow, running up behind her. Shaking off the thought, she slid her feet to the floor. She had an aching pain in her knee and it hurt to straighten her leg. Tom mumbled in his sleep and rolled over.

Memories of the previous night came rushing back and she tried to put them out of her head. She could hear Tom's friends moving around in the kitchen below. She wasn't sure if she should go home or if she should just keep busy and try to forget about the whole incident. She didn't want to face any of the people downstairs and have to talk about what happened. Maybe she and Tom could head over to the mountain and that would help her keep her mind off things. She felt a wave of gratitude that Tom was there. She didn't want to be alone.

* * *

The wind blew fiercely as Tom and Emily skied past the chairlift and came to a stop at the bottom of the slope outside the lodge. Emily released her boots from their bindings and stepped out of her skis.

"Sorry I couldn't ski very well, my leg is hurting a little," Emily said, turning to Tom. "I think I'll just hang out in the lodge for now."

In reality, her knee was throbbing, but she didn't want to let Tom know. He had asked her that morning if she would rather not ski today, but Emily had convinced him that she really wanted to.

"Don't worry about it," Tom said. "Why don't we head back to the camp and relax?"

"Are you sure you don't want to ski a little longer?" Emily asked. "I can wait here."

"I'm ready to go. It's too windy today. I also don't want to leave you alone."

Emily wanted to argue but she really didn't want to be alone. She nodded and they lapsed into an awkward silence. She knew that Tom was feeling responsible for what had happened to her and wanted to do something to make her feel better. He had told her the night before that he felt like he was to blame for her getting attacked and that he should have met her somewhere easier to find and brought her to the camp instead of giving her directions. She had tried to tell him that was ridiculous. He had no way of knowing that some random stranger would come after her in the middle of nowhere. Besides, she never should have stopped in the first place.

"Let me help you with your skis." Tom bent down to pick them up.

"Tom, I'm fine." Emily reached for her skis. She winced in pain as she bent her knee.

"None of this would have happened if you hadn't come to meet me."

"Stop," Emily said. "Let's just try to forget it."

She was glad to be leaving the slopes. She really didn't want to be around a lot of people who she didn't know. It didn't sound like the police had any real hope of finding the man who attacked her. Emily couldn't give them a good description of the truck he was driving or what he looked like. All they had found at the scene were tire tracks and a little bit of blood in the snow. For all she knew, the man could be here at the mountain today. She felt sick at the thought.

They carried their skis to Tom's car and loaded up their gear. Emily was quiet on the short ride back to the camp. As they drove past the spot where she had stopped the night before, she turned on the radio and tried to think about anything else. They pulled into the driveway of the Miller's camp where Emily's car sat with a flat tire.

After the state police had examined it the night before, they had been kind enough to get the car out of the ditch and John had driven it over to the Miller's for her. She was very grateful for all of John and Anne's help. They had been remarkably kind and she'd have to find a way to thank them someday.

Tom drove up the winding driveway past Emily's car and she spotted a red pickup truck parked near the camp.

"Oh no, it's my parents," she said. "What are they doing here? They've never even met you. This is not good. They must have found out what happened."

As they pulled to a stop, Jane and Ed Parker came bursting out of the front door of the cabin. Her mother ran up to them. "Are you all right? Where were you, and what in the world is going on?"

Emily's father fixed a furious glare on Tom.

"Mom and Dad, this is Tom," Emily said. "I'm all right, really. I didn't call because there isn't a phone here. I didn't want to call you last night when I was with the police and tell you what happened because I didn't want you to worry. I was going to wait until I got home."

"You didn't want us to worry? We've been sick with worry. The story has been on the news and everyone has been calling,"

Emily's mother said. "We've been in shock; we didn't even know how to find you up here. Luckily you had left me the address for this place."

Jane put her arms around Emily and hugged her tightly. "Never mind any of that, the most important thing is that you are all right. You're coming home with us, and you can tell us all about what happened later."

"We need to change this tire. I'll drive your car back," said her father.

"I'll help sir," Tom said. "I'm sorry, I didn't realize that it had gone flat."

"Come on in and I'll get my stuff," Emily said. "I'm really sorry."

Emily and her mother walked to the cabin as the men turned toward the car to change the tire.

Emily was relieved to be headed home and away from Sugarloaf. She stared out the window and tried to describe what happened to her mother. Guilt and shame washed over her again as she thought about how stupid she had been to stop and ask a stranger for directions on a dark, deserted road. She almost deserved to have something bad happen for showing such poor judgment, and it could have been much worse if she hadn't gotten away.

She turned to her mother. "Mom, I really am sorry that I didn't call you. I wanted to come home but I also thought that I should stay and try to forget about it. I didn't know that you would hear about it and get upset."

Jane glanced over at her daughter as they drove down the snowy roads. "I understand, sweetheart, but we were so worried. The story was on the news last night and then again this morning. The report said that Emily Parker of Orleans, Maine, was attacked up at Sugarloaf. Your father and I were going out of our minds and we came here to get you as soon as we heard."

Emily sat in shocked silence. Why would they say her name on the news? Now the man who attacked her would be able to find out her name and where she lived. What if he tried to come after her? She wished she could go straight back to Boston where he wouldn't be able to find her. If she stayed home she wasn't going to be safe.

CHAPTER FOUR

Emily returned to Boston a couple weeks later. She was happy to be back for the last semester of her senior year at college. At home in Maine, everyone had treated her differently and she couldn't wait to get away. She wanted to put the whole incident at Sugarloaf behind her. The problem was, she couldn't get it out of her mind. She didn't want to talk about it with anyone because she was ashamed and embarrassed about letting herself get into such a situation. The memory of being touched by the man who attacked her that night continued to fill her with disgust. Her confidence was rocked and she didn't know what to do about it.

Tom had called her every day and she found herself relying on his support. Now that they were both back in town, he made a point to come by and see her whenever he got a chance. Emily had never planned to get involved in a serious relationship, but Tom's comforting presence was growing more important to her as the weeks passed.

With the start of classes, she had tried to get her life back into a routine. Things might never go back to the way they had been, but Emily refused to let the events from that night continue to get the better of her. She had always been proud of her independence and it bothered her that now she was frightened to be alone at night. She knew on a rational level that she was safe. Even so, she didn't like being alone. She was reluctant to admit it, but she was relieved that one of her roommates was usually around in the apartment when she got back from class.

Their apartment was in a busy neighborhood near Fenway Park and it was only a short walk to classes. Emily had found that she couldn't stand to have anyone walking behind her. She stepped to the side and let people pass so that she could keep a distance between herself and anyone approaching from behind. This proved difficult when walking through crowded corridors between classes, so she got into the habit of waiting till the halls were less crowded, which meant she was often late to class.

On a cold Friday afternoon in February, Emily climbed the stairs to her third floor apartment after her last class of the week and opened the door. "Anyone home?" she called.

"Hi, how's it going?" Her roommate Jess looked up from her seat on the couch. "How was class?"

"It was okay," Emily said. "I'm glad it's Friday. What're you up to?"

Jess brushed her curly red hair back from her eyes. "I have a date tonight. We're going to hit that new club on Boylston Street. Why don't you come with us? We're meeting a bunch of people."

"No thanks, I don't think I'm going to go out. I have too much to do."

Walking through the dark streets and going to a crowded bar full of strangers didn't sound appealing at all. Emily had met Jess, a pretty, outgoing girl from the West coast, during their freshman year and they had become good friends. Emily often tagged along with Jess and her friends. They always had fun meeting people and dancing in the clubs. Jess made no secret of her lesbian lifestyle, and Emily admired her for standing up for herself. Lately though, Emily just wanted to stay at home and avoid people. Tom would probably stop by later and keep her company, so she wouldn't be alone.

"You sure? I miss going out with you," Jess said, with a worried look at her friend. "I had some people I wanted you to meet. We can have a few drinks and I can make fun of your dancing," she teased.

"I bet," Emily answered with a laugh. "You know I have a boyfriend so stop trying to fix me up."

"Tom is great, I really like him. It's just, I know you met some girls last semester that really liked you and I think you liked them, too. I worry that Tom might not be the right one for you."

Emily shrugged and didn't answer. She thought about one of Jess's friends she'd met the last time she went out with her before Christmas break. Kerri had been really interesting to talk to, and Emily had found herself thinking about her for a while after they met. She wanted to forget about all that though. She had nothing to offer to anyone at the moment and she needed to get herself back on track. She couldn't even walk after dark without getting scared, for crying out loud. Who would want to get involved with someone like her? Not to mention that her parents would never understand if she started dating women—that would not go over well.

She shouldn't be thinking about that anyway. She was really lucky to have Tom. He was smart, sweet, and good-looking, and he made her feel safe and loved.

"Thanks, but I'm really not feeling that great tonight. I should stay in and study. I've got a ton of homework. Tom is probably going come over to hang out with me."

* * *

Six months later, Emily stood in the doorway of the apartment and took one last look around. All of her things had been packed up and loaded into the moving van that was waiting outside. She thought back on the past few months and how much her life had changed. She and Jess had graduated and were ready to start their lives. She'd had some of the best times of her life here in Boston. She'd made some great friends along the way, like Jess, and she had fallen in love with Tom. Maybe they should have taken things a little slower, but she was full of hope for their future together. They were going to be married in a few weeks, at the end of the summer, and had a big wedding and reception planned with all of their friends and family. Her parents had ended up loving Tom once they got to know him and had welcomed him into their lives.

It had been pretty surprising and a little difficult at first when she found out she was pregnant, but she and Tom both felt that getting married would be for the best for both of them. Emily had never been one to look forward to a big wedding. She had never really given much thought to getting married. Her future plans had been more focused on what type of job she might want to get. Now it looked like she would put that on hold for a while and work in the office for Tom's family's company. Tom was going to work for his father for the time being. He planned to have his own business someday.

With the wedding date fast approaching, Emily had let her mother take over most of the arrangements because she knew her mother enjoyed it. Emily would have just as soon eloped and not been involved in the whole spectacle, but it meant so much to her mother that Emily went along with it all. She didn't want to let her parents down. There would be plenty of time to figure it all out. She knew that Tom loved her and he would keep her safe.

PART TWO

CHAPTER FIVE

Twenty-five years later

Emily looked up from her computer screen at the chubby young man fidgeting in her doorway. He adjusted his smudged glasses as he stared down at the floor, managing to look sweaty in the cool office climate.

"Hey, Sam, do you need something?"

"We've had a few users calling in with problems from yesterday's code rollout," Sam said. "Some people are hitting an error and I'm not sure what's causing it. I think it may be something that you updated."

"Okay, I'll take a look and let you know what I find." Emily opened up a screen and connected to the database for the online app that had been released the previous day. She brushed her sandy blond hair back from her eyes and rolled her shoulders, settling in to try and identify the latest problem. There was never a shortage of issues to deal with at the State Bureau of Identification (SBI) where she was employed by the Maine State Police. It was a fast-paced environment that demanded all of her attention and kept her from getting bored. She spent most of the day solving puzzles with her code and she enjoyed coming up with the best methods to process and analyze data.

Her experiences all those years ago with the Maine State Police when she had been attacked had left Emily with a curiosity about law enforcement. The police had been professional and courteous at the time, but she had never heard anything more from them about her case. They had never arrested anyone or even found a suspect, as far as she knew. She sometimes wondered if the man who attacked her had ever done it again to anyone else.

Emily had spent several years in various roles with information technology companies when she decided to apply for a technical opening with the state police. It had been a good fit for her and had allowed her to continue in the field of computer technology, which she liked, while learning more about how the police track their cases. She also liked the idea of being able to contribute to solving crimes.

She now had a position with the SBI as a systems analyst and had worked with the state police internal databases, along with a team of other developers, for over ten years. She enjoyed her job. The databases that she and her team oversaw were tied in with crime statistics from all over the world, which was a far cry from how things had been done twenty-five years ago.

Emily leaned back in her chair and powered off her laptop. She had identified and corrected the problem that Sam had brought to her. She was back to focusing on another project that had an upcoming deadline. She stood and stretched, reaching for her black ski jacket. One thing that she particularly liked about her job was that she could wear whatever she wanted to the office. This usually consisted of jeans and a button-down shirt. She had maintained her athletic figure as she had gotten older and she knew she did not have the most feminine appearance.

When she was a child, Emily was often mistaken for a boy. Kids used to tease her about it frequently when she was growing up, but she had never had trouble making friends and she hadn't let it bother her. Her older sister had long blond hair and was the ladylike daughter, while Emily had always been the tomboy. There had been a few years in college when she grew her hair out and had tried to be more girlish, but that didn't last very long. She had always been more focused on keeping fit than on being fashionable. She was comfortable with herself and didn't have much insecurity about her appearance these days.

She and Tom had a good life together for the most part. They had devoted themselves to raising their two sons and she was very proud of her boys. For the past twenty-five years her focus had been on her family. She and Tom made sure that both of their sons got good educations and reached for their dreams.

Ben, the oldest, was now twenty-four, living in Portland, and was employed with an engineering firm. She and Tom had been young and overwhelmed when Ben had been born, but they had been united in their love for their son. Ethan had come along a year later and had completed their family. He had graduated from college the previous spring and was now working in Boston and living happily with his girlfriend. Emily wouldn't have changed any of it for the world. Her kids were her life and filled her heart.

The SBI office was in a building that was shared with the state's Office of Information Technology, located in Augusta. They were down the street from the Augusta troop of the state police and worked with the Major Crimes Unit. Detectives and state troopers often stopped by to check on various requests for information.

She walked down the hallway toward the reception area. Her boss, Alex, called out to her as she passed by his office door, "Emily, have you got a minute?"

Emily turned and entered Alex's office. "Sure, what's up?"

Alex was sitting at his desk and a woman Emily had never met before sat in the chair across the desk from him. She tucked her short, dark hair behind her ears and unbuttoned the blazer she was wearing. When she turned, her blue eyes caught Emily's attention.

Emily found herself staring for a moment. Giving her head a quick shake, she wondered if the woman might be good at softball since she looked pretty athletic. Emily was the coach for the office softball team, which was perennially bad. She was always on the lookout for new talent. The woman's attractive face was set in a serious expression. Her stern demeanor could definitely be good for the team's intimidation factor.

"This is Detective DeLorme. She's with the Major Crimes Unit. She needs us to compile data reports on some of the traffic stops that have been made on I-95 over the past few years, along with some of the drug arrests throughout the state."

Detective DeLorme rose from her seat and extended her hand toward Emily. The detective appeared to be in her forties and was a couple inches taller than Emily. "Call me Kay. Pleased to meet you."

Emily shook her hand. "Hello, I'm Emily Stratton. I'd be happy to set up some reports to look through the database for whatever you need. Let me give you my card so you'll have my email. I can take some notes about what you're looking for."

Kay sat back down and Emily took a seat in the chair next to her. Emily reached into her bag to pull out a pen and notebook and glanced over at Kay who was watching her closely. She had a moment of self-consciousness then shrugged it off. She was confident that she would be able to provide the detective with whatever data she would need. Emily opened her notebook and started writing.

"Can you tell me what time frames and locations you are looking for?" Emily asked, smiling politely at Kay.

After gathering the requirements for the reports that Kay was looking for, Emily said good night to her and Alex and walked out of the building to her silver Toyota pickup truck. She tossed her bag onto the passenger seat and climbed in. The sun had set early on this cold January day. This time of year it was often dark when she got to the office and dark when she left. The good news was that the days were going to keep getting longer now that December was over. She put the truck into gear and headed home.

Tom owned and ran a local electrical business. Most days he left a little later in the morning than she did and he usually got home a couple hours after her in the evening.

Emily pulled into the driveway of their cape-style home in a quiet neighborhood in the small town of Orleans, Maine. She opened the door and called out a greeting to Sally, their Siberian Husky. Sally was happy to see her and gave a welcoming howl as she ran over to Emily.

"How's my girl? Have you been good today?" Emily scratched Sally's chin as she put down her bag and reached for a leash. "Let's go out and take a little walk, sweetie."

Emily waved to the cars that passed by as she and Sally walked along the side of the road. Absentmindedly thinking about what to cook for dinner, she turned and started to guide Sally back to the house as her phone rang. Her best friend Julian's name showed on the screen.

"Hi, Julian," Emily said.

"Hi, Kitten. How are you?" Julian loved teasing with nicknames whenever he could. He owned a successful hair salon in Augusta and they had been best friends since high school. They had gotten along so well that they briefly tried dating back when they were teenagers, but quickly realized that they were meant to be friends. Julian had always preferred men. He had been in a long-term relationship for the past ten years with his partner, Mark, whom Emily also loved dearly.

"I am not a kitten, that's how I am. Are you at the salon?"

"Yes, I wanted to see if we're still on for dinner tomorrow?"

Julian and Emily had a standing weekly date for Wednesdays at a local restaurant that held trivia games on that night. Julian, in typical fashion, was obsessed with going each week and threw himself into the game whenever they went.

"I'll be there, but I'm not sure if Tom will want to go."

"That's okay, I want all your attention. Tom never wants to go anywhere."

"True, he doesn't like to go anywhere when there's a hockey game on, which there usually is. Either way, I'll meet you at the pub at around six."

She said good-bye to Julian as she and Sally reached the house. They walked in and Emily hung up the leash in the entryway and headed into the open kitchen. She took out some plates and set the table. Julian was right—Tom never wanted to go anywhere. He also didn't like it if she went somewhere without him. Her evenings with Julian were often a source of aggravation. This time of year could get depressing with nothing to do besides go to work, so Emily went in spite of Tom's objections. She also made it a point to get to the gym early each morning to make sure that she got plenty of exercise prior to sitting at a desk all day. Cold winter months always made her look forward to the warm weather when the softball league would start up.

Emily thought back to her meeting with Kay that afternoon. She hadn't wanted to ask her if she played softball till she got to know her a little better. She looked like she was pretty athletic and they really needed some good players. She hated being the worst team in the league. They had a few good players, but the majority of her tech coworkers were not very athletic. Kay seemed friendly. Maybe she would ask her about it when she sent her some of the data that she was looking for.

Emily walked over to the stainless steel refrigerator and started getting things out for dinner. She usually prepared some sort of dish with meat for Tom, with lots of vegetarian side dishes for her since she hadn't eaten meat for many years. She reminded herself to give Ben a call tonight and check in. She hadn't spoken with him in a few days and wanted to hear how he was doing. She and Tom had talked to Ethan the night before and were planning to visit him in a couple weeks.

With their sons grown and living on their own, life had changed over the past few years. She and Tom had gone directly to parenthood from college. Without the boys living with them, it was nice to have more freedom and less responsibility. Having more time on her hands also gave her more time to think about her relationship with Tom.

One thing Emily readily admitted was that she wasn't the easiest person to live with. She definitely had a tendency to fly off the handle. While she sometimes got emotional and overreacted, Tom was very laid-back and seldom even raised his voice. She did get frustrated at times at his lack of emotional response, but she had gotten used to it over the years. Tom loved her in his own quiet way and they shared a comfortable life together.

As they got older, Emily had to admit that she did question some major things about their marriage. She would never do anything to break their marriage vows, but something was missing. She loved Tom, but not in the way that a wife should love her husband. For quite some time she found herself faced with the fact that she was no longer attracted to her husband. Over the years it was clear that Tom was still drawn to her because he often told her so, but she didn't feel the same. It wasn't that she was attracted to other men, either. Although she would never act on it or ever share the thought with another soul, she knew that if she were ever to get into another relationship, it would not be with a man.

CHAPTER SIX

After dinner, Emily and Tom sat together on the couch in the living room. A cozy fire blazed in the fireplace and Sally was curled up on the rug. Emily set down the book she was reading. "Julian wants to get together for dinner and trivia tomorrow night. Do you feel like going?"

"No thanks, I think there's a Bruins game on. You can go ahead if you want." Tom turned on the television and switched on the sports channel.

Emily picked up her book and started reading again, refraining from telling him that she didn't need his permission. She glanced at Tom as he read the paper while watching the latest hockey analysts discuss the Boston Bruins. The noise from the television set filled the silence after their brief conversation. Their evenings were often fairly quiet. Tom had never been one to talk very much. Emily had often wished over the years that Tom would talk a little more. They never discussed much other than upcoming plans or whatever their sons were up to. After spending the day sitting alone in her quiet office, Emily missed having someone to talk to now that neither of the boys was around.

The newspaper rustled as Tom set it down on the coffee table. "How about we get comfortable?" he asked with a smile as he slid his hand along her thigh and up under the loose cotton shirt that she was wearing. His strong, rough hands scratched her skin and she slid back into her side of the couch. Emily looked into Tom's eyes and tried to relax.

He was still a handsome man. A little gray was showing in the curly brown hair around his temples, but that was really the only sign of aging that she could see. He kept very fit and active. In the summer months they enjoyed running together and usually entered a few 5K races for fun.

Emily didn't want to hurt him but she really wasn't interested. He deserved to have a wife who appreciated him and enjoyed having sex as much as he did, and she didn't want to fake it. She loved him, but he felt more like a friend or brother to her. She put her hand on his and stopped it from moving any further. "I'm sorry, I just don't want to do anything tonight."

"You never do," Tom muttered in exasperation, standing up and walking from the room.

* * *

The next evening Emily gave Sally a quick ear rub as she headed out the door. The dog had been fed and dinner was in the fridge for Tom. Her daily duties had been completed and she was free for the night.

She drove down the street and headed to the pub to meet Julian. She parked next to his car and hurried to the door, shivering in the cold night.

Julian was sitting at a table chatting with their usual waitress. "About time you got here."

"I know, I had to work late and then I wanted to make sure to leave Tom something for dinner. Hi, Debbie." Emily turned to their waitress. "Is he bothering you again?"

Debbie laughed. "I'll be right back with your usual drinks."

Julian was dressed perfectly, as usual, in a royal blue sweater with a scarf wrapped around his neck. His dark brown eyes twinkled at her. He was the best-looking man in the place, and he knew it. His skin-tight clothes accentuated the muscular physique that he trained daily at the gym to maintain. He had a way of getting on people's nerves. Many people found him rude and arrogant and they instantly disliked him. Beneath that sarcastic, outspoken exterior, however, he was actually a very kind and generous friend to those who knew him well.

"Tom should have come with you. You guys never go anywhere."

"I know, but it's kind of nice to hang out just with you anyway." She looked around the busy dining room, but didn't see any familiar faces. "I swear all we do is eat dinner, watch television and go to bed."

"Well, I bet Tommy likes going to bed," Julian teased.

"Zip it," she said. "That's the last thing that I'm interested in."

"You never were one to get all that excited about sex, were you?"

"That's enough about that topic. Tell me about the vacation that you and Mark are planning. I'm jealous. When are you going?" Julian had hit a nerve with his comment about her sex life. What was wrong with her? She had a handsome, successful husband who treated her with love and affection. They had two wonderful children who she was very proud of. She loved Tom, but she had never shared the same desire for him that he felt for her, and it was getting worse. Would she ever get a chance to feel more fulfilled in her life or was it downhill from here on in?

Julian told her about his upcoming vacation plans. They settled into a comfortable conversation and waited for the next round of trivia to begin. Soon they were caught up in the competition with the other regulars sitting around the room. Between rounds of trivia Julian asked, "Did you hear about that drug bust in Orleans? One of my clients was telling me about it. I guess there is some big drug ring that the police are trying to break up."

"No, I hadn't heard about that."

"I thought you'd have more info for me. You're with the state police after all."

"Well, I wouldn't be able to talk about anything I was working on. I just deal with data anyway, you know. I have heard that there are a lot of problems with drugs being brought into Maine by dealers from New York. That's always in the news."

Julian nodded. "I heard that the latest drug of choice is heroin. Can you imagine? I bet Chris Brooks is in on the whole thing. He has a hand in everything that goes on in Orleans."

Julian made no secret of the fact that he could not stand Chris Brooks, a rival salon owner from Orleans who had insulted Julian and his sisters many times to his clients. Emily nodded and then turned her attention back to the trivia screen. "What is the world's second most commonly spoken language?"

"I think it might be Spanish."

Emily returned home by nine. Tom was already in bed and Sally was sprawled out in the living room. Emily gave the dog's upturned belly a pat as she went by and headed up the stairs to brush her teeth. She slipped quietly into bed after changing into a T-shirt.

"Did you have a good time?" Tom mumbled.

"Yes, it was fun. Sorry I woke you up. Good night."

"I have to go to a job site out at Long Pond tomorrow so can you make sure I'm up when you leave?"

"Sure." She turned over and went to sleep.

CHAPTER SEVEN

Emily reached for her keys and gym bag the next morning and headed out the door, giving Sally a quick pat as she walked past her. She was about to get in her truck when she remembered Tom's request to make sure he was up. She turned around to go back in the house and jogged up the stairs.

"Are you up?" she called into the bedroom. "Sorry, I almost forgot to wake you. You know I forget everything in the morning if I don't write it down."

"I'm up. Have a good day, Em."

"Bye. I'll talk to you later." She headed back downstairs.

After her morning workout, Emily drove from the gym to her office and settled in at her desk, eager to get busy with her projects. There was an email in her inbox from Kay with more details about the dates and locations that she needed to look for. Kay's request sounded interesting. The email had been sent last night. Kay apparently kept late hours.

Emily logged into the network and launched the first batch of reports that she would need that day before turning her attention to Kay's data. She had time to start looking up Kay's information while she waited for her reports to finish running. Alex gave the developers plenty of autonomy as long as they managed to meet their deadlines, which meant that she would have the flexibility to work on Kay's data while managing her other projects.

She set up a query that would look for traffic stops on Maine's highways and compiled data on all the drivers and passengers involved, along with any information that might have been collected for additional offenses such as drug possession. Once that was ready, she turned her attention to the data that had been gathered from drug busts over the past five years. She would send all of these statistics to Kay in a report that would give details on any correlations between the data.

The morning passed quickly. Emily finished all of Kay's reports and sent them to her in an email. She included a note to let Kay know that she would be happy to give her more information if she needed it. Emily pushed back from her desk, stood up, and stretched her stiff shoulder muscles. She walked into the break room and took her lunch out of the common fridge. While she was waiting for her frozen Weight Watcher's meal to heat up in the microwave, she saw Kay walk by.

"Hi there, Kay," she called to her. "Did you get my email?"

"Hi. I was looking for you actually. I got your email and had a couple questions. I was headed this way anyway, so I figured I would stop in and see if I could catch you."

Emily once again found herself looking a little too long into Kay's blue eyes. They were a remarkable color. She caught herself and stepped back, embarrassed. She wanted to get out of the messy break room and get a little more control over herself.

"Let's go to my office and we can go over the data," Emily said. "Have you eaten? I could heat one of these up for you."

"I'm all set, thanks," Kay said. "I didn't mean to barge in on your lunch."

"It's no big deal. I usually eat at my desk." She took the container out of the microwave and walked back to her office, Kay following behind her.

Kay sat down in the spare chair while Emily placed her lunch on the side of her desk and opened up her computer. Emily's office was very neat and organized. She couldn't stand to have paperwork and other distractions piling up on her desk.

"First, I want to thank you for getting back to me so quickly," Kay said. "I really appreciate it. I know the turnover for data requests can sometimes take weeks. I hate to push my luck, but is there any way that you could expand the search a little more?"

Emily pulled up one of the reports on her screen. "Which parameters were you thinking about?"

"I was hoping we could include other traffic stops from a list of the state roads in this area. Is that possible? We're trying to find a pattern of names and locations from some of these stops. We want to identify drivers and routes that are being used to bring drugs to central Maine. I might also see if you can refine things by looking at their plates."

"Sure."

They both became engrossed in setting up queries and generating reports. Emily found herself surprisingly comfortable working on her laptop with Kay looking over her shoulder. "Do you have a partner?" she asked.

Kay gave her a startled look. "Uh, what do you mean?"

Emily laughed. "I meant, aren't you teamed up with another detective on this?"

"Oh, right. I thought you were talking about something else," Kay said. "Yes, I am on a team with a few other people. I'm actually fairly new to the Augusta barracks. I used to be down in Southern Maine. My partner is Pete Harris. Do you know him?"

Alex suddenly appeared in the doorway with an anxious look on his face. "Excuse me Emily, I am afraid I have to tell you some really terrible news."

Emily looked at him in surprise. She had never seen Alex so upset. Her mind raced, thinking of all the things that could be wrong. She didn't want to hear his news, but forced herself to ask through lips that were suddenly dry. "What's wrong, what happened?"

"Tom has been in an accident and he's being life-flighted down to Portland."

She jumped up, grabbed her purse and headed to the door. "I've got to get down there."

"You shouldn't drive yourself," Alex said. "Let me find someone to bring you."

"I'll take you. Let's go," Kay said.

"You really don't have to—" Emily started to say.

"I want to, it's fine. I have my car right outside and I can put the lights on to get us down there faster."

Emily gave Kay's arm a quick squeeze of appreciation. She struggled to hold back tears as she grabbed her coat. "Thank you. Let's go."

The drive to Portland normally took about an hour. Kay assured her that she would get them there much faster than that. Emily tried to hold herself together as the highway flew by. She called the hospital to get an update on Tom's condition, but the nurse she spoke with couldn't give her much information other than the fact that Tom was in surgery.

Please let him be all right, she repeated to herself as they drove down to Portland. She had called Ben and Ethan and let them know that there had been an accident. Ben was going to meet her at the Maine Medical Center, which was not far from the office where he worked. It would take Ethan a little longer to drive up from Boston. Emily reassured him as best she could that she would call him as soon as she knew anything.

"I still don't even know what happened," she said to Kay.

"I'm sure that they will be able to tell you a lot more once we get there. I can try to reach someone at the office and get more information, too."

"It is really nice of you to drive me down here like this. We just met and you barely know me. I can't thank you enough." Emily ran her fingers through her hair distractedly.

Kay nodded. "I'm glad to help and I'm so sorry that this has happened. Let's just get you there so you can be with your husband."

When they finally reached the hospital, Emily took some deep breaths and tried to stay calm while Kay found a parking space at the main entrance.

"I'll come in with you and wait to see if you need a ride back," Kay said.

"Thank you," Emily said, but she was too distracted to think about getting home.

Emily rushed in and made her way to the surgical floor with Kay following close behind. They stepped out of the elevator and Emily caught sight of Ben. He walked over and she pulled him into her arms. "Have you heard anything?"

Ben was the spitting image of his father, with Tom's curly brown hair. "Hi, Mom. I've been waiting for the doctor to come out of surgery and tell me something."

Emily gestured to Kay. "This is Detective DeLorme. She gave me a ride down from Augusta."

Ben nodded to Kay as they stepped into the waiting room. Just as Emily was about to say good-bye to Kay and thank her again for the ride, a doctor entered the room.

"Are you the Stratton family?" he asked.

Emily stepped forward. "Yes, can you tell us how Tom is?"

The doctor met her eyes and she knew. The hope she had been holding on to disappeared as he answered. "I am very sorry. We did everything that we could but his injuries were too severe."

Emily sat down as she felt her world collapsing around her. What would she do without Tom? There must be some mistake. She tried to follow what the doctor was saying to Ben about Tom's injuries, but she kept thinking back to that morning. She didn't even kiss him good-bye. She'd been having such awful thoughts about their relationship lately. If only she had handled things differently. Maybe she couldn't have stopped this from happening, but at least she could have made sure that Tom knew how much she loved him.

She had to hold it together for the boys, but right now she didn't know what to do. Tom had been there for her for over twenty-five years. How was she going to make it without him?

The doctor quietly left the waiting room. Ben hugged Emily close as they both sobbed. Emily felt like she was in a dream and she wanted to wake up.

"I'm very sorry," Kay said softly. "I'll leave you two alone."

Emily nodded through her tears and Kay turned to go. Before she had a chance to leave, a state trooper appeared in the doorway. Kay stepped back as he entered the room.

"Emily Stratton?" the trooper asked.

"Yes." Emily let go of Ben and straightened her shoulders. "Can you tell me about the accident? What happened?"

"I am very sorry, ma'am. It appears that your husband, Tom Stratton, was going at a high rate of speed on the North Road in Winchester when he went off the road on a sharp turn. The road was icy and that may have contributed. We have called in the crash reconstruction unit to try to determine more details. His truck was severely damaged and we have transported it back to the Troop A Barracks garage in Augusta. I am sorry to tell you that your dog was also in the vehicle and she was killed on impact."

"No, not Sally too," Emily cried. Why on earth would Tom have been speeding on an icy road? He was always a safe driver and had never been in any traffic accidents. This just didn't make any sense.

The trooper nodded in sympathy and turned to go, Kay following close behind, leaving Ben and Emily alone in the waiting room to deal with their loss privately.

Ben put his arm around his mother just as Ethan walked in. Ethan looked more like Emily with his sandy blond hair, but he had his father's easygoing temperament. Emily fought to keep in control as she tried to tell him what had happened. It was almost impossible to get the words out as she looked into his tear-filled eyes and knew that she was going to break his heart.

CHAPTER EIGHT

The next several months passed quickly. The funeral had been an ordeal, but it had given Emily and her sons some comfort to see how many people had loved Tom. The church had overflowed with friends and family members. Tom's parents had returned to Massachusetts afterward and her sons had both gone back to their homes in Portland and Boston. They were all learning to live without Tom's strong and loving presence in their lives.

Emily had been surprised to find how much it meant to her to have all of her friends and coworkers come to the funeral. Even her old college roommate, Jess, had come all the way from New York, where she now lived. It had been good to catch up and hear about what she had been up to for the past few years. They had managed to stay in touch, but the frequency had dropped off as the years went by. Before she returned to New York, Emily had promised to go visit and Jess had also promised to come back and see her soon.

Kay had also been at the funeral. Emily was touched by how incredibly supportive she had been to her throughout everything. It had been so kind of Kay to drive her down to the hospital on that terrible day. Emily had spoken with her frequently since then. They had formed a bond on the day of Tom's accident. She felt a tremendous amount of gratitude for how Kay had helped her and her sons deal with all of the details at the hospital. Kay had kept in touch and given her steady support during the heartbreaking days and weeks that followed. She knew she had found a caring and loyal friend.

Emily hated sitting home alone in her quiet, empty house. She was filled with a terrible sense of guilt that she hadn't been a better wife. She had never broken her vows and she never would have, but she knew there were times that Tom's love had been a lot stronger than hers. If only she had appreciated Tom more. She had felt trapped in her marriage but now she missed Tom terribly. She also missed her daily walks with Sally and having her there to greet her with unconditional love when she got home. She had been such a sweet girl.

Emily had spent many sleepless nights worrying about what she could have done differently and why Tom had gotten into the accident. The first few weeks she had found herself waking up with tears in her eyes before she even knew what was wrong. She would lie there for a moment and then the realization would hit her all over again.

Since Tom's death, she had become uncomfortable talking to most people, as questions had inevitably been asked about the accident. Emily still found it difficult to believe that Tom had been driving so fast on an icy road. It just wasn't like him to do that. Because of the circumstances of the accident, she was sure that a lot of people felt that Tom's death was caused by his own recklessness. It bothered her to see that her sons were hurt by the thought that their father had been so careless.

She had been forced to spend a lot of time dealing with the insurance companies for Tom's truck and for his life insurance. It had been painful to keep repeating a description of the accident to them. She needed to make sure that their insurance policies were honored but she was still waiting for the official report from the state before the life insurance policy would be paid. Kay had given her contact information for tracking down the troopers who were investigating Tom's accident. She was hoping that they would finish their report soon so that she could finally get everything straightened out. It was taking a lot longer than she had expected.

She had been working from home for the past few months and was planning to return to the office full time the next day, which was a Monday. She could have continued doing her job from home if she wanted. Alex had assured her that she could adapt her schedule to whatever she needed. There were several people in her office who worked from home full time, but she preferred to go back to the office where she could put aside distractions and concentrate. Spending more time alone was going to drive her crazy. She had too much time on her hands and not enough going on to keep her mind occupied. She felt like it was definitely time to try and return to a structured schedule and a more normal life.

Emily's thoughts were interrupted by a call on her cell phone. She glanced at the screen and saw that it was Julian. He had been a good friend to her since the accident. He had called her or stopped by almost every day. His crazy sense of humor had distracted her from her grief and kept her from falling into depression.

"Hi there. What's up?" she greeted him.

"Mark and I went to brunch. You should've come with us. It was delicious. Anyway, we saw that creepy Chris Brooks. He definitely looks like he is on something."

"I would have come, but I had some things to do to get ready for tomorrow." She hadn't felt like greeting people at the busy restaurant where they often went to brunch. She almost always ran into people she knew there and she just didn't want to deal with their sympathetic questions.

"That is a very lame excuse. Mr. Creepy asked about you."

"That's weird. He barely knows me."

"I know, I think he just wanted us to dish on Tom and get details on the accident, the jerk. I told him you were doing fabulous."

"Thank you. I'm sure people are curious, but I really don't feel like talking about it."

"Of course not, cupcake. People are just nosy. Are you sure you want to go back to work tomorrow?"

"Yes," she said. "Looking forward to it actually."

The next morning Emily couldn't help but remember the last time she had headed to the gym before going to the office. She had still been going to the gym while she worked at home, but it had been kind of nice not to have to go so early. Glancing at the corner where Sally used to sleep, she grabbed her keys and headed out the door.

It was her normal arrival time of seven a.m. when she walked through the door of the office, too early for the receptionist and many of her coworkers to have arrived yet. She was grateful to be able to walk down the hall and not have to greet anyone just yet. She put down her bag and hung up her coat, then sat at her desk. Thankfully, she'd kept up on everything while working at home, so she wouldn't be too swamped today. She powered on her laptop and settled into her chair, reminding herself to stay tough and focus on her projects. No one was going to see her cry. It was good to be back.

* * *

Kay pulled up to the SBI office. She'd decided to stop by and check on Emily this morning on her first day back in the office. They had spoken frequently since the funeral. She wanted to check on her and show her support. Kay was impressed with how Emily had handled herself. She must still be hurting but she didn't want any sympathy. Now she was getting back to her regular routine, and Kay could see that she was determined not to let grief get the better of her.

Kay entered the building and walked down the hall to Emily's office. Knocking on the doorway to announce herself, she looked in. "Good morning, welcome back."

Emily looked at her with a smile. "Hi there. It feels kind of strange but good to be here. I'm glad to be back. I really don't like working from home all that much. When I'm there I spend too much time thinking about everything."

Kay felt her heart rate speed up. She couldn't help but notice that Emily looked a little thinner and her hair had gotten a little longer, but this made her look even more attractive. Shutting those thoughts down immediately, Kay reminded herself that she was here to support her friend. She and her last girlfriend had split up well over a year ago and she hadn't met anyone since who interested her. She found Emily to be very intriguing and appealing but she was definitely off limits.

"I'm sure you have a lot to catch up on," Kay said. "But if you do find that you want something interesting to look into, I'm still trying to identify different patterns for drug arrests. At least, *I* think it's interesting."

"I do, too. I love analyzing data and finding ways to make it useful. Some people would think it sounds boring, but I enjoy it. I would love to help you with the traffic data and whatever else you think might be useful for the investigation that you're working on. I welcome the distraction."

"That would be great. The investigation is focusing on a drug ring that we think is being run from here in the Augusta area. There've been a few small arrests, but we think it's part of a much larger ring that has ties with a supplier from out of state."

"I did hear something about a drug bust in Orleans a few months ago," Emily said.

"Yes, that was related. The governor is trying to come down hard on the drug problem in Maine, so we're under some political pressure to get results. My partner is focusing on tracking down the locals while I'm trying to identify some of the suppliers. Your data could be very helpful."

"I'm really glad that I can try to help," Emily said. "I have your cell number so how about I give you a call after I get a chance to run some more reports?"

"Oh you don't have to rush. I know you must have a lot to catch up on. Just let me know when you get a chance." Kay hesitated. Would Emily want to be alone later or would she rather have company? It was hard to tell and she didn't want to overstep the boundaries of their new friendship.

"Thanks, I will." Emily smiled at Kay.

"Well, I guess I'd better get going," Kay said, still not sure if she should say anything about getting together sometime. "Have a good day."

"Listen, if you wanted, maybe we could go over the reports and get something to eat for dinner at the same time?" Emily said. "I know you're busy and I don't want to impose. I really don't want to go home to the empty house tonight, though."

"Sure, that would be fine." Kay tried to play it cool, but she was surprised how much she did want to go to dinner later. "You're not imposing at all. I don't have any plans."

"Great," Emily said. "I'll call you when I'm done with the reports and we can decide where to go."

* * *

Kay and Emily were seated at a table by a window overlooking the river. Warm weather was finally here, so it was still light enough to look out across the water. The Riverside Restaurant was a popular spot, even on a Monday evening. They had briefly gone over the report that Emily brought with her. Not wanting anyone to overhear their conversation, they put the report aside as the restaurant filled up with people.

"How are you liking the area?" Emily asked.

"I love it. I moved here to Orleans last fall and it's been great."

"I live in Orleans, too. I grew up here," Emily said. "It's a fun place to be. With all the restaurants and cafes, you can find live music playing somewhere most nights of the week."

"What I like about it is how open-minded and tolerant most of the people that I've met seem to be," Kay said. "I was surprised that there's such a diverse population for a small town, with so many local artists and musicians."

Emily nodded. "I think there's always been a general spirit of acceptance here."

"Emily, I feel like I need to be upfront with you about something. I'm not sure if you realize that I am a lesbian."

Emily looked startled. "I thought you might be, but I didn't think it mattered in any way."

Kay felt relieved yet disappointed. She didn't think that Emily was going to be judgmental, but she had wanted to be sure. At the same time, she now had confirmed that Emily did not feel any interest toward her. It was ridiculous of her to feel that way, she knew. Emily was a straight woman who had just lost her husband. Of course she didn't have any interest in her. Their relationship was strictly platonic. It was just hard to keep remembering that when they were together.

"Are you seeing anyone?" Emily asked.

"No, I've been single for almost two years now. I haven't met that many people outside of work as I mostly stay home in the evenings. I've gone out a few times in Orleans, but I didn't really feel comfortable going by myself."

"I'll have to introduce you to some friends of mine. Someone as gorgeous as you won't be single for long." Emily's face flushed and she looked away. "Sorry, I haven't been out of the house much lately and I didn't mean to say anything awkward. I always talk too much when I get nervous."

"Thanks for the compliment," Kay said with a smile. So, Emily thought she was gorgeous?

The waiter came by and asked if they were ready to order. They each ordered one of the locally brewed beers.

"Do you like trying the different local beers?" Kay asked.

"I do. There are some great beers in Maine and I like trying the new ones. The problem is that I can never remember which ones I liked. I've never been much of a wine drinker and I hardly ever drink mixed drinks, either."

"Same here. I'll have to bring you some beer that I love from a place I sometimes go to in Portland."

The waiter delivered drinks and they ordered their meals—Emily decided on a portobello burger and Kay got the pasta primavera.

"Do you like to cook?" Emily asked.

"I love cooking," Kay replied. "It's usually just me and I make something simple, but when I have someone to cook for, I really enjoy it."

"I'm finding that I don't feel like making the effort now that I'm just making meals for myself. I used to try and have a nice dinner for Tom every night, but now I really don't feel like it."

"I try to cook extra things on the weekends to have during the week," Kay said. "I don't like to order out much. Once in a while I'll get pizza, but I try to eat healthy stuff most of the time."

"I'll have to try to plan ahead on the weekends. I used to make dishes with meat for Tom, but I'm a vegetarian, so I won't be doing that anymore unless one of the boys comes over for dinner."

"Hey, that's interesting, I'm a vegetarian, too."

They continued to find interests that they both shared as the night went on. Kay was surprised by how much they had in common.

"I have been meaning to ask you, do you like softball?" Emily asked.

"Are you kidding me? I love it. I used to play shortstop for a team in South Portland up until a couple years ago when I got too busy at work. Now I'm worried that I'm getting too old."

"You're not too old! We have an office team that plays in one of the leagues in Augusta. I'm the coach actually, mainly because no one else wanted to do it. We have a wide range of abilities on the team—some of our players are pretty good and others not so much. Would you be interested in playing? We start soon."

"That sounds great. It would be a good way to meet people, too. What position are you?" Kay was not surprised to hear that Emily played softball. She looked very athletic.

"I play second base and sometimes pitch," Emily replied. "I'm a decent player but not great. In fact, I always secretly wished that I could be an awesome softball player and be a power hitter. I also wanted to be a great singer. Luckily, you don't have to be a super talented player to be a superstar on our team."

After dinner, Kay turned to Emily. "That was very good. I'll have to come back here."

"I'd better check on the time and make sure that it's not getting too late," Emily said. She took her phone out of her bag and looked at the screen. "Looks like I missed a call from Ethan. He and Ben check up on me every day."

"Your sons seem like very nice young men, by the way," Kay said.

"Thank you, they really are. Of course I'm a little biased. Do you have any children?"

"No, I focused on my career. I was always busy with my job and I never took the time to stay in a long-term relationship or have kids. I do regret that sometimes," Kay said.

"You obviously have had a successful career so far. I can see that you've worked hard to get where you are."

"Thanks. I guess we better get going." Kay was reluctant to leave. The evening had flown by and she couldn't remember when she had enjoyed a dinner more.

"You're right. We've both got another early day tomorrow." Emily stood and put on her jacket.

Kay reached down for her bag, which had slid under the adjoining chair. She grabbed it and stood up, turning for the door just as Emily stepped back and turned quickly in the same direction, running straight into Kay and bumping her face into Kay's neck.

Emily jumped back. "God, how embarrassing. Sorry, I wasn't paying attention and I didn't realize you were right there."

Startled by Emily's touch, Kay stepped back and raised her hands. "My fault. I was trying to get my bag and I didn't see you. Are you okay?"

"I'm fine." Emily laughed nervously. "I hope I didn't hurt you. I'm not the most graceful person.

They walked out to the parking lot. Kay waited by her car while Emily unlocked the door to her truck. "Thank you, Kay. I had a good time, although I feel so guilty saying that. I miss Tom terribly, but I really couldn't stand the thought of sitting home by myself tonight."

"It must be very tough. I was happy to have something to do, too. Any time you feel like you want someone to hang out with, just let me know."

Kay got into her car and watched Emily drive away. She put her hand to her neck and wondered what she was going to do to stop these feelings she was having about her new straight friend.

CHAPTER NINE

On Friday evening Emily pulled into her driveway and parked her truck. It had been a long week at the office. She had a lot of projects going on, but she had made it through. She had even gone to trivia with Julian earlier that week. Ben and Ethan sounded like they were doing better, too. She was starting to feel hopeful for the first time in while.

She sat for a minute thinking about Kay and wondering if she might want to go to dinner again this weekend. She certainly didn't have any plans herself. She had been a little worried that Kay might have agreed to go to dinner the other night out of pity, but they had ended up having such a good time that she wanted to spend more time with her.

She had told Julian about her evening and he had raised his eyebrows. "Better be careful, the gossips are going to think you're out on a date."

Of course it was nothing like that, but she and Tom knew a lot of people in town and she wouldn't want any of them to think she cared so little for Tom that she was already over him.

She missed him every day, but she was so confused. She knew that any passion that they had shared had been long over, but it still felt like a betrayal to think about ever being with anyone else. Not that she thought of Kay that way, of course. She did enjoy listening to Kay talk, though. She really had a beautiful voice.

She got out of the vehicle and walked to the side door, unlocked it, and went into the house. She flipped on the kitchen light and gasped when she realized that someone had been in her home. Her normally tidy kitchen had been ransacked. The cupboards and drawers were open, the contents jumbled about. She looked into the living room and saw that the cushions on the couch and chairs were upended and everything on the shelves had been tossed to the floor. Not sure if she was alone, she quickly turned and ran back to her truck, reaching for her cell phone and dialing 911.

The Orleans police arrived quickly. Emily wasn't sure if she should call anyone else. She didn't want to alarm her sons until she knew more about what was going on. She tried reaching Julian but he didn't answer his phone, as usual, and she didn't leave a message. Emily knew some state troopers through the office, but not well enough to call them outside of work. Besides, what were they going to do that the Orleans police couldn't do? Still, she didn't want to be alone at the moment. She quickly tapped a number into her phone. "Hello, Kay? It's Emily."

"Hi there, how are you?"

"I'm fine, thanks," Emily said. "Actually, I'm not fine. I hate to bother you, but it looks like someone has broken into my house."

"What's your address? I'll be right there."

Emily gave her address to Kay and waited in her truck. Kay hadn't hesitated to come over. Emily knew she would have done the same thing for Kay if the situation had been reversed, but it was nice to know that Kay was there for her. A short time later, Kay's car pulled into the driveway and parked behind her truck. Emily got out and walked back to her. "Hi. Thanks for coming over so fast."

"I was on my way home so I wasn't too far away. What happened?"

Emily started to answer as one of the Orleans officers came out of the house. "The house is clear. We need to have you come in and see if anything is missing."

"Officer, this is my friend Detective DeLorme. She's with the state police Major Crimes Unit."

"Hello, Detective DeLorme." The officer nodded to Kay. "I'm Officer Sullivan."

Kay shook the officer's hand.

They walked into the house and Emily started looking around. The television was still mounted on the wall. Her laptop was still sitting on her desk in the office, although the desk drawers were all opened. She went into her bedroom and looked around. Her bureau drawers were all ajar and the clothes were in messy piles. The closet door was open. She checked the jewelry chest on top of her bureau and didn't see anything missing. Her sons had helped her to pack up most of Tom's clothes a few weeks after his accident, so his bureau and closet were almost empty. She checked in the two spare bedrooms, which each contained a bed and bureau, and didn't see anything missing. She went down the stairs to the living room where Kay was conferring with the two officers.

"I don't see anything missing," she said. "I don't have any idea why someone would break in and then not take anything. It doesn't make sense."

"It looks like they got in through the door off the deck," Officer Sullivan said. "We found the lock on the French doors had been pried open."

Officer Sullivan and his partner, Officer Tate, completed an inspection of the house with Emily. She still didn't find anything missing. The police told her that they thought perhaps someone had interrupted the break-in and the burglars left before they were able to take anything. That really didn't made sense to Emily, but she didn't have a better theory. The officers finished their paperwork and left.

Emily turned to Kay. "I'm sorry that I bothered you. I'm sure you had better things to do tonight, but I just got scared. "

"I'm glad you called. Someone broke into your house, for crying out loud. Anyone would be scared. I don't agree that they just got interrupted, though."

"I know. If whoever was here took the time to go through every room in the house, then they definitely had time to take things if they wanted to. I don't have a lot of valuable stuff, but they didn't even take my jewelry. I have some pretty nice gold chains and earrings."

"I think they were looking for something. Any ideas about what it could be?"

"No, not at all. I really can't think of anything. Listen, it's getting kind of late. Do you need to get going or do you want to order a pizza or something?"

"I am kind of hungry and pizza sounds good," Kay said. "Why don't we get something to eat and try to think about what they might have been looking for? It seems strange that nothing was taken."

"All right. Hopefully I'll think of something while we eat."

Emily called and ordered a veggie pizza. She grabbed two bottles of beer out of the refrigerator and carried them into the living room where Kay was putting the cushions back on the couch and chair.

"Can I help you pick up?" Kay asked.

"That would really be great, thank you. I ordered dinner and here's a beer for you."

"Thanks." Kay took a swallow. "Mm, I like this."

Emily swallowed. She watched Kay's lips on the bottle and the way her silky, dark hair slipped back to frame her face. It suddenly hit her how much Kay was affecting her. Her heart was racing and she had a sudden urge to run her fingers through Kay's hair. "I'm going to try to straighten up the shelves."

What was she thinking? Kay was here to help her as her friend. Kay wouldn't be interested in someone like her anyway. She had just lost her husband and should not be thinking like this. It was wrong.

Kay and Emily picked up the books that had been taken off the shelves and tossed to the floor. They placed them back on the waist-high built-in bookcases that ran along the wall.

Emily stopped to look at some of the family photos that were on display. They showed her and Tom in various scenes with their two sons through the years. The pictures reminded her that in spite of any issues that she and Tom may have had, they'd been a happy family and done a lot of fun things together.

"It's really nice of you to help me, Kay, thank you again," Emily said. She looked at Kay, standing by the bookcases, and reflected on how much her life had changed since those pictures had been taken. Her husband was gone and her kids were grown up and on their own. At this point in her life she didn't have to answer to anyone.

The doorbell rang and Emily went to the kitchen door to greet the deliveryman. Setting the pizza box down on the table, she went to the cupboards where the napkins and plates were kept. She quickly straightened up the stacks of napkins and grabbed a few. The plates were still in place. The intruders apparently hadn't touched anything in the cupboards.

"Ready to eat?" Emily called to Kay.

Kay came into the kitchen, carrying her beer. They sat at the table and Emily served them each a big slice of pizza. They ate quietly for a few minutes. The silence stretched out.

Emily spoke up quietly. "I truly appreciate your help. You really don't need to stay though. I'm fine now."

"I don't mind staying," Kay replied. "I hope you actually wanted me to and weren't just being polite."

"Not at all," Emily said. She didn't want Kay to feel any pressure to stay. "I just thought you might have had other plans and I don't want to take advantage of your friendship."

"I don't have any other plans," Kay said. "I think you need to be careful. It's possible that whoever broke in might come back for something."

Emily had been thinking the same thing. "I wish I knew what they were looking for."

"Could it be something to do with Tom's business?"

"I don't know. He never kept anything valuable here. I gave most of his tools to the boys after the accident. We don't have any money hidden here or anything like that."

"Has anything happened recently that you can think of?"

"Well, some troopers from the crash reconstruction unit brought back all of the things that were in Tom's truck. They're hoping to have the accident report completed next week, so they finally released everything. It was mostly a couple jackets and some tools. Also all the things that he kept in the console of his truck, like his wallet and phone. He didn't like to keep things in his pockets. It was hard to go through it actually. I just took a quick look and then I put the box in the office."

They got up from the table and went into the office. The box was sitting open on the floor next to the desk. The contents were jumbled up, the shirt and jacket that had been in the box had been tossed to the floor.

Emily knelt down and looked through the contents. A wave of sadness hit her as she saw the papers, Post-it notes, business cards, gum, and other little remaining pieces of Tom's life. She found his wallet and held it for a moment, thinking about how much she missed him.

Emily looked up at Kay. "Hey, I don't see his cell phone. I remember seeing it the other day when they brought the box over. The battery was dead, so I was going to charge it and look at his messages. I just hadn't done it yet."

"Any idea why someone would want to break into your house and steal Tom's phone?"

Emily shook her head. "The whole thing is really strange. Why would someone come take his phone months later? Why would anyone want his phone in the first place?"

"The timing of it makes me wonder if someone knew that it was just returned to you."

Kay and Emily looked through the rest of the office, straightening up as they went along. They put books and folders back into place and tidied up the drawers. Not finding anything else missing, Emily and Kay returned to the kitchen.

"Do you want any more pizza or something to drink?" Emily asked.

"No, thanks. Listen, I really don't think you should stay here alone tonight. You need to get the lock on your French door fixed."

Emily leaned against the counter. Kay was probably right but it was getting late and she really didn't feel like calling Julian or anyone else to see if they could come over. She was always welcome at Julian's, so she could go stay there tonight, but she was tired of bothering her friends with her troubles all the time.

"It's getting pretty late, I'm sure you want to get going. Thank you so much for helping me. I owe you big time." Emily was getting nervous and talking too much. "Don't worry about me. I can call one of my friends and see about going over."

"It's late and I'm not convinced that you're going to call anyone," Kay said. "I've had a couple beers and I probably shouldn't be driving. How about if I sleep on the couch and help you keep an eye on things?"

Emily was relieved. That would be much better than going over to Julian's and she didn't want to be alone. "Sure. But I'll put you in one of the spare bedrooms. That will be much more comfortable than the couch. I'll go get it ready and find you a toothbrush."

Kay sat down on the couch and Emily turned on the television for her before going upstairs. The living room, like the rest of the house, was filled with comfortable furniture with a few antiques mixed in. Emily liked to keep things simple so there was no clutter. The house had been built to let in plenty of natural light during the day, and there were several windows throughout the kitchen and living room.

Emily came back down the stairs and sat next to Kay. "Can I get you anything?"

"I'm all set. Let's try and see if we can come up with any reasons why someone would want Tom's phone."

Emily brushed her fingers through her hair. "Tom was the most honest person I know. If he knew that someone was doing something wrong, he wouldn't have stood by and let it go."

"Do you think he knew about something?"

"He never mentioned anything to me. I think that he would have told me if there was something going on. I know you never met him, but you would have liked him. He was very easygoing and got along with everyone. I grew up here but he knew more people than I did. He loved talking with people. He was much friendlier than me."

Kay smiled at her. "I think you're pretty friendly."

Emily smiled back. "You have no idea how difficult I am in the mornings. I'll try to be civil tomorrow."

"Thanks for the warning."

"I feel like you know all about me, but I don't know too much about you. Where did you grow up?"

"Let's see. I grew up in Freeport then I went to UMaine for college. My mother died from cancer when I was a teenager," Kay said.

"I'm sorry. It must have been hard to lose her when you were so young."

"It was. I still miss her."

"What made you decide to go into law enforcement?"

"My father was a Portland cop. He died a few years ago. He was my idol. I always wanted to be like him. The state police had openings after I graduated from college, so joining worked out perfectly for me. It gave me the chance to be a cop and I've been able to advance to where I am now. Like I told you, I've always been very focused on my job and I haven't really taken the time to stay in a relationship for long."

"Did your parents know that you're a lesbian?" Emily asked.

"By the time I figured it out when I was in high school, my mom had already passed away. I always figured that my father knew, but we never talked about it. I never tried to hide anything, but my dad and I didn't talk about things like that."

"No brothers or sisters?"

"Just me."

It sounded lonely to Emily. She had been so young when she and Tom had gotten married that she had never lived alone until now. She was getting used to it, but it would have been hard if her friends and family hadn't been there to support her. It sounded like Kay didn't have a lot of people in her life.

Emily spoke. "I want to tell you something that I have never told anyone. I feel like you won't judge me and it's been on my mind a lot lately."

"What is it?"

"It's hard to explain. Ever since college I have felt attracted to women but I never did anything about it. I think I just denied it to myself, but it was always there. I met Tom and he was my best friend. He was there for me and we could always count on each other."

Emily continued, "I got caught up in raising the boys and helping Tom with his business. I was always busy with my job and I just kept going forward. We had a good life. I would never have broken my vows with Tom. I never was actually interested in another particular person. I just have always had this longing that I could never do anything about."

Emily saw Kay's shocked expression and worried that she was going to think she was making a pass at her. Was she making a pass at her? With her looks, Kay probably got hit on all the time. "I didn't mean to put you on the spot. I just thought that since we were getting to be friends, you might have some advice for me."

"No, I was just surprised," Kay said. "This must be a very confusing time for you."

"No, I'm not confused. I feel guilty, like I wasn't faithful to Tom, even though I never looked at another person that way while he was alive."

"What about now? Is there someone that you've been looking at that way?"

Emily stared into Kay's beautiful eyes. She wanted this so much it scared her. "Uh, I think there is."

Kay leaned toward her and kissed her gently. Emily closed her eyes and her lips returned the kiss. She felt her heart pounding. She sat back and took a deep breath, speechless.

Kay smiled at her.

Emily leaned back toward Kay and their lips met again. Kay's tongue teased its way past Emily's lips. She reached up to touch Kay's short, glossy hair, running her fingers through it. She felt Kay's hands caressing her back.

Kay pulled back. "I think we should probably slow down a little. You are very special and I don't want to rush this."

Emily's head was spinning. She hadn't expected anything like this to ever happen to her. She didn't want to stop now, but maybe Kay wasn't as interested as she was.

"I understand." Emily stood up and offered a hand to Kay. "Let me show you where your room is."

Kay took Emily's hand and they walked up the stairs together. Kay released her hand and said good night.

Emily watched Kay go into the guest room before turning to enter her own bedroom. She brushed her teeth and got ready for bed, distracted by the thought of Kay in the room nearby.

Lying in her bed, Emily was unable to sleep as she thought back on the events of the day. She should probably be nervous about the break-in, but she couldn't stop thinking about Kay. She had never kissed another woman. She hadn't kissed anyone other than Tom for over twenty-five years. Her lips and skin had been so soft. She closed her eyes as she thought about Kay.

Kay brushed her teeth and changed into the T-shirt that Emily had given her. Her mind filled with thoughts of Emily as she got into bed and tried to get to sleep. Kay lay thinking about the kisses that they had shared. She had been so busy fighting her attraction to Emily that she hadn't realized that Emily might be attracted to her as well. Had Emily really meant to kiss her or was this was just an impulsive experiment for her? She hoped that Emily wasn't going to be embarrassed and regretful in the morning.

At dinner the other night she had started feeling a strong attraction to Emily and she had been telling herself to be careful. They seemed to have a lot in common, but she had wanted to be sure not to misread the situation. Her plan had been to back off and protect herself from getting too involved. In spite of her good intentions, her attraction to Emily was too strong and she hadn't been able to hold herself back earlier.

The family photos in the living room had reminded her that Emily's life had been much different from hers. The photos showed a picture-perfect family, but she had never met Tom and there may be more going on here than she was aware of.

Kay hoped for Emily's sake that the cell phone theft didn't have anything to do with Tom being mixed up with something illegal.

Kay closed her eyes again. She needed to stop thinking and get some sleep. As she drifted off, she vowed that she was going to be very careful. She didn't want to get hurt if Emily changed her mind.

CHAPTER TEN

Emily got ready quietly the next morning. She didn't want to wake Kay. She took a shower, got dressed, and went downstairs. She went into the kitchen and tried to think of what she could make Kay for breakfast. She usually just had a bowl of cereal in the morning and she didn't have many other choices on hand.

She heard Kay moving around upstairs. She was apprehensive about seeing her after last night. It could be that Kay thought Emily threw herself at her. Maybe Kay was just being polite last night. She may not be interested in her at all. Kay had a confident, charismatic personality that drew Emily to her. She wished she knew what she should do. This whole situation was so perplexing that she was starting to get irritated with herself. She decided that she was going to try to stop being nervous. She would act like nothing had happened.

Kay walked into the kitchen and over to Emily. She smiled and gave her a hug and a quick kiss. "Good morning."

"Hi. Good morning." Emily was flustered. Her heart raced again at the sight of Kay. She was relieved that Kay seemed happy to see her.

"What do you want for breakfast?" Emily asked. "I have cereal and toast, but we could go get something if you want."

"Cereal would be great. I thought you were going to be scary in the morning? You seem fairly normal. Or was that just a bluff?"

Emily laughed. "No, I really am crabby in the morning. I just was so happy to see you that I forgot to be grumpy."

Kay's smile grew. "I was worried that you might be embarrassed or uncomfortable this morning and I'm glad you're happy to see me."

"I may be a little nervous, which can be embarrassing," Emily said. "But I'm definitely happy."

They sat down at the table and shared the newspaper while they had breakfast. Emily kept stealing glances at Kay who smiled at her whenever she caught her looking.

"I'm going to call the locksmith as soon as they're open. I want to get the back door fixed. I'm thinking about calling an alarm company, too. What do you think?"

"I think that's a good idea. Maybe they were just after the phone and it won't happen again, but I think it would be good to have a little more security since you live alone."

"I wish we knew why someone would want to get Tom's phone."

Kay paused for a moment before replying. "One thing that I can think of is that he might have seen some criminal activity. I know you said Tom wouldn't have stood by if he saw anything illegal going on, so possibly he saw something and there was a message or photo on the phone that someone wanted to get their hands on."

"So what do we do next?"

"I could try and get his phone records."

"I'm sure you have a lot going on with your other investigations, but if you have time to get the phone records, we could see if there are any strange calls. He talked to clients and vendors all day long, so it might be hard to tell if there is anything unusual, but it's worth a try."

"I agree. I'll try to be really discreet and get the records this week. It's probably a good idea to keep this quiet till we find out anything concrete."

"Thank you for all your help."

"I have to get going," Kay said. "I've got some errands to run this morning. Let me know how you make out with the locksmith."

"I think I'll give Ben and Ethan a call and let them know what happened. I don't want to worry them, but I know they'd be upset if I didn't tell them. I bet Ben will want to help me with the alarm."

"What do you think your sons would think of me?" Kay asked.

"I think they could be upset if they thought that I'd moved on too quickly from their father," Emily answered quietly. "It's really not like that, though. Tom and I loved each other, and even though he's gone I will always love him."

Emily put her hand on top of Kay's. "On one hand, I do worry that my family and friends might think that I was betraying Tom if I met someone else. On the other hand, I want to find out what we might have between us and it has nothing to do with anyone else."

Kay nodded. "Let's just take this slowly and see what happens. I feel like we could have something special going on here. I really like spending time with you and talking with you, but I don't want to rush you into something that you aren't ready for."

After Kay left, Emily finished picking up her house and waited for the locksmith to arrive. Ben came over in the afternoon and helped her set up motion-activated cameras near both entry doors. She planned to call an alarm service on Monday.

Ben was reluctant to leave. "Are you sure you're all right here by yourself, Mom? I'd be happy to stay with you this weekend."

"I feel very secure now and you don't need to worry. The police are keeping an eye on the neighborhood and my friend, Kay DeLorme, is going to stop by, too. Do you remember her, she's the detective from the state police?"

"She seems nice, and I'm glad you won't be alone. Call me if you need anything."

After Ben left to return to Portland, Emily sat in the kitchen and made a list of possible reasons that someone might have broken in and taken Tom's phone. She hadn't gotten very far when her phone rang.

"Hi, Julian," she answered.

"Hello, kitten, how are you? I just got your text. I can't believe someone broke into your house. How awful."

"Everything's fine. Like I said, nothing was taken except for Tom's phone. Isn't that strange?"

"Why didn't you leave me a message when you called last night? I would have called back. You should have come over here. In fact, why don't you stay with us tonight?"

"The locks are secure and Ben installed some cameras for me. I'm not going to be scared out of my own home." Emily avoided telling him that Kay had spent the night. She didn't want to get into all the details on the phone.

"I want to hear all about it. Let's do brunch tomorrow."

Emily was dying to tell Julian about Kay. She wasn't entirely sure how he would react, but they had always told each other everything and she wanted to talk to him about it. Just not on the phone.

"Sounds good, I'll see you at noon tomorrow."

Emily hadn't heard from Kay all day and was debating whether she should call her or give her some space. It would probably be a good idea to have a quiet evening and get some rest. She hadn't been able to sleep much last night. Maybe she'd give Kay a quick call to say hello.

She dialed Kay's number. "Hi."

"Hi there. Hold on while I turn down my radio. Okay, that's better. I'm in my car, driving toward the office. I was going to give you a call but I haven't had a chance. It's been a crazy afternoon. Have you heard the news today?"

"No, what happened?" Emily walked into the living room and grabbed her laptop. She opened it up so that she could check the local news site as Kay continued talking.

"A trooper was shot on the interstate near Augusta. He stopped a van for speeding and the driver pulled a gun out and shot him. My partner and I got called in because they think the driver might be connected with the drug ring in Augusta that we've been investigating."

"Is the trooper going to be all right?"

"No. He died instantly."

"That's terrible. Did they catch the shooter?"

"Not yet. We're trying to track down the van. There was some good footage of it from the trooper's dash cam. The theory is that this guy was transporting some drugs and didn't want to get caught. We've got everyone in the state out looking for the vehicle."

"Sounds like you have your hands full. Be careful."

"Did you get your lock fixed?" Kay asked. "I feel bad that I haven't checked in with you."

"I did get it fixed, and the door is all set now. My son came up and helped me put in some cameras, too. I think I have plenty of security for now, although I am going to get an alarm system this week."

"That's a relief. Sorry that I didn't stop by. I meant to but I haven't have time."

"That's sweet of you, but I'm fine. I know you must have a lot to do. I don't want to keep you from getting back to work."

"You aren't. I'm driving back to the office now. Pete and I are going to meet with some of the other guys on the task force and try to see if we can help find out more about the shooter or who he might be working for."

"Is there anything I can do to help?" Emily asked.

"We might need to run some more reports on Monday and see if we can tie any of this in with the data we've been looking at. The plates on the car haven't showed up in anything so far."

"I'd be happy to check into that. Just let me know what you need."

"I've been thinking about you today," Kay said. "I was hoping we could spend more time together this weekend, but it isn't looking good."

"I'm looking forward to spending more time with you, too." Emily heard Kay's car come to a stop. "I'm sure things must be really busy right now."

"Yeah. I'm back at the office. I'm going to have to get going."

"I hope you catch the shooter," Emily said. "Take care, Kay. I'll talk to you later."

"Bye."

CHAPTER ELEVEN

The next morning Emily checked the news as soon as she got up. The shooter hadn't been caught but the van had been found stripped and abandoned on a deserted dirt road. The shooter was the target of a statewide manhunt, but so far it didn't sound like the police had many leads. The news showed a photo of the trooper. His name was Joshua Williams. He had been married and had a young daughter. The media was going crazy with the story.

Emily thought of Kay and wondered how the Major Crimes Unit was handling all of this. Even though it was a bureau of the state police, the SBI was not often called on in emergency situations, and she hadn't had any involvement in the case.

Emily took extra care getting dressed because Julian noticed everything and she didn't dare show up looking messy. She had on her usual button-down shirt and jeans, but she made sure to select a shirt that was a little more form-fitting than she usually wore to work. She chose a tight pair of jeans, knowing that Julian would give her a hard time if she wore anything baggy.

She put on some earrings and a little perfume. Ready to face the world, she headed out the door.

She pulled her truck into the restaurant parking lot and took a deep breath before getting out. She wavered about telling Julian about Kay. He was always supportive and she needed to talk to someone about it, but he was going to be shocked.

She walked into their usual brunch spot and requested a table for two. The hostess seated her near a window and she had a good view of people walking by on the sidewalk outside. A short time later Julian showed up, just as she was getting ready to send him a text asking where he was. He was wearing a blazer with a vibrant red tie.

"Good morning, darling." Julian wrapped her in a big hug.

"Hi there." She slipped free and sat back down. "Glad you could make it."

"You were early, and I'm right on time."

The waitress came over and they ordered drinks. Emily got a Diet Coke and Julian got a Bloody Mary.

"So tell me about your break-in," Julian exclaimed. "You need to get a big gun."

"There isn't much more to tell. The house was messed up but the only thing missing was Tom's cell phone," Emily replied. "I don't know why anyone would want it."

"Do you think he had some messages or pictures that someone didn't want anyone to see?"

"It's a possibility. I really don't know, and he never mentioned anything out of the ordinary."

"I bet he saw something." Julian paused as the waitress delivered their drinks. "I can't imagine Tom letting it go if he saw anything illegal. He was honest to a fault."

Emily nodded. "He definitely would have reported it if he saw anything going on. But what could it have been? It's so frustrating not to know."

"Maybe he had pictures of someone that was having an affair," said Julian. "What if he told the person having the affair that he was going to expose them and they wanted to get the photos back?"

"Why wouldn't he have mentioned it?" asked Emily. "I don't think Tom would take pictures like that anyway."

"Good point," Julian said. "This is very intriguing."

"I had just gotten the phone back from the police, along with all the other things in his truck. They're finally finishing up the crash investigation." Emily glanced around the table to make sure no one was listening. "Don't you think it's funny that someone broke in to get the phone right after I got it back? How would they know that I didn't have it before?"

Julian's big, brown eyes widened dramatically. "This is our own mystery investigation. I feel like Jill Munroe in *Charlie's Angels*."

In spite of the seriousness of the situation, Emily couldn't help but laugh. Julian's crazy sense of humor could always get her.

"You wish you were Jill Munroe."

"What are we going to do?" Julian asked.

"Do you remember my detective friend Kay who I told you about?" Emily asked cautiously.

"Yes, the one you went to dinner with the other night." Julian looked at her curiously.

"She is going to help me look up the phone records. She's been a big help." Emily shifted in her chair as she tried to think of a good way to explain her new friendship to him. She could hardly explain it to herself at this point.

"I didn't realize you were so friendly with her."

"Well, she's really nice. I want you to meet her. She's hasn't been in town long, so she doesn't know too many people."

Julian gazed at her inquisitively.

She tried to fill the silence. "I'm working with her on some data for an investigation that she has going on. She happened to stop by the night that the house was broken into and helped me pick up."

"Oh really?" Julian finally answered. "You seem to be a little bit flustered, darling. Is there anything else you want to tell me?"

"What do you mean?"

"I know you, Emily," Julian said. "I've never seen you smile like that or blush when you're talking about someone. What's going on?"

She should have known that Julian would be perceptive. He had always been very good at reading people, while she was often oblivious to such things.

"It's not easy to explain. I started feeling this intense attraction to her. I know I probably shouldn't. It hasn't been that long since Tom died. I can't seem to help it, though." Emily wasn't sure what Julian's reaction would be, and she didn't want him to be upset with her.

Just then the waitress brought their meals and set them down. They thanked her and started eating. Emily glanced around again to make sure that no one was listening in to their conversation.

Julian set down his fork. "I don't want you to take this the wrong way. I loved Tom dearly. He was a wonderful guy, but you haven't seemed happy together for quite a while. I always worried that you weren't all that well suited for each other."

Emily defended Tom. "He loved me very much and I loved him, too. We had a good life together with the boys."

"Yes, but I always wondered if you would have made different choices if you hadn't gotten pregnant and rushed into marriage."

"It really doesn't matter. I made the choices that I did and I am happy about how my life turned out. I have two great kids."

"I'm sorry," Julian said. "I didn't want you to take that as criticism. It's just that I sometimes got a vibe from you that you may not have been altogether satisfied with the status quo, if you know what I mean."

"No, I don't know what you mean."

"Based on hearing you and Tom talk, you never seemed all that into sex to put it bluntly. You aren't very feminine, either. I think I'm definitely more feminine than you."

Emily wondered how long Julian had been thinking this. She didn't realize that it had been so apparent.

He continued, "You dress rather mannishly, I'm sorry to say. You love sports and working out. You have always worked with men. You drive a truck and you love beer. I could go on, but it's leading me to the conclusion that I am not surprised that you are attracted to a woman. There, I've said it."

Emily had several retorts on the tip of her tongue. Plenty of women drove trucks and worked with men. That was no basis for judgment. He happened to be right in this case, but she hated labels and stereotypes.

"Your reasoning is ridiculous. You work with hair stylists. Your sisters are not comparable to the average woman. Just because I don't wear heels and makeup, you can't classify me as a lesbian."

"I don't classify you as anything. It's just a vibe, like I said." Julian smiled charmingly at her.

She decided to pursue her point. "That's like saying just because a man likes show tunes and dresses nice, he must be gay."

"I call them like I see them."

Once Julian believed he was right, there would be no reasoning with him. He was one of the most judgmental people she knew and it could be infuriating at times. She gave up the argument and tried to dismiss her irritation and get back to the subject.

"Anyway, I'm hoping that Kay can help me figure out something with Tom's phone messages."

Julian touched her hand. "If she makes you happy, then I'm glad you have this new friend. Does she know how you feel about her?"

Emily shrugged, not wanting to go into details. "I think so."

"Has anything happened?" he asked.

"We kissed, actually, but that's all."

"Oh my God, you kissed a woman!" Julian gasped.

"Shh. I know. It was kind of shocking." Emily smiled, remembering it.

"Well don't forget what we talked about the other day. This town is full of gossips, so you might want to be discreet. Not that there is anything wrong, but if you don't want the whole world to know, be careful."

"You're right." Emily didn't care what people might say about her, but she didn't want anyone to say anything negative about Tom. She knew people had already done plenty of gossiping about him after the accident, speculating on how recklessly he had been driving.

Julian nudged her foot under the table. "Don't look, but here comes that awful Chris Brooks."

Emily casually leaned back and glanced around. She saw Brooks talking with some men at the bar. "He's hanging out at the bar. It doesn't look like he's coming over."

"Good, I don't want to have to try and be polite," Julian said.

"I don't think I have ever seen you be polite when you didn't want to be."

"Very true. I wouldn't put it past him to come over here and ask you all about Tom's accident like he did to me and Mark last time we were here."

"It's really none of his business," Emily said. "I can't stand that man."

Julian leaned forward. "You know, I've been hearing things about Brooks dealing drugs out of his salon."

"Really?" She didn't know Chris Brooks very well, but Tom had done some work on his salon and he had told her that Brooks's behavior was very erratic. Some days he would be very friendly and courteous and other days he would be angry and impossible to please. Tom decided he was too hard to deal with and had tried to avoid working with him after that.

"Like I always say, if you want to know what's going on, ask a stylist. People tell me everything."

Thinking of Kay's drug investigation, she wondered if she should mention the rumor about Chris Brooks to her. Julian probably would be a good source, now that he mentioned it.

"Keep your ears open about my break-in. Maybe someone will know something about it. I would love to find out who did it. I haven't heard anything from the Orleans police."

"I definitely will. This angel is now on the job."

"What's Mark up to today?" she asked, taking a last bite of her breakfast burrito.

"He went to the gym. I'm going to go later. It takes a lot of work to maintain this." He gestured to himself with an exaggerated bow of his head.

"Spare me, please."

They finished their meals and waved to the waitress. On their way out they carefully avoided the bar area and Chris Brooks. Julian gave Emily a hug as they walked over to their cars.

"I'm glad you're doing so well. I would be a mess if someone broke into my house. Call me if you want to talk or if you want to come stay at my place."

"It's made me think about possibly moving to a smaller house. I'm not worried about another break-in, but I don't know if I really want to live there anymore. Too many memories and I really don't need all that space by myself."

"Don't rush into any decisions. You have plenty of time to think it over."

"See you later." She waved to Julian as she got in her truck.

"I'm going to be watching and listening for clues," he exclaimed through his open window as he drove off, radio blasting.

CHAPTER TWELVE

Emily was home in the office looking through the notes in the box of Tom's things when she heard a knock. She went to the door in the kitchen and looked through the window. Kay was standing there. She had sent a message to Emily earlier saying that she would try to come over, so Emily had been expecting her. She opened the door with a smile.

"Hi, hope you don't mind me dropping in on you." Kay grinned at her.

"I'm glad you did, I've been thinking of you all day." Maybe she shouldn't be so obvious. She wasn't sure how this was supposed to work. All she knew is that she couldn't get her mind off Kay.

They walked into the kitchen and Kay leaned back against the counter.

"Can I get you something to drink?" Emily really wanted to touch her but she was suddenly feeling jumpy and her heart was racing again. Her eyes were drawn to Kay's lips.

"No thanks. I just wanted to stop by and see how everything was going." Kay smiled. "Come here for a second."

Telling herself there was nothing to be nervous about, Emily swallowed and took a step toward Kay. She felt Kay's arms slip around her waist, pulling their bodies together. Emily looked into Kay's eyes as she moved closer and their lips met in a kiss. Emily reached up and wrapped her arms around Kay's shoulders, sliding her fingers up the back of her neck and into her silky hair. Kay nibbled on Emily's lower lip, then slid her tongue into her mouth.

Emily felt Kay's solid body pressed up against her own. It was a new sensation for her. She felt the firmness of her muscular arms and shoulders while the softness of her breasts pressed against her. It felt so good that she could hardly breathe.

Kay gently released her and pulled back. "Glad I stopped by."

Emily tried to collect herself. She took a deep breath and smiled back at Kay. "I don't know how you do that to me. I've never had anyone kiss me like that."

"Oh, we're just getting started," Kay said, reaching for her hand. "One step at a time though. I don't want to rush this."

Emily was all for rushing at the moment, but she knew that Kay was right. She wasn't ready to jump into anything too quickly. When they did progress past kissing, she was going to be completely clueless. What if she messed everything up? The thought of it filled her with so much anxiety that she had to push it out of her mind and think about something else.

"Do you want to stay for dinner?"

"Sure, that would be nice. It's been a long weekend. We haven't been able to tie the van that we found to any of the people that we've been keeping an eye on. There's a guy named Kevin Pomerleau who's one of the local bosses. We believe he works with a supplier named Mike Martin from New York. Pomerleau and Martin grew up together here in the Augusta area and we know they keep in touch."

"I haven't heard either of those names," Emily said.

"They stay under the radar, but we've been trying to keep tabs on them for the past six months or so. They have drivers bring drugs up here from New York and we're pretty sure that this was what was going on Saturday when Trooper Williams was killed." Kay sat down at the table.

"Maybe I can find something useful in the data tomorrow."

"That's what I'm hoping, too. Meanwhile, I haven't forgotten that we want to pull those phone records."

Emily smiled. She had been hoping that Kay wouldn't forget about helping her find out more information about Tom's phone.

"How about veggie burgers for dinner? It's a nice night to cook outside. I can throw them on the grill and maybe cut up some potatoes to cook with them."

"That sounds great. What can I do to help?"

"You can set the table. Since you helped me pick up the house the other night, you probably know where everything is. That's one good thing about the break-in."

They worked together companionably, setting the table and preparing the meal. Emily set the plate of burgers down on the table and sat down.

Kay moaned appreciatively as she took a bite of her burger. "This is really good."

Emily's mouth had gone dry at that moan. "Thanks. I make them myself and keep a batch in the freezer."

"I'll have to get your recipe."

"I had brunch with my friend Julian today. I told him about you."

Kay's eyes widened in surprise. "What did you tell him?"

"I told him that you were helping me figure things out with Tom's phone. I also told him that I was intensely attracted to you."

Kay smiled at her. "Intensely attracted, huh?"

"Yes, definitely intensely." Emily slid her chair closer to Kay's.

Kay put her hand over Emily's on the table and stroked her fingers. "You're making it really hard for me to remember why I didn't want to rush."

Emily saw the look in Kay's eyes and she felt a flutter of panic. Changing the subject quickly, she said, "I also wanted to talk to you about tomorrow."

"What about?" Kay asked.

"I was wondering how you felt about having people at work know that we're anything more than friends. I just wanted to know how I should act if I see you in the office."

"It's no reflection on how I feel about you, but I don't think we should let anyone know," Kay said. "I don't think my boss would be happy about it. He is very strict and I wouldn't want it to undermine his view of my professionalism."

"Even though we're in totally separate areas, there would still be talk, especially with the guys I work with," Emily said. "They love to gossip."

"I don't think the guys that I work with would care all that much, but I wouldn't want my boss to hear about it and turn it into an issue."

Emily was glad that she'd asked. She didn't want to upset Kay by being too affectionate if she saw her at work. Now she also knew that it wouldn't hurt Kay's feelings or insult her somehow if she didn't broadcast their relationship to her coworkers.

They finished dinner and Kay helped Emily pick up the kitchen. Emily rinsed off the dishes and put them in the dishwasher while Kay cleared the table.

"You're a good cook," Kay said.

"That's sweet of you to say, but I really only have a few dishes that I'm good at. I have to say that it's nice to cook for someone who doesn't eat meat."

* * *

Once the kitchen was clean, Kay followed Emily into the living room. She knew she should get going soon, but she wasn't quite ready to leave. Emily sat on the couch and Kay took the seat next to her. They sat together quietly for a moment.

Emily shifted to face Kay and rested her elbow on the back of the couch. "Softball practice starts next weekend and then we have a game the week after, if you're still interested."

"Of course I am. In fact, I can't wait to impress the coach." Kay looked into her eyes.

"Believe me, you won't have to do much to impress the coach. Our team is pretty terrible." Emily tapped her fingers on her leg restlessly and kept talking. "We have a few decent hitters, but no good outfielders at all. A couple of the guys' wives play so that we can keep the co-ed quota, and they're much better than their husbands."

"Emily, how about I impress you right now?" Kay leaned in and started placing light kisses on her mouth. She could tell that Emily was nervous and she wanted her to relax. Kay kissed her way over to Emily's ear and whispered, "Do you think I'll make your team?"

Emily gasped and turned toward Kay's lips. She kissed Kay back, running her hands down her arms and tracing her muscular biceps.

"I think you might be a power hitter," she said softly to Kay. "We'll definitely have a place for you in the lineup."

Kay laughed. She ran her hand softly along Emily's side, up and over her breasts to her neck and stopping at her cheek. "You are so lovely, I could just sit here with you all night."

Emily looked into her eyes with a smile. "I love listening to your voice, Kay."

Kay liked hearing Emily say her name. She had a way of saying it that made it sound special. She really needed to be careful that she didn't get in over her head here.

Kay reluctantly sat up. "I probably should go. I know you get up as early as I do and we both have a lot going on tomorrow."

Emily squeezed her hand. "I'm not going to keep letting you off the hook so easily."

Kay looked at her with concern. "I hope you know that it's not that I want to leave. I don't want to push you into something that you aren't ready for. I think you're wonderful and I love spending time with you. I'm just not sure that you are ready to jump from a long-term marriage with a man into something with me."

"I appreciate that, I really do," Emily said. "But this feels right to me. I'm not being pushed into anything. I have never felt like this with anyone before. I've lived long enough to know what I want and what I don't want. I'm not fragile and you don't need to worry."

Kay was reassured to hear that, but she still planned to take her time. She didn't want to open herself up to heartbreak if Emily were to change her mind.

Emily continued to hold Kay's hand in hers. "I want to explain something to you. Remember how I told you that back in college I was starting to feel attracted to women, then I met Tom and we got married?"

"Yes." Kay nodded.

"Well, it really wasn't that simple. I mean, those are the basic facts, but there were things that led up to Tom and I getting together and staying together like we did. Some events in our lives can have consequences that affect everything else that happens to us, even if we don't realize it at the time."

"You mean like fate?"

"Not really. I guess some people might believe in fate, but I don't think that things that happen are predestined. Life is all about the choices we make. What I'm trying to explain is that sometimes I look back at the big events that took place in my life and I think of the path that my life has taken as a consequence of some of these events."

Emily explained. "When I was on Christmas break from college my senior year, I had just started dating Tom. I drove up to meet him to go skiing at Sugarloaf. I was pretty young and I was stupid enough to stop and ask for directions from a stranger at night. I ended up getting attacked by the guy, and then I got away."

"My God, Emily," Kay said softly.

Emily nodded. "It was one of those events that I was talking about. It was just a short encounter in my life but it had a major impact. One of the consequences was that I really lost my confidence and Tom was there for me. We never talked about it, but there was a time that I really relied on him and he never let me down. I would never have wanted to let him down either, even though I often wondered how well we were actually suited for each other. Do you know what I mean?"

"Yes. I think I can understand how you got married when you were so young."

"Exactly. I have no regrets. Tom and I had a lot of happy times. I was lucky enough to have my two sons as another consequence.

"The reason that I'm telling you all of this is that I want you to understand that I am not experimenting with you or playing some sort of game. I'm finally going for what I really want. I know what I'm doing. Well, I don't completely know what I'm doing, but I know that I want to be with you and it's not just some passing fancy that I'm having."

Kay was touched by Emily's story and the fact that she trusted her enough to tell her. She realized that the perception she had been having of Emily's life and marriage was not entirely accurate. People's lives were always a lot more complicated than they looked to others from the outside. She had been judging Emily and thinking that this might be her way of experimenting with having a relationship with a woman, but it really wasn't as simple as that.

Kay squeezed Emily's hand. "Thank you for telling me all that. It helps me understand where you're coming from. Did they ever catch the guy who attacked you?"

"No, I never heard another thing about it. Records weren't kept as well then as they are today. I suppose it could be a possible data project for me someday."

They sat quietly for a little while, and then Emily stood up and held out her hand to pull Kay up. "It's getting really late, I didn't mean to keep you so long."

"I guess I'd better get going," Kay said. "Thank you for dinner and for trusting me with your story."

They walked to the door and shared a soft kiss before Kay stepped outside. She smiled as she slid into her car and looked back to see Emily wave to her through the window.

CHAPTER THIRTEEN

Requests for information had started coming in to the SBI office over the weekend and they continued to be overrun with them throughout the week. The slain trooper's killer had still not been caught and the state police were doing everything they could to try and track him down. Emily's boss had asked her and Sam to concentrate on working with the detectives that were focused on the investigation. Emily looked up from her desk to see Sam standing in her doorway. He stared intently at a spot over her shoulder, avoiding eye contact.

"What's up, Sam?"

"I set up some jobs to look through the driving records database and I wanted to run it against some federal data. Can you help me set up the connection?"

Emily was surprised that Sam had come to her with this. Like most of the men she worked with, he was usually unwilling to ask for help, especially from a woman. Alex must have told him to. Sam was a young guy and seemed to be good at writing code, but his social skills were lacking. He had an annoying habit of pointing out problems whenever she talked to him. He was probably just insecure, so she tried to be patient.

"Sure, I'll show you how I do it." She closed the screen that she was working on and opened a new one. She called up the connection information and pointed to the lines that Sam would need. "You're going to need to do this."

As she explained the login information to Sam, she couldn't help but notice that he smelled like he hadn't had a shower that day. There were little bits of popcorn caught in his collar. After he left, she started thinking about what might be the best way to track down information about the shooter's abandoned car. Sam had given her an idea.

* * *

Kay sat back in her chair, rolled her stiff shoulders, and stretched her neck. She had been glued to her desk all day, sifting through the tips that had been coming in and trying to find a lead on a connection to the trooper's shooting and the Pomerleau drug ring.

Her mind drifted to thoughts of Emily, wondering what she was doing. She had been working late and had been too busy to see Emily since the weekend. They had been sending each other texts and had found time to call each other in the evening, but she really wanted to go over to Emily's office and visit her. It was going to be hard to act like they were just business associates when she saw her in public.

She kept thinking about how sweet it had been to kiss Emily and how comfortable she felt being around her. She had never been so distracted like this by another person. She kept reminding herself that it wouldn't be smart to get carried away too quickly. She didn't want to act foolishly. But she couldn't help wondering if Emily was thinking about her and feeling this surprising connection, too.

Kay forced her mind back to her work. She was picking up the phone to check in with Pete when she remembered her promise to try and track down Tom's cell phone records. It had been so busy this week that she had almost forgotten, and she wanted to do it as discreetly as possible. Kay found it hard to believe that anyone connected with the state police had been involved in the break-in at Emily's but it was too coincidental for her comfort that the phone had been stolen right after it had been returned.

Kay called her friend Terry, a fellow detective that she used to work with at her old unit in Portland. She gave her Tom's number and asked her to run a report on all calls and messages for the month leading up to his accident.

Terry promised to run it that week and told her she would email her the results as soon as she got them.

"Thanks Terry. I appreciate it," Kay said.

"How are things in Augusta? Any breaks on the shooting?" Terry asked.

"Lots of leads."

"Well, good luck. I'll be in touch soon. We should get together some weekend."

"Sounds good, I'd love to come down." Kay hung up. She wondered if Emily might like to go with her to Portland some time. There she went again, thinking about Emily. She tried to put her mind back on her work as she dialed Pete's number to check in with him.

Kay had been assigned as Pete's partner when she transferred to Augusta last year. So far, they had worked well together. Pete was an army vet and had done two tours in Afghanistan. He was outgoing and had a fun-loving, macho attitude. At first she had been worried that he might be a male chauvinist and that their personalities would clash, but she had found him to be a very tolerant and open-minded person.

"Hey Pete, where are you?" she asked.

"I'm downtown, trying to find one of my contacts."

"Did you have any luck tracking down Pomerleau's brother?"

Kay and her partner had spent the last several months working with the Maine DEA on their investigation into the drug ring that Kevin Pomerleau was running in the Augusta area. It was the Major Crimes Unit's goal to link Pomerleau with the violent crimes that they suspected his group was responsible for in the area. Pomerleau himself had proven difficult to track. He owned a large compound on a local lake in Rome and was seldom seen in public. They knew that Pomerleau had several family members who were working for him. Rumor had it that his younger brother, Troy, was a hothead and that he was a heroin user himself. Pete had been investigating all the local connections and was convinced that getting to Troy would lead them to information that they could use against Kevin Pomerleau.

"I've got some leads on it. A few of my contacts were telling me that Troy left town in a hurry and went to some camp they have up north. I'm trying to find out more information on an exact location."

"That sounds interesting," Kay said. "Maybe he knows something and he's hiding out. I'll see if I can find property listings for anything that the family might have up north."

"I'll keep checking with people around town. I'd really like to find out where he might be," Pete replied. "Have you had any luck with any of the tips that have come in?"

"A lot of people have called in, but so far there isn't any new information. At this point we really don't have anything that ties the van to Pomerleau or Martin, other than the fact that it was in this area."

Kay could hear Pete's car pull over and come to a stop.

"They're the main suspects in my mind, but we still need some evidence," Pete said. "That's why I really want to find out where Troy Pomerleau is and see why he left town."

"I'll get started on the property search. I think I'll get in touch with someone I've been working with at the SBI office and see if she can help us. That might speed things up." Kay hung up the phone. Time to check in with Emily.

* * *

The day had flown by before Emily had a chance to call Kay. She was hoping to have some good data for her and she was just wrapping up a report when she heard a knock on her doorway and looked up. She couldn't keep the happy smile from lighting up her face when she saw Kay standing there.

"Hi, Emily," Kay said softly.

"Hi yourself. Come on in." Emily walked over and shut the door, turning to face Kay. "I was just…"

Kay slipped her hand around Emily's waist and drew her toward her. "I've been thinking about you." She gave Emily a kiss and pulled her closer.

Emily breathed in Kay's scent and relaxed in her arms for a moment. She stepped back so she could tell her about the reports she was running. "I was just going to call you. I think I found some information that will be helpful."

"What did you find?"

"Well, you know we've been trying to find out more about who was driving the vehicle. We know who it was registered to but we seemed to hit a dead end when we found out it was stolen?"

"Yes, the VIN matched a New York registration for a van that was reported stolen. It belongs to a plumber who had no ties to Martin and has a legitimate plumbing business in New York. He had reported the van as being stolen a week before it showed up in Maine. The New York police have checked him out pretty carefully."

Emily nodded. "One of my coworkers was looking up some federal data on driving records and it made me think that we might be able to find out more information if we broadened our vehicle search parameters and dug into more federal info. I accessed the federal databases that hold vehicle and personal information and did some analysis on Mike Martin and his family. When I looked into the Martin family, I wanted to find out what businesses or property they owned to see if there were any connections.

"It took a little while to get a list of his relatives and find out where they worked and lived. I found that Martin has an aunt and uncle on his mother's side that own a plumbing supply business in New Jersey. I have a list of the employees that work there. I've been running reports on the employees to see if there's anyone who stands out. I found a couple of possible suspects that have previous convictions for car theft and drug trafficking," Emily said.

"That's exactly what we need to start tying the van to Martin," Kay said excitedly. "Great thinking to look at relatives and businesses."

"I know this doesn't create a strong link yet, but hopefully you can get some more information to tie it together."

"Yes. I'll need to get in touch with the New Jersey police and find out more about this aunt and uncle and their plumbing supply business. We'll need to tie the plumber's stolen van to the business. The plumber sounds like he may be a legitimate customer who was targeted by one of Martin's guys who works for the aunt and uncle."

"That's what I was thinking," Emily said. "Of course we don't know for sure, but hopefully this could at least give you some names to check out."

Kay gave Emily an appreciative smile. "This is great, thanks. I'll start following up on these names."

Emily squeezed her arm. "Let me know what you find out. I can get more information about these guys or others if you find you need it."

"I probably should get back to my office and get working on this." Kay turned to leave. "Oh, wait, I came over here for a reason."

Emily sat down at her desk. She had been hoping that Kay had stopped by because she wanted to see her.

Kay sat in the chair next to Emily's desk. "We're trying to locate Kevin Pomerleau's brother, Troy. We think he left town after the shooting and we want to question him. I was hoping that you might be able to help me get a list of property that the Pomerleau family owns up north."

"Oh, okay, I can do that. Do you have a list of names that you want me to look for specifically or should I put together a list of relatives? I'll be able search for property tax records and motor vehicle records and get some addresses."

Emily opened a screen and they created a list of names and areas that Kay wanted to check. Emily was struck once again by how comfortably they worked together. She turned to look at Kay, who was studying the data on the screen. Their faces were inches apart and Emily couldn't resist leaning closer and brushing her lips against Kay's.

Suddenly, Emily's door swung open and Sam peered into the room. "Uh, Emily, I was just looking for you."

Emily jumped back guiltily. "Maybe you should try knocking. I'm meeting with someone right now." She was completely flustered and irritated that Sam may have seen her kiss Kay. Knowing him, he would be sure to tell someone.

"Uh, okay, I'll come back." Sam backed out of the room, leaving the door open.

"Sorry about that," Emily said, conscious of the fact that Kay wanted to keep their relationship private at the office. Hopefully Kay wasn't upset, but she had hadn't meant for Sam to see anything. Meanwhile, Emily didn't want Kay to leave. She had been meaning to ask her if she wanted to go to trivia with her and meet Julian. "Do you want to get some dinner later?"

Kay stood up abruptly. "I would, but I really need to get going on this Martin lead you gave me. I'll probably be working pretty late tonight."

"All right." Emily looked at Kay who was clearly anxious to leave. "Well, I'll let you know as soon as I get a property list together for the Pomerleaus."

"Thanks, I appreciate your help."

"You know I'm happy to help you any time." Emily was careful to keep her hands to herself in case anyone might walk by. She wanted to kiss Kay again, but suddenly it all felt too awkward.

Kay walked to the door. "I guess I'll talk to you later."

Emily didn't want her to go. "Bye."

Emily watched Kay walk away down the hall. She had acted very cool to her after Sam had seen them. Was she feeling some regret for having gotten involved with someone from work? She knew that Kay was not one for staying in relationships.

She'd probably had her choice of women all her life. She had wondered why Kay was attracted to her in the first place. Maybe she was having second thoughts.

* * *

Kay passed Sam as she walked down the hall to the entrance. He was staring at his computer and glanced up nervously as she walked by. She considered Emily's reaction to Sam seeing them kiss as she walked to her car. Kay knew that she had told Emily that she didn't want anything getting back to her boss, but Emily seemed awfully embarrassed about having someone see them together. Emily may have told her friend Julian about them, but it appeared that she still wasn't ready for the world to know.

Maybe Emily had simply been worried about protecting her from having her coworkers become aware of their relationship. It still hurt though, to think that Emily might be ashamed to have people know that they were together. She knew that part of it was that it hadn't been very long since her husband's death. She couldn't help but worry that Emily might be having some regrets.

CHAPTER FOURTEEN

Emily was busy refining the Pomerleau property list the next morning when her phone rang. "Hello, this is Emily."

"This is Trooper Johnson with the crash reconstruction unit. We have completed our investigation of your husband's accident that took place last January and we would like to go over the results with you. Is there a particular time that you would be available?"

"Yes. I'd like to hear your results as soon as possible. Can I come over today?"

"Certainly, would you like to stop by this morning at eleven?"

"That would be fine."

The office was located in the same building as Kay's. That would give her a chance to see if she could go by and bring Kay her report at the same time.

Emily called Kay to let her know she was coming. She wasn't sure if Kay would be in or if she might not appreciate having Emily intrude at her office. They hadn't spoken since the previous afternoon and Emily was a little worried that Kay was upset with her about their encounter with Sam.

* * *

Kay was busy writing up a report when her cell phone rang. She looked at the screen and saw that it was Emily. "Hello, there."

"Hi, Kay, it's Emily. I have the list of properties for you and I was wondering if I could bring it over to your office?"

Kay found herself feeling a surprising rush of happiness at hearing Emily's voice. Try as she might to stop herself from caring too much, she couldn't help but want to see her.

"That would be great, thank you," Kay said. "You know where my office is. Just call when you get here and I'll come out front and sign you in."

A text from Emily showed up on her phone a short time later, letting Kay know that she had arrived at the barracks and was waiting in the reception area. Kay walked out to meet her at the front desk. The receptionist turned back to her work after handing Emily a visitor's pass.

"Thanks for bringing this over," Kay said.

"I emailed you a copy, which will probably be more useful. I did want to go over the results with you, though. And I also just wanted to see you." Emily stared into Kay's blue eyes.

Kay looked back at her with a pleased smile. "My office is this way."

She led Emily into a large area filled with several rows of cubicles. There was a general hum of activity from the various officers and agents talking on the phone and working on their computers.

They walked along a hallway and around a corner to Kay's section. Her desk was piled with tidy stacks of folders. There weren't any pictures on display, but there was a quote from Buddha on her desk, *"Have compassion for all beings, rich and poor alike; each has their suffering. Some suffer too much, others too little."*

Kay sat at her desk and gestured to the chair beside her. "Have a seat. I'm envious of your office and how you have your own private space. It's not very quiet here."

Emily sat down. She spoke softly so that no one would overhear. "About that. I'm sorry that Sam came barging in yesterday. I know you don't want anything to get back to your boss. Hopefully Sam didn't even notice anything, but if he did, I'm really sorry."

"Well, I thought that maybe I had embarrassed you in front of one of your colleagues."

"God, no. I think you misinterpreted. I have no reason to care what Sam thinks about me personally. I was just worried that you would be upset about it."

Kay felt a wave of relief. She had been wrong to believe that Emily was embarrassed. She had decided long ago that she was proud of the way she lived her life and it had hurt to think that Emily might be feeling regretful or ashamed.

Emily touched her knee. "Hey, I would never be ashamed or embarrassed about being with you. If anything, I'm going to have to be careful that being around you isn't going to make me too conceited. You're incredible looking."

Kay was surprised by how much she cared about what Emily had just said. She cleared her throat. "I really wish we were somewhere a little more private right now."

Emily's face relaxed into a smile. She opened the folder with the property list. "Okay, back to work. There are a bunch of properties in this area and further south, but there aren't that many up north."

They went through the list and found two potential northern locations that Troy Pomerleau might have gone to. One was near Moosehead Lake, which was about three hours north from them. The other was closer to Canada in Jackman, Maine.

"I need to get these to Pete. Hold on for a minute while I check to see if he's here." Kay picked up her phone and dialed Pete's number.

Pete answered, "What's up?"

"Hey, I've got some addresses that you'll want to see. Are you in the office?"

"Sure am. I'll be right there."

Kay hung up and swung her chair back to face Emily just as Pete came around the corner. His size was intimidating, but his friendly eyes and open smile made him a lot less formidable. Emily stood up and Kay introduced them.

Emily offered her hand to Pete. "Pleased to meet you. My name is Emily and I work in the SBI office."

Pete shook her hand. "Thanks for helping us out with this. I know there's usually a longer wait for data and this could give us a real break."

"Kay's a good friend of mine and I'm happy to help." Emily smiled at Kay.

Pete glanced back at Kay and gave her the thumbs-up gesture behind Emily. Kay wasn't sure what to think. Was he noticing a vibe between them or just happy about the data?

Kay spoke up quickly to cover her tension. "Here are two family-owned properties that turned up. One in Greenville and one in Jackman."

Pete nodded enthusiastically. "The Greenville address could tie in with some of the talk that I've been hearing. From what I have been able to find out, the family has a cabin at Moosehead that's pretty private. I'll check with my contacts up there and see if we can locate the place and check it out discreetly. If they see signs that anyone's around, then I want to go up."

"The locals should be able to put the camp under some level of surveillance," Kay said. "Just make sure they don't tip Troy off if he is there."

"I'm going to make a few calls. Looks like we might be headed to Greenville this afternoon, Kay," Pete said.

"Sounds good," she answered.

"Thanks again, Emily. Nice meeting you." Pete hurried off to make his calls.

Kay turned to Emily. "We're waiting to hear back from the New York police. They're looking for the two men that you identified. According to the contacts that the detectives from New York have spoken to, the men's names both came back as known associates of Martin. They're working on tracking each of them down. We need to find out if they left the area and possibly travelled to Maine.

"One of those two men could be the shooter. Their prints are on file and we're hoping something turns up in the van that can be used to link them. The van was stripped down, but you never know."

"I'm glad to hear that you're making some good progress on the case," Emily said. She glanced at her phone. "I need to make another stop while I'm over here."

"For what?" Kay asked.

"I got a call from the crash reconstruction unit and I spoke with Trooper Johnson. Do you know him?"

"No, I don't. Is the report finally ready?"

"Yes. I'm going to go review it with him in a few minutes."

Kay was concerned. She knew that Emily had been waiting for months to find out what had happened to cause Tom's accident. Now she was going to have to relive the whole thing again.

"Listen, I'd be happy to go with you. It might be helpful to have someone with you to ask questions and help keep track of everything they tell you. Of course, if you would prefer to do this privately, I completely understand."

"I would love to have you come with me. I know you're really busy and I didn't want to ask, but I would love to have the support. I'm dreading hearing the report."

* * *

Together they went to the section of the building where Emily was supposed to meet Trooper Johnson. Emily was happy to have Kay with her as she gave her name to the receptionist. Johnson came out to meet her a few minutes later and she introduced Kay. "This is Detective DeLorme. She's a friend of mine and I wanted her to hear the report as well."

Johnson shook their hands and escorted them into a conference room. Emily sat down nervously. She steeled herself for the upcoming description. She had thought about the accident every day since it had happened and she still did not believe that Tom would have been speeding. In all the time that they had been married he had always been a good driver. He would not have driven recklessly on slippery roads.

Johnson opened up a laptop that was set up to project a PowerPoint presentation on a screen along one of the walls. He began by displaying a map of the area where the accident had occurred.

"On the day of the accident, road conditions were very icy in Winchester. There had been a fresh snowfall early that morning. We did not find any evidence of alcohol consumption or drug use. All medical tests came back negative."

Emily spoke up. "Tom didn't do drugs and of course he hadn't been drinking. Why would you be thinking that?"

"I didn't mean to upset you, ma'am," Johnson said. "We are required to investigate all possibilities and we had to rule these factors out.

"We spoke with several of Mr. Stratton's associates and determined that he had been in the area visiting a job site on Long Pond. As you can see, the job site is several miles from the accident. We examined the site and found tire tracks in the snow that matched your husband's truck as well as paw prints that would probably have been made by your dog. However, the homeowner who was planning to meet your husband at the site said that he was not there at the time they had been scheduled to meet."

Several photos were displayed, showing the home that was under construction. The photos revealed tire tracks in the driveway as well as in the turnaround area behind the home. Footprints and paw prints were also displayed. Emily's heart ached at the thought of Tom and Sally walking through the snow, unaware of the tragedy ahead.

Johnson resumed his report. "We interviewed people in the area to find out if anyone had seen anything. We did have reports from multiple residents along the route that they had seen a gray pickup truck matching the description of Mr. Stratton's truck being followed closely by a black pickup. The vehicles caught people's attention because of the high rate of speed that they were travelling."

Emily stared at Kay. This was the first she had heard of another vehicle. She listened intently as Johnson spoke.

"This is the location on the North Road where the accident occurred. We determined that the truck was travelling at a rate of approximately 75 miles per hour when it hit a patch of ice on the corner and lost control. The truck left the pavement, then went over the ditch and struck a tree."

Johnson pointed out the corner on the map and displayed photos from the accident scene. The front of Tom's mangled truck was crushed against a large maple tree. The bed of the truck had come to rest on a stone wall that ran along the ditch behind the tree.

Emily couldn't bear to look. The shattered glass and twisted metal made her feel sick to her stomach. She tried to hold back her tears. She felt Kay's hand take hers and squeeze it comfortingly. Emily was praying that Johnson wouldn't show any photos of Sally. She didn't think she could take the sight of her sweet little puppy in the wreckage.

Johnson pulled up a photo of the back of Tom's truck. While the front of the truck had been destroyed, the back was relatively unharmed. Johnson continued to the next view, which showed a closer view of the back driver's side of the truck. There was a clear image of multiple dents along the back panel and the back bumper showed a distinct depression.

Emily realized she needed to stay strong and pay attention. There would be time for her to fall apart later, but she had to find out what happened to Tom and Sally. There was clearly more going on than she had been expecting.

As he showed more views of the dented back panel and bumper, Johnson gave her details. "We have found evidence of black auto paint on the back panel and the back bumper of the truck involved in the crash. It became clear to us during the crash reconstruction that the back of Mr. Stratton's truck was struck multiple times by another vehicle.

"In conclusion, the determination of the investigation is that Mr. Stratton's crash was caused by another vehicle. We believe that another vehicle striking Mr. Stratton's truck caused him to increase his speed and lose control on the icy road."

Emily couldn't believe it. After all these months of having everyone think that Tom had caused the accident with his own carelessness, they now knew that it had been purposely caused by someone else and was no accident at all. Why would anyone want to run Tom off the road? Her first thought was that she was going to have to tell Ben and Ethan that their father's crash was not his fault. Would that bring them any comfort or would the thought that someone caused his death make them suffer even more?

Kay spoke up. "Have you been able to identify the type of auto from the paint?"

"This particular paint comes from pickup trucks manufactured by Ford. At this time, we are looking for a Ford pickup truck. Unfortunately, we have not been able to track it down."

Emily listened to Kay asking a few more questions while she thought about what she should do next. She was going to do whatever she could to find the driver of that truck.

CHAPTER FIFTEEN

Emily's brain was overloaded by all the questions she had racing through her mind. She and Kay had thanked Trooper Johnson and walked outside after they finished talking. They were sitting together in Emily's truck in the parking area next to the office building.

"I'm not sure what I should do next," Emily said. "I need to find out who did this to Tom."

"I think the break-in at your house and Tom's missing cell phone have to be related. Johnson gave me the name of the homeowner that Tom was supposed to be meeting that day. We should start there and see if we can find out what he was doing there and why he left."

Emily looked at Kay. "You're going to help me?"

"Of course I am. I have to go to Greenville this afternoon, as you know, but once I get back I'm going to make sure that our unit starts looking into Tom's death. I'll talk to my sergeant as soon as I go back inside."

"I know this is going to hurt the boys. I wish I didn't have to tell them. At least they'll know that the accident wasn't Tom's fault."

Kay reached over and held her hand. "I'm waiting to hear back on the records from the cell phone. I called a friend of mine and she should be getting back to me any day now. I wish I wasn't so busy with the Pomerleau case, but I'm going to help you as soon as I can."

Emily wrapped their fingers together and looked at Kay. "Thank you for helping me. It means a lot. You'd better get back inside. Pete is probably ready to leave for Greenville."

"I'm aching to kiss you right now, but I wouldn't want anyone to see us here." Kay gave Emily a quick hug. "It will probably be pretty late when I get back. I'll call you tomorrow and we can start figuring out a plan."

Emily sat in her car and watched Kay go back inside the building. She picked up her phone and dialed Ben's number. It was time to break the news to him and Ethan.

Ben's phone went to voice mail, so Emily left a message for him to give her a call. Next she dialed Ethan's number in Boston.

"Hi, Mom," he answered.

"Hi, sweetie," Emily said. "How are you doing today? I hope I'm not bothering you at work."

"'Course not. Is anything wrong?"

"I wanted to let you know that the accident report is back from Dad's crash." Emily took a deep breath and continued. "It's really hard to tell you this Ethan, but you need to know that the police have determined that the crash wasn't an accident. There is evidence that another truck ran your father off the road."

"What? This is crazy. Why would anyone do that?"

Emily could hear Ethan struggling for composure and instantly regretted calling him in the middle of the day. She should have waited until he got home. He would have been upset with her for not telling him immediately, but she still should have waited.

"I'm sorry sweetheart, I just don't know, and I can't think of any reasons why it happened. My friend Detective DeLorme, the one you met, is going to help get an investigation started and try to find out some answers."

"I feel like I should come home and do something."

Knowing that Ethan would want to find out who did it as much as she did, she said, "There really isn't much you can do right this minute. Once they start the investigation, I'm hoping that there might be something for us to actually do, although I'm not sure what it would be."

"It's kind of a relief that it wasn't his fault, you know," Ethan said. "But on the other hand, now it's worse because someone took him away from us."

* * *

Kay went directly to Pete's desk. "When do you want to head up north?"

Pete looked up. "I got in touch with the Greenville PD. They called me back and let me know that there is definitely someone staying at the camp. I also got in touch with Troop C and they are sending over some troopers to help keep an eye on the place until we get there. I just need to make a couple more phone calls, then I'll be ready."

"Sounds good. I have to check with the Sergeant and then I'll be ready."

Kay went to her desk, answered a couple emails and then shut down her laptop. Before meeting with Pete she wanted to talk to her boss like she had told Emily she would. Sergeant Hixon had always been tough but fair in her dealings with him, so she was hoping he would agree to let her investigate Tom Stratton's crash. She knocked on his door.

"Come in DeLorme," Hixon said.

"Sir, I wanted to talk to you about a homicide that has been brought to my attention."

Hixon looked up from the paperwork he was reading with his usual stern expression. He took his glasses off and put them on top of the open folder on his desk. Running a hand across his gray crew cut, he asked, "Is this related to the Pomerleau investigation?"

"It's related to recent results from a crash investigation. One of the SBI data analysts that I have been working with lost her husband in a car crash several months ago. The reconstruction unit came back today with a finding of vehicular homicide. Apparently another truck forced him off the road."

"I see," Hixon replied. "This sounds like something that we do need to look into. I would certainly approve opening up a case."

Kay nodded. "I would like to be assigned to it. We're working some good leads on the other cases, but I think that Harris and I could fit this one in, too."

"Trooper Williams's shooting takes top precedence, as you know. If you think that you'll have time to manage that and still be able to handle this crash case effectively, then I will support you on it."

"Thank you, sir." Kay nodded and headed back to Pete's desk.

She considered the possible details that could be checked out once they started looking into Tom's crash. The first thing she planned to do was contact the homeowner of the project Tom was working on and go see the building site. She wished she didn't have to make the trip to Greenville, but she wouldn't want to say that to Pete. She returned to Pete's desk to find him ready to go.

Kay walked with Pete out to his car. She would have preferred to drive, but if they took his car, she would hopefully have time to follow up with the New York police and see if they had any more information on their suspects. They got in the car and headed for the northbound highway.

"I was just talking to Hixon about a vehicular homicide case," she said.

"Whose case is it?"

"Ours."

"Are you serious?" Pete asked. "How are we going to have time for another case with all the time we need to put into tracking down Pomerleau and Martin?"

"I'm sure we can fit it in. You know Emily Stratton who I introduced you to?"

"The SBI lady?"

"Right. It was her husband. He got killed in a car accident last January."

"Wow, she didn't look like a married lady. I thought she might have been a friend of yours."

Kay glared at him. "What is that supposed to mean?"

He gave her a grin. "Hey, no offense. I thought she was very cute and seemed nice and all. I just thought by the way she looked at you that maybe she was your girlfriend. Sorry, I may have misjudged, but I usually have pretty good insight on these things."

Kay was so surprised by what Pete was saying that she didn't know how to respond. "I have no idea what you're talking about."

Pete laughed. "Oh really? You think I might not have noticed that you prefer women? Come on, I'm your partner. It's not like you have to hide it from me. I tell you all about my girlfriends."

"Well, all right then. I'll be sure to let you know."

"All right yourself. Now, tell me about this crash that we're going to be investigating."

"Someone ran Tom Stratton off the road. There were paint traces from another truck ramming the back of his pickup. Last week his cell phone was returned to Emily and someone stole it from her house a couple days later."

Pete raised his eyebrows. "Hmm, interesting. It could be tough to track anyone down after all this time, but maybe we'll get lucky once we start looking."

They continued on their way up to Greenville.

* * *

Emily had decided to take the afternoon off. She had too much on her mind to be able to concentrate on work. She let Alex know and headed home. Once she got home she decided to go for a run to try and organize her thoughts. It was a warm, sunny day. Perfect weather to be outside. She and Tom had both loved to go running on days like this. She hadn't gone running since he died, but today seemed like a good day to start. She changed into shorts and a T-shirt and headed out the door.

She headed down the trails in the woods near the house. It felt good to be out in the fresh air. Some of the tension left her body as she made her way down the path. Memories of the many times she and Tom had taken Sally down this path filled her thoughts. Tom had taken Sally out for a five-mile run almost every evening in the summer and fall. When she went with them, Emily usually couldn't keep up and met them back at the house. She thought about how tough Tom had been. He never gave up on things. He was dedicated to running and never got lazy about it. He didn't care if it was too hot or he had other things to do. He was a good person and he was dedicated to her and the boys. She wasn't going to give up on finding out who killed him. They may not have had the perfect marriage, but she would always love him in her own way. He deserved justice and so did their sons.

A half hour later Emily jogged back up her driveway. She was gasping for breath. Her lungs ached and her legs would probably be sore the next day, but she felt energized and ready to face the challenges ahead. She was trying to think of ways to find out more about what had happened to Tom that day. Kay was going to help her, but she wasn't going to leave it all up to someone else. Like Kay had said, they needed to go the job site and talk to the person that Tom had been working for. They also needed to get the phone records and see if there had been any calls that day that might have been made after he saw something.

The only thing that made sense was that Tom had seen something illegal and someone had tried to stop him from reporting it. He and Sally had been at the job site that morning. Was it something they saw there? Or had he seen something on another day and someone had come looking for him and found him there? Maybe one of the neighbors had seen someone else at the site.

Emily walked into the kitchen and contemplated the various possibilities. She washed her face then filled a glass of water and took a big drink before sitting at the table and checking her phone. She had missed a call from Ben. She wanted to put off calling him. It was so hard to break this to him, but she knew he would want her to tell him right away. She dialed his number.

"Hi, Mom," Ben answered. "I talked to Ethan and he told me about Dad."

"Oh, sweetie, I'm so sorry. I found out earlier and tried to call you."

"I know. It's all right. I wish I could have gone to hear what the accident reconstruction people said."

"I have a copy of the report. Why don't you and Ethan come over this weekend and we can look at it together."

"Yeah, I think I'd like to do that. I just can't believe that anyone would want to hurt Dad, though. Why?"

"That's what we all want to know. Did Ethan tell you that Detective DeLorme is going to be helping us with the investigation? Do you remember her?"

"Yes, I remember her. That's good," Ben said. "I want to do something, too."

"I know. I'm just not sure what we can do right now. Maybe we can go over some ideas this weekend."

"All right. I'll talk to Ethan and we'll make plans to come up on Sunday. Would that be good?"

Emily wished she could be with him and give him a hug. "That would be great. I can't wait to see you guys. I'll probably check in with you again before then, but please call me if you want to talk about anything. I love you."

"I love you, too."

Emily realized she was going to have to let her family and Tom's family know about the report. She tried to think of anyone else she should call. If word got around town about the cause of the crash it might remind someone who lived along that road about it. Maybe someone had seen something and would come forward.

She decided that she would give Julian a call. That was one way to get the word out. He might be busy with a client, but she figured she'd try calling.

"Hello, butterfly," Julian answered.

"Hi, are you in between clients?"

"Yes, I have a nice little break for a few minutes. What are you doing? Come see me and bring me a coffee."

"Sorry, I can't right now. Want to get a bite to eat later?"

"You know I'm always up for a night of trivia. Meet me at six thirty?"

"See you then," she answered. "Bye."

CHAPTER SIXTEEN

Kay had been trying to reach her contact with the New York police during the drive up to Greenville. She'd left messages with the detective that she had spoken to earlier. Phone service was not reliable in the wooded areas that they were driving through, but she was hoping she would be able to speak with him. They were still about an hour away from Greenville when she saw that her phone had service and she had a message. She listened to it and turned to Pete.

"I heard back from the detective I've been working with in New York. The two men that turned up in Emily's report from the plumbing supply business are nowhere to be found. We know they worked for Martin's aunt and uncle in New Jersey and that the van used in the shooting was stolen from a plumber who was one of their customers. The two men are John MacNamara and Nathan Jackson and they both have prior records.

"The New York detective left a message saying that they verified that the two were known to have worked with Martin. It sounds like they're good candidates to have been the drivers of the van. They most likely were on a run delivering drugs. The New York police have checked on their home addresses and contacted family members and no one has seen them since last week."

Kay punched a number into her phone. "I'm going to call Hixon and the MDEA and let them know. We need to put out an APB for MacNamara and Jackson."

Kay and Pete arrived in Greenville and stopped by the local police department. They planned to get out to the Pomerleau's camp as soon as possible but wanted to make sure that they went to the right location. There were many seasonal roads in the area and their directions weren't clear. They went inside the small building that was located in the center of town. The police chief was waiting for them.

"Hello, I'm Chief Fortin."

"Hello, Chief, I'm Detective DeLorme." Kay shook his hand.

"Detective Harris," Pete said, shaking the chief's hand.

"I understand that you are trying to locate a suspect that you believe may be hiding out at a camp on Lily Bay Road?"

"Yes. We've been investigating last week's shooting death of Trooper Williams. We have reason to believe that this suspect may have information and we want to bring him in for questioning," Kay said.

"I know where the property is located. I drove by when you called earlier. There was a vehicle in the driveway. I could lead you out there and stay back while you go in, if you like."

"We'd appreciate that. Thank you," Pete said.

They got back into Pete's car and followed Chief Fortin through town and out to one of the main roads that ran along the east side of the lake. Several gravel roads branched off as they drove along and Kay was glad that Chief Fortin was guiding them. Pete radioed the troopers that were maintaining surveillance on the camp to let them know they were on their way.

"Detective Harris here. Have you seen signs of anyone at the property?" he asked.

"We've been here for about three hours and haven't seen much of anything," the trooper on the radio answered.

"We should be there in a few minutes," Pete said.

They took a left off the main road and followed the chief down a wooded gravel side road. The thick forest of pine trees blocked the view of any buildings. They drove slowly down the rutted road for another mile before they caught site of a state police car pulled over toward the ditch near a small driveway.

The camp wasn't visible from the road, so they would not be noticed by anyone inside. Pete pulled up behind the troopers' car and they got out. The chief had parked a little further back behind them. He got out of his car and closed the door quietly before joining Kay and Pete. They walked over to the troopers who were standing next to their car.

Kay nodded to the men. "I'm going to take the front door and Harris is going to go around back," she said softly. "You two come behind us and keep us covered. Chief, please stay here and keep an eye on the driveway. We don't want anyone slipping away."

The men nodded in agreement. Kay pulled out her weapon and started down the winding driveway. She and Pete had both put on their bulletproof vests. If Troy was involved with the men that had shot the trooper, they had to be very careful.

They walked around a corner and the camp came into view. A red Jeep Cherokee was parked in the driveway near the door. The camp was small, with two windows in the front and a single step leading to the front door. The back of the camp faced the lake. She could see a dock protruding from the rocky shoreline. She walked quietly toward the front door and stepped to the side of it. Pete crept along the brush and trees that ran along the building and made his way to the back.

After giving Pete a few minutes to get in place, Kay rapped on the door. "Maine State Police, open up."

She didn't hear any sounds from inside the camp. Dozens of discarded cigarette butts were lying on the ground near the steps. She knocked again. "Maine State Police. We're coming in."

The knob turned with no resistance when she reached out and tried it. She picked up her radio to let the others know. "No answer from inside the camp. The door is unlocked and I am proceeding to enter."

She carefully turned the knob and pushed the door open gently, staying back to the side. There was still no response from inside, so she swung into the doorway with her handgun raised. The camp was a smelly mess. The layout consisted of one large room with a bathroom on the first floor and a sleeping loft upstairs. There were beer bottles and cigarette butts strewn all around. Trash littered the floor in the living room area.

Pete entered through the back door. She pointed to the left-hand side of the room. The bodies of two men lay slumped over on each end of the grimy couch. They had both been shot in the forehead and were clearly dead. Used hypodermic needles were scattered on the coffee table in front of the couch. Kay and Pete put on gloves and proceeded to look around cautiously. It didn't take long to determine that there was no one else in the camp.

"Pete, is one of those men Troy Pomerleau?" Kay asked.

"No. I've never seen either of them."

"We may have just found MacNamara and Jackson. We've got to find out if Troy was here. Do you know if that's his car outside?"

"I've seen him driving one just like that around Augusta and Orleans. We'll have to check the registration, but I bet it's his."

They went outside to secure the scene and speak with the troopers and the chief. Kay filled them in on what they had found in the camp. Pete called for backup and requested the Evidence Response Team.

The first of many questions that they needed answers for was the location of Troy Pomerleau. They had to find him. At this point, they had no idea how long the two men had been dead. The troopers assured them that they hadn't seen or heard anything during the time that they had been watching the driveway. The chief said that he had pulled into the driveway just far enough to see the car and then backed out when he had checked earlier in the day. It was possible that someone had seen him.

"If that's his car, how do you suppose he got away?" Pete asked. "Why would he leave his car here?"

"He must have seen the police car," Kay answered.

"They were obviously doing drugs," Pete said. "He certainly wouldn't want to get caught with those two guys if they're the ones we're looking for. He probably shot them and took off. He's not smart enough to think it through and realize we were going to know it was him and come find him."

Kay agreed. "Right. If he thought someone was out here watching, he probably didn't dare drive. The first thing that comes to my mind is that we're here on the lake. What's to stop him from taking a boat somewhere?"

The chief spoke up. "If he took a boat, he probably headed to the boat landing back in town. There are usually plenty of cars around. He may have gotten a ride with someone or stolen a car. I'll send one of my officers to the boat ramp and check on things."

Several hours later, Kay and Pete were finally able to leave the crime scene. The Evidence Response Team was busy processing the scene both in and around the camp. The Jeep did indeed belong to Troy Pomerleau and there was still no sign of him. The two dead men did not have any identification on them. Their fingerprints had been taken and sent to the lab for processing.

The crime scene techs had given Kay photos to send to the New York police in the hope that they could identify them as MacNamara and Jackson. It had been after business hours by the time she sent them, so she wasn't expecting a reply until the next morning.

She and Pete decided to get rooms at the local motel rather than make the three-hour drive home in the middle of the night. They checked in and went to their separate rooms. Kay lay down on the lumpy mattress and tried to sleep. Every time she closed her eyes, her thoughts went to Emily. The news from Tom's accident report must have come as a huge shock. She wished that she could be there to give Emily some support.

It was frustrating that she was going to be so busy working on the Pomerleau case. Hopefully they would be able to track Troy Pomerleau down quickly. If they could identify the two dead men and tie them to the van, it would be a huge break in the case. There was a lot of work to be done to link any of this to Kevin Pomerleau and Mike Martin. In the meantime, she would take whatever extra time she had to help Emily try to get some leads on her husband's case.

Kay had never felt so strongly about someone before. It was a strange sensation for her. She had been in several relationships throughout her life. None had ever lasted more than a year or so and she had never been all that devastated when they ended. Her previous partners had often complained that she was emotionally unavailable. Something she blamed on her job.

This time was different, and she wasn't sure why. She and Emily shared a deeper connection than she had experienced before. They worked well together and had a lot of the same interests. She also felt a major physical attraction to Emily, even though they had only kissed. Judging from Emily's reactions, she was feeling the same. It scared her to put her happiness in someone else's hands. She was afraid she wasn't being cautious enough about the whole thing. She hoped that she wasn't setting up expectations that Emily was never going to be able to meet.

CHAPTER SEVENTEEN

Emily pulled into a parking space outside the pub at six thirty. She saw that Julian's car was already there. She walked in and waved to Julian as she went over to the table. He jumped up and squeezed her in an exaggerated hug. She laughed and slid out of his arms.

"You know that you overhug sometimes," she said.

"I can't help it. I just want to give you a big squeeze."

"You're going to mess up your outfit if you aren't careful," she teased. "You look nice tonight. I like that tie."

Their waitress came over to the table. She always laughed when Julian flirted with her. He stroked her arm and smiled at her. She pulled free and asked, "What can I get you guys?"

"Hi, Debbie," Emily said. "I'll have a Sam Adams Light and Caesar salad with no meat."

"Emily, don't you ever get tired of having the same thing?" Julian asked. "I'll have a margarita and a turkey club."

Their attention turned to the trivia screens as they joined in the next round.

"Name a plant that grows at the North Pole?"

"Lichen," Julian said.

After the round of trivia ended, Debbie brought their meals over and they started eating. Emily finished a bite of salad and turned to Julian. "The accident report came back today and I wanted to tell you about it."

"Finally. Why did it take so long?"

"I'm not sure. The thing is, the report determined that Tom's crash wasn't an accident."

Julian was speechless for a moment. "What? Oh my God."

"Let me explain. You know how I've been saying all along that Tom was a safe driver and it didn't make sense that he was going so fast?"

"Yes."

"It turns out that he was being chased by someone in a black pickup truck. The state police found dents and paint that proved someone rammed into the back of Tom's truck a couple times. That's what caused him to go out of control and off the road."

"Emily, this is mind-boggling. Who on earth would want to hurt Tom? Unlike me, he got along with everyone."

"All I can think of is that he saw something he shouldn't have and someone wanted to make sure he didn't tell anyone."

"This is exactly what we talked about the other day when you told me about the stolen phone," exclaimed Julian.

"Yes, and I think the phone being stolen must be related."

"Do the police have any idea who might have done it?"

"No," Emily replied. "Kay is going to help me open up an investigation."

"I need to meet this woman," Julian declared. "You are getting involved with her and I haven't even gotten a chance to approve. I'm glad she's helping you, of course."

"I want you to meet her. It's just that everything has been happening so fast."

"How are you doing, muffin? This must have blown your mind."

"It did, but the whole thing is making more sense to me now," Emily said. "I never agreed that Tom had been driving recklessly. He certainly wasn't perfect, but he didn't drive like an idiot."

She took a sip of her drink. "This gives me something to focus my anger on. I'm tired of feeling sad and guilty. I want to find out who did this and make them pay."

"I'm all for vengeance," Julian said. "Wait, why do you feel guilty?"

"Because I should have been a better wife. Don't argue. You said it yourself that we didn't always seem like we were all that suited for each other. That was totally my fault."

Julian put his hand on hers. "You were a good wife to Tom. You never gave him any reason to doubt you and you dedicated your life to making him and the boys happy. Neither of you were without your faults, but you didn't do anything wrong."

"Thanks."

Julian sipped his margarita. "I've been keeping on high alert for any gossip about your break-in. I haven't heard anything helpful yet, but I'm listening. If people hear about the accident, maybe someone will have some information for us."

"I'm hoping you do hear something. Right now, we don't really have much to go on."

"I will be back on the case. Jill Munroe, at your service."

"Thanks, Farrah."

* * *

Emily spent the next morning catching up on projects at work. She was hoping to hear from Kay. She wasn't sure if she had made it back from Greenville yet. There had been a sweet text on her phone that Kay had sent during the night. "*I can't sleep because I'm lying here thinking about you. See you tomorrow.*"

A knock drew her attention to the doorway. She looked up and saw Sam standing in the doorway looking down at the floor.

"Hi, Sam. What's up?" She hadn't seen him since the other day when he walked in on her and Kay. Was he going to give her a hard time?

"I wanted to find out about softball. Alex said that practice starts this weekend. I think you were supposed to send information out about it."

"Oh, no. I totally forgot to send an email to everyone."

With everything that had been going on, softball practice had slipped her mind. She needed to send information out to everyone and make sure that they knew about practice the next day.

"Thank you for reminding me, Sam. Do you want to be on the team this year?"

"Yes."

She was surprised. He was short and chubby and very pale. It looked like he didn't spend much time outside. Still, she was always looking for players.

"That's great. We are supposed to meet at the field tomorrow afternoon at two. What position are you?"

"I like to play in the outfield."

"Okay. I'll be sending out an email with the schedule and directions. See you tomorrow afternoon."

Sam disappeared back down the hall. Emily was excited to think that softball started tomorrow. She knew there was a lot going on, but it wouldn't hurt to take a little time out. She hoped Kay wouldn't be too busy. She organized the information and sent an email to everyone. Once that was done, she returned to her work.

Another knock sounded on her doorway. She looked up and saw Kay smiling at her. She jumped up and shut the door and gave her a hug.

"I feel like you've been gone a long time. I missed you." Emily looked into Kay's blue eyes and forgot where she was for a moment.

Emily felt Kay's arms go around her, pulling her closer. Her self-restraint dissolved as their lips met. Emily kissed Kay back hungrily, parting Kay's lips with her tongue and tasting her mouth. She felt light-headed with longing.

Kay slid her hands up Emily's sides and stroked her down to her waist. Emily let out a soft groan as Kay pushed her back against the wall and pressed their bodies together. Kay stepped back with a surprised look on her face. "I didn't mean to get carried away like that."

Emily gave Kay a happy grin. "I guess you missed me, too."

"I did." Kay took a second to catch her breath. "I also wanted to get back and tell you all about what's been going on with the men you identified from New York."

They sat in the chairs next to Emily's desk. Kay described the trip to Greenville and told Emily about finding the two bodies at the camp.

"We stayed over at a motel in Greenville and came home this morning. There's a lot going on and I'm going to be crazy busy, but I wanted to see you for a minute."

"I'm glad you did. Anything I can help with?"

"Not at the moment. We should be hearing back any time now from New York on the photo identification for the two men. Meanwhile we're looking for a match on the dead men's fingerprints with the ones on record for Jackson and MacNamara."

"Any sign of Troy Pomerleau?"

"Not yet. Chief Fortin from Greenville called this morning. They got a report of a stolen car from a house near the boat ramp. People from another house also called because they noticed that someone left a boat tied up to their dock. The crime scene techs are checking out the boat and that will help us put the pieces together against Troy. The guy must smoke like a fiend. He leaves cigarette butts everywhere he goes."

"Has anyone talked to Kevin Pomerleau yet?"

"Pete is headed out to his house now. Troy lives with Kevin, who owns a big place out on Long Pond in Rome. It's very secluded and it's a tough place to keep under surveillance."

"So Troy might be there?" Emily asked.

"It's possible. Pete went there with a warrant and a team to search for him," answered Kay. "Troy would have to be pretty stupid to go there, but he isn't known for his intelligence. We could get lucky."

"I hope he turns up soon."

"Yeah. Also, I want you to know that I'm going to get going on Tom's case as soon as I can. Sergeant Hixon, my boss, approved the investigation. I'm going to get in touch with the people that own the home in Winchester that Tom was supposed to be meeting with that day. Their names are Paul and Sherry Bartlett. I want to try and set up a time to go out there. Do you want to come with me?"

"Of course. Thanks for letting me go. I know it must be hard to find time to work on Tom's case, and I really appreciate it."

"I'd better head back to my office. I need to get in touch with the crime lab techs that are working on the van from Trooper Williams's shooting. I want to see if they found anything that we can use to try and match up with the two dead men."

Emily touched Kay's arm. "Good luck with everything today. Don't forget about practice tomorrow. I hope you aren't too busy, but I understand if you are."

Kay looked at her in confusion. "Practice?"

"Softball practice, remember?"

"That's right. I had forgotten that it was tomorrow. What time?"

"It starts at two." Emily was really wishing that Kay would go, but she was trying not to get her hopes up. Kay was busy and she might not be that into it.

"Unless some emergency comes up, I'll be there. I'm looking forward to it. It's been a couple years since I played, so I'm probably pretty rusty."

"Believe me, you'll be fine. In fact, I hope you don't quit the team once you see how bad some of the players are."

"I would never quit your team," Kay said, meeting her eyes with a smile.

Emily felt a shiver run up her back. Kay's eyes were mesmerizing. Did Kay have any idea what she was doing to her every time she looked into her eyes like that?

"Do you want to ride together?" Emily asked. Not wanting to pressure her, she said, "You probably have a lot to do, and it might be easier for you to just meet there."

"I would love to ride together," answered Kay. "We haven't done anything together just for fun yet, have we?"

"That's true. I'll plan to pick you up tomorrow. You'll have to tell me where you live."

"Sounds great. I'll give you a call later and let you know what's going on with everything." Kay opened the door and walked down the hall.

Emily sat at her desk and tried to get her mind focused back on work and away from thinking about how fascinating Kay's voice was. It was addictive. She felt like she could listen to it all day.

CHAPTER EIGHTEEN

Kay sat at her desk, writing up notes from the previous day's events. The New York police had confirmed that the photos she had sent them of the dead men in the cabin were similar to photos they had on file for MacNamara and Jackson. Final confirmation had been made when the fingerprints collected at the crime scene matched as well. Now they needed to tie the two men to the van with some physical evidence.

The Evidence Response Team had turned up fingerprints and DNA for Troy Pomerleau on some of the beer bottles, cigarettes and empty needles at the crime scene. There was currently a warrant out for his arrest. Any additional evidence would help them put him away once they were able to track him down. The murder weapon itself was probably somewhere at the bottom of Moosehead Lake.

She was waiting to hear from Pete when her phone rang. It was her friend, Terry, from the Portland unit.

"Hi, Terry. How are you?"

"Hi, Kay. I've got those phone records for you. I'm going to send them in an email. I just wanted to let you know they were coming."

"Thanks, I appreciate it," Kay said. "The accident case is now officially open. This could be very helpful."

"What kind of case is it?"

"The phone records are from a stolen cell phone that was owned by someone who was a vehicular homicide victim."

"Glad to have been of help. I hope you can find something in the records."

"Thanks again. I'll talk to you later, Terry"

"Don't forget to come see me sometime. Bye."

Kay checked her email and saw that Terry's message had arrived. She downloaded the file and started looking through it. The list of numbers called was extensive. They would begin by focusing on the day of the accident. This was something that Emily could work on. She could help her to identify the numbers and they could contact the people that Tom had called if necessary.

She came to the day of the accident and saw that a call had been made to 911. It appeared that the call had only connected for a second and then been interrupted. Maybe the signal hadn't been good from the location Tom had called.

Kay was interrupted by another phone call. It was Pete.

"Pete, how's it going?"

"No luck at the Pomerleau place in Rome. We looked around the property and didn't find Troy. They weren't too happy to see us with the warrant, but they didn't seem very surprised. I think they were expecting it and they had gotten rid of anything they didn't want us to see."

Pete continued, "I'm sure they've been in contact with Troy. They must have known about the shooting and that we would be out there looking for him."

"What about Kevin?" Kay asked. "Were you able to ask him any questions?"

"Yes, I asked if he had heard from Troy and of course he said that he hadn't."

"I wonder if Kevin has heard from Mike Martin since Troy shot his two guys."

"It will be interesting to see what happens with that. I would expect that this could cause some major problems."

"Troy was obviously helping MacNamara and Jackson hide out after they shot Trooper Williams," Kay said. "When Martin finds out that Troy killed them, if he hasn't already, he might go after him."

"Although, if those two hadn't killed Williams, none of this would have happened. So Martin might not feel a need for payback."

"It's hard to say. We're dealing with a group of people that has no regard for human life. All they care about is money."

"They're a bunch of sociopaths with no consciences," Pete agreed. "I'm going to keep looking for Troy. I'll keep you posted."

"All right. I was planning to check with the crime lab and see if they've turned anything up from the van."

Kay hung up and decided to drive over to the crime lab. It would be easier to get an answer if she went there in person. The crime lab was also located in Augusta, and was a short drive from her office. She headed out to her car and drove over. When she got to the lab she gave the receptionist the case number for Trooper Williams' case and waited for the technician that was working the case to come out. Entry to the lab was restricted and visitors had to meet in the outer conference rooms.

A young woman came out to greet her. "Hello, I'm Jennifer Adams. I'm one of the technicians processing the evidence found on the van involved in the shooting. Let's step into this room."

They entered a small room off the reception area and sat down at a round conference table.

"Hello, I'm Detective DeLorme. Please call me Kay. Have you turned up any fingerprints or other evidence that we could use to identify the driver or drivers?"

"As a matter of fact, we have."

Kay leaned forward, eager to hear more. "That's great. I had heard that the van was stripped and that there may not be much useful evidence."

"The plates were taken off and the van was cleaned out. Someone had attempted to wash it down but it's not that easy to clean something up completely. Trace evidence was found throughout the van. A lot of what we found might not be related to the shooting, since the van was stolen."

"I'm interested in fingerprints. Were you able to find any?"

"The main areas had been wiped down, but there were some places that were missed. We got some prints from the door handles, the glove compartment, the rearview mirror and a couple other places."

"Have you had a chance to find out if there are matches for any of them? Earlier today I sent over the names of two suspects that we have."

"We started running a search this morning, actually. The police in New York gave us the van owner's prints, so we are eliminating those. That left us with a few other unidentified sets. The search that we run looks at everything in the national database including the two suspects."

"How long before you know if there are any matches?"

"I expect that it could be done soon, if not already. It usually takes a few hours and it's been at least that long. I can go take a look if you don't mind waiting."

"Please. Should I stay right here?"

"Yes. I'll be back shortly." Jennifer exited the room.

Kay stood up and paced the floor while she waited. If they could link MacNamara and Jackson to the stolen van with physical evidence it would be a major step. The MDEA would need to work on getting evidence tying the two dead men to Mike Martin. The New York police might be able to help them with that.

The shootings at the camp in Greenville tied Martin's men to Troy Pomerleau. They still had work to do to link Kevin Pomerleau directly to the case against Troy. Finding Troy Pomerleau was vital. Especially before he hurt anyone else.

Jennifer came back to the conference room and handed Kay a printout. "Good news, Kay. It looks like we found matches to both of your suspects."

Kay felt a surge of adrenaline. She thanked Jennifer profusely and headed back to the office. It was time to fill Sergeant Hixon and Pete in. Maybe the sergeant would allow some of the officers on the task force that was investigating Trooper Williams's death to help her and Pete locate Troy Pomerleau.

Kay called Pete on her way over and had him meet her at Hixon's office. He was waiting outside Hixon's door for her and they went in together. Hixon gestured to them to take a seat.

"Sir, we've heard back from the crime lab on the Williams case," Kay said. "They were able to get some fingerprints from the van."

Kay described the crime lab's findings, along with the fingerprint matches.

"Excellent. I'll let the colonel know that we have verified identification of the suspects," Hixon said. "He'll want to send out a press release immediately."

Hixon paused as Pete's phone buzzed. Pete shut off the notification and studied the screen while Hixon turned to Kay.

"The two suspects were initially discovered through analysis done by someone at the SBI, correct?" Hixon asked.

"Yes, sir. Emily Stratton has been working with us on this."

"This shows how important it is that we work closely with the people at the SBI," Hixon said.

"I agree, sir," Kay said. She tried to suppress a smile when she glanced over at Pete and saw him grin at her with his eyebrows raised.

"Is this the same data analyst that you were telling me about with the vehicular homicide case?" Hixon asked.

"Yes, sir. Her husband was the victim."

"All right. Now that the case is open, let's make sure we do our best to find out who was responsible for her husband's accident. In the meantime, the priority is to locate Troy Pomerleau."

Pete spoke up. "Sir, I just received word that the car that Pomerleau stole in Greenville has turned up in Waterville.

There were no weapons or drugs in the car. They did find some cigarette butts, but no other evidence was visible. The car is being brought in to the crime lab to be checked out."

"What about Pomerleau?"

"We have an APB out on him. No sightings reported as of yet."

"I want to know as soon as you have any new information," Hixon said. "I'll make sure that some of the officers that were investigating the Williams shooting are put on the team that's tracking Troy Pomerleau."

"Yes, sir," Pete said.

Kay and Pete left Hixon's office. It was getting late and most people had left for the day. Kay had a couple more phone calls to make before she went home. She stopped at her cubicle.

"How long are you staying, Pete?"

"Not sure. I wanted to stick around a little while and see if anything turned up with Troy Pomerleau. I'll let you know if I hear anything. Do you have anything going on this weekend?"

"I'm going to start looking at the phone records in the Stratton case. I also got recruited for the SBI softball team."

"Doing your part to work closely with the people at the SBI?" Pete laughed. "One person in particular?"

She gave in and raised her hands in defeat. "Okay, I admit it. Emily and I are sort of in a relationship. We're more than just friends."

"I knew it," Pete said triumphantly. "I can always tell. Why so secretive?"

"I'm not sure how people would react, especially Sergeant Hixon. Not just because she's a woman, but she's also someone who I work with."

"I don't think that you work closely enough that it would be a problem at all. I know he's old school, though. He may have some personal feelings about the whole thing. You're right, it's hard to tell."

She nodded. "There's also the fact that her husband's death wasn't that long ago. I don't want to make it harder for her by having people gossiping."

"I've got your back, partner. These lips are sealed. I don't think you have anything to worry about, though. You two aren't doing anything wrong and you shouldn't feel like you have anything to hide."

"Thanks, Pete. That means a lot."

"Good luck with the SBI softball team. I hear that they're really bad."

Kay sat at her desk and watched Pete walk off down the corridor. The more she got to know him, the more grateful she was that she had gotten such a good partner.

CHAPTER NINETEEN

Kay woke early and went into the office. Even though it was a Saturday, she wanted to catch up on everything so that she would be able to spend the afternoon with Emily. There was still no sign of Troy Pomerleau. Police departments all over the state were looking for him and the state police were keeping the Pomerleau's property in Rome under surveillance.

Kay was working with the MDEA on linking the case against MacNamara and Jackson with Mike Martin. They knew that the two dead men had been delivering drugs from Martin when they shot and killed Trooper Williams, but they had no hard evidence to prove it. The New York police had been helpful in providing information. The arrest records for the two men showed a pattern of ties with Martin, but nothing to prove conclusively that he was the one that sent them to Maine.

She decided to turn her attention to Tom Stratton's case. She opened up the file that Trooper Johnson from the crash reconstruction unit had sent her. She found the contact information for Paul and Sherry Bartlett, the people who owned the home that Tom had been working on. She dialed their home number.

"Hello," a woman's voice answered.

"Hello, I'm trying to reach Paul and Sherry Bartlett," Kay said.

"This is Sherry Bartlett speaking."

"This is Detective DeLorme with the Maine State Police. I'm investigating an automobile accident that took place last January. The victim was Tom Stratton, who was an electrician that was doing some work on a home you were building. I'm trying to put together a timeline for the accident and I would like to set up a time to talk to you and your husband."

"We've talked to the police already."

"I have a few more questions for you, if you don't mind."

"You'll have to speak with my husband. He was supposed to meet with Tom that day. I really didn't have anything to do with it and I'm quite busy."

"Please have your husband give me a call." Kay gave the woman her number and hung up. Feeling a bit irritated at Sherry Bartlett's lack of cooperation, she turned her attention to the phone records. She planned to get Emily to help her track down the numbers that Tom had called and texted. She looked at the list of text messages that Tom had sent out for the month prior to the accident.

Unfortunately, the length of time since the accident meant that the actual texts and any photos that had been stored on the phone were long gone from the cell phone carrier's servers. Carriers generally only saved that information for a limited time, usually not more than a month. Kay looked at the numbers showing up in the report, wishing she could see the actual messages that Tom had sent or received.

Kay was contemplating what the next step should be when her phone rang. She saw that the call was coming from the Bartlett's number.

"Hello, this is Detective DeLorme," she answered.

"Hi, this is Paul Bartlett. I understand that you have some questions about Tom Stratton."

Kay was somewhat surprised that he had called her. She had been doubtful that Sherry Bartlett would give her husband the message.

"Yes. I was hoping that I could meet with you at the house where Tom was working and ask you a few questions."

"That would be fine. We finished the house and we live here now."

Kay decided to see if they could meet on Monday. There might not be enough time today and most people did not like to be bothered on Sundays.

"Could we meet some time on Monday? I can be there during the day or the evening, whichever you prefer."

"How about at four on Monday afternoon?" asked Paul.

"That would be fine."

Paul gave her his address and they hung up.

Kay decided to get some lunch and get ready to meet up with Emily. She drove home to the apartment she was renting. She was within walking distance to the shops and restaurants downtown but was far enough that it was fairly quiet in the neighborhood she lived in. She liked living in Orleans and was thinking about looking for a house to buy at some point.

She went inside and changed into jeans and a T-shirt. She made herself a sandwich and took it out on her deck so that she could look out at the river while she ate. The day was warm and comfortable. There was a pair of eagles that lived in the woods behind her apartment that liked to soar in circles above the buildings and down around the river below. She watched one of them and was grateful that she had taken the chance to relax for a few minutes. Winter in Maine was cold and sometimes miserable, but summer made up for it.

She finished her sandwich and gave Emily a call. "Hi, there."

"Hi, how are you?" Emily asked.

"I'm good. I'm psyched for softball and I can't wait to see you."

"Me, too. I'll come pick you up. Can you give me directions to your place?"

* * *

Using the directions that she had gotten from Kay, Emily headed over to pick her up. It was a little early, but that would give her time to get a look at Kay's apartment. She found the place easily and parked next to Kay's car. She saw Kay standing in her doorway and walked over. It was the first time she had seen Kay wearing casual clothes and she looked good. She had on a tight-fitting black T-shirt that showed her slim, muscular build. She was wearing a Red Sox hat. The closer she got, the more flustered Emily became. They had always had something from work to talk about when they got together. She didn't know how to handle the attraction she was feeling, so she started talking, hoping that Kay wouldn't notice.

"Hi. I guess I found your apartment. It looks like you have a nice place."

She knew she might be talking too much, but Emily was too nervous to stop. "I like your hat. You look really good in a hat. I am one of those people who looks ridiculous in a hat. I always have. It's embarrassing really. Are you a Red Sox fan?"

"Yes, I like the Red Sox."

Emily's embarrassment grew. She was probably making a fool of herself. She needed to calm down before Kay ran screaming back into her apartment. She would try a new topic. "So, where did you get your shirt? It's nice."

"Uh, I got it online," Kay answered. "Would you like to come in for a minute?"

Emily nodded and followed her into her apartment.

The apartment was situated on two levels. The downstairs had one large open room with the kitchen along the back and the living room area in the front. There was a bathroom in the back corner. The living area had a comfortable linen colored couch and chair with an oversized ottoman. Kay had some colorful prints of nature scenes hanging on the walls and the apartment had a very relaxed, peaceful look.

"This is it," Kay said. "There are two bedrooms upstairs and a bathroom. I use one of the bedrooms for an office."

"This is really nice. I love the view you have of the river."

"There's a deck off the kitchen. I like to sit out there when the weather is good. Do you want to have something to drink and sit for a minute with me?"

Emily's mouth was feeling very dry. "Sure, that would be good."

Kay got them each a glass of water and they sat out on the deck. "We should probably leave soon, huh?"

Emily took a sip from her glass. Her hands were shaky and she dropped her glass, spilling water down the front of her shirt and onto the deck. She jerked back and looked at Kay apologetically. "God, I'm really sorry. I think I told you before that I'm not the most graceful person."

"It's not a big deal. It's just water." Kay stood up. "Hold on and I'll be right back."

Kay went into the house and came back onto the deck a moment later with some paper towels. She handed a couple to Emily so she could dry herself off. Emily wiped ineffectively at her shirt while she watched Kay kneel down and mop up the small puddle on the floor.

Kay looked up at Emily from where she was kneeling. "Do you want to borrow a dry shirt?"

Emily shook her head. She tried not to think about how foolish she must look to Kay. It was obvious that she was not good at this. She should not have come over early. They should have gone straight to practice.

"You seem a little nervous. Is everything all right?" Kay asked.

"I'm sorry. If you want to go now, that might be good. We don't have to be there for another half hour, but we could get there early."

Emily stood up and picked up their glasses, anxious to leave. They went back into the kitchen. Kay grabbed her bag and they headed for the door. They got into Emily's truck and drove toward the softball field.

* * *

Emily's attention was focused on the road and Kay was able to study her carefully. Emily looked mouthwatering in her shorts and T-shirt, which were still pretty damp. The sculpted muscles of her legs were fantastic. Kay had no idea what the hat talk had been all about earlier.

Kay wasn't sure why Emily was acting strangely. She had seemed awfully uncomfortable at her apartment and now she wasn't talking. Kay was a little worried and confused. Things had never felt awkward between them before. Maybe Emily was having second thoughts about spending the afternoon with her. Finally, she couldn't stand the silence any longer.

"Are you sure there's nothing wrong?" Kay asked. "If you would rather have me drive over in my own car, that would be fine."

"No, I'm happy to give you a ride."

"You don't seem it."

They reached the parking area for the field and pulled into a spot in the back corner, away from the other cars. There was another team practicing and the field was busy with activity, but the parking lot was deserted. Emily turned the engine off and they both stayed seated in the truck.

Emily turned to Kay. "I'm sorry. I'm just embarrassed. I saw you at your apartment and you looked so good that I didn't know what to do. I realized how bad I am at this. I really like you, a lot, and I'm really attracted to you and I just don't know what I'm supposed to do."

Kay was astonished at Emily's admission. She had never considered that Emily might be feeling that way. She took it for granted that Emily would realize that Kay wasn't expecting her to act in any certain way. Emily had surprised her once again.

"I was worried that you were having second thoughts," Kay admitted.

"No, please don't think that. If anything, I'm the one worried that you'll have second thoughts. I can't even manage to drink a glass of water when I'm alone with you. It's pathetic."

"Look, I know this is all new to you. I want you to be comfortable with me and I don't want you to think that I expect anything from you. Let's just take it slow and see what happens."

Kay reached for Emily's hand and held it. She could see the tension in Emily's face slip away as she relaxed back into her seat and looked over at Kay. "You really do look good in your softball clothes."

Kay smiled. "I have to say that I like seeing you in your shorts. I had no idea you were hiding those awesome legs."

She slid her hand from Emily's and stroked her leg.

Kay felt Emily's body respond to her touch. She shifted in her seat and looked out the window to see if anyone was near. Their corner of the lot was still empty.

Emily reached her hand over to Kay and touched her cheek. "You're so soft. It feels so nice."

Kay's hand continued to caress Emily's leg, travelling from her well-developed calves up to rub the muscles in her thigh, then gliding up under the edge of her shorts. She could tell that Emily couldn't sit still, sliding as close to Kay as her seat allowed. Emily's hand slid down Kay's cheek to her neck and down to her shoulder, stopping just short of Kay's chest.

Kay swallowed hard. If Emily didn't stop touching her, she wasn't going to be able to restrain herself from caressing more than her leg. Expecting their teammates to be arriving at any minute she said, "We probably ought to head over to the field soon."

Emily nodded. "We should go warm up."

Their faces were inches apart. Kay gave Emily a lingering kiss and pulled back, looking in her eyes. "All right, let's go warm up, Coach."

CHAPTER TWENTY

They carried the equipment from Emily's vehicle over to the field. The other team was finishing up their practice and packing up. Emily said hello to the players as they walked by. She and Kay put on their gloves and started tossing a ball back and forth. Emily was delighted to find that Kay had a good arm. She threw the ball hard and fast to Emily.

Kay called over to her, "I hope you're not going to do any sliding in those shorts."

"No, I won't do any sliding at practice. I don't wear shorts to games, though, usually we all wear jeans and our team shirts."

Cars with the SBI players started arriving. Emily greeted her coworkers and their spouses and friends. She paired them up as they arrived and had them warm up by playing pass with each other.

When it looked like everyone had arrived, Emily called them all over to home plate. "Hello, team, thanks for coming. We've got the field for about two hours. We're going to start by doing some fielding practice, then we'll give everyone a chance to take a few hits."

She began introductions. "I think that most of us know each other from last year, but let's go around the group and introduce ourselves for the people who are new. Be sure to say what position you play. My name is Emily, and I play second base and sometimes pitch."

She nodded to Kay, who spoke next. "My name is Kay. I'm a detective with MCU and I play shortstop."

Sam was standing next to Kay. He was clearly uncomfortable speaking before the group and mumbled, "I'm Sam. I play outfield."

The introductions continued as everyone in the group said their names. The final player was Alex. "Hello everyone, I'm Alex and I play first base."

Emily had been hoping that Alex wouldn't show up to play this year. He was a dismal first base player. He had a habit of closing his eyes when the ball was thrown to him and it often bounced off his glove. Since he was her boss, she really couldn't replace him. He didn't seem to have any idea how bad he was. He talked about softball all the time at the office and loved to describe great plays that he thought he'd made. He had treated her well when Tom died and she vowed to try and think kinder thoughts about him.

"All right everyone, we're going to do some fielding practice. Go to your positions and I'm going to hit you some balls," Emily said.

She carried the bucket of balls along with her favorite bat over to home plate. She started off by hitting a ball to third base. Their third baseman was one of the software developers. He bent down to get the grounder she hit to him and missed. The ball bounced off his shoulder and rolled away. He chased after it and threw it to Alex at first base. The throw was a little wide and Alex missed it.

"Okay, that's fine," Emily called. She hit a sharp grounder to the shortstop area. Kay reached for the ball and snagged it effortlessly. She turned and snapped it to first in one smooth motion.

Emily was glad to see that Kay made a good play but she wanted to stay cautious in her enthusiasm. She was really hoping that Kay would be good. They desperately needed some talent on their team. "Nice job," she called.

The fielding practice cycled through the positions. Sam made a decent catch when she hit a pop fly to him. The rest of the team managed to catch some of the balls, but the majority had been missed. Not to worry; it was only their first practice.

It was Kay's turn again. Emily hit a swift line drive in her direction. Kay leaped up gracefully and caught it. Emily's heart pounded at the sight of it. Kay was very distracting. She had to keep reminding herself to focus on practice. Her mind kept returning to thoughts of sitting with Kay in the truck.

After a few rounds of fielding practice, Emily called over to their pitcher who was warming up on the sidelines. Her name was Kelly and she was one of the project managers who Emily worked with.

"Okay, team, Kelly is going to throw you each a few pitches. I want you to try and get three good hits each. We'll go in the same order as we used for fielding."

Emily jogged over to second base. Kay looked over and gave her a smile. She looked so good that Emily felt a wave of heat flash through her body. She had never had this happen to her before and it was very disconcerting.

Kelly was pitching the ball softly, trying to allow the hitters to get an easy ball to hit. The third baseman hit a couple grounders and a pop fly. Kay was the next one up. She stepped up to the plate and pounded her first hit out to Sam in left field. He didn't have to move too far to catch it and he fielded it easily.

She hit a hard line drive that whistled over Emily's head on the next pitch. Emily was a little relieved that it hadn't come closer. When Kelly threw the third pitch, Kay crushed it. The ball went over all the outfielders' heads. Emily was ecstatic. Not only was she incredibly turned on by watching her, but Kay might actually help them to win a game or two.

Emily was up to bat next. She managed to get a couple balls into the outfield and had one strong grounder that went through Alex's legs. She returned to second base and tried to concentrate on watching the ball instead of Kay for the rest of the practice.

Another team arrived at the field and their time was up. The SBI players gathered up their equipment and brought it over to Emily's truck. She thanked them all and reminded them about their upcoming game.

"We have our first game next week. I have everyone's game shirt here, so be sure to pick it up before you leave. We won't get another chance for a formal practice, so try to get a little practice in on your own, if you can."

Emily and Kay leaned against Emily's bumper and watched the other players go to their cars. Some of them were getting together to have drinks and dinner.

Alex shouted over to them, "Are you two coming with us?"

"Do you want to go have a drink with the team?" Emily asked.

"Sure, if you do," Kay answered.

Emily called back to Alex, "Yes, see you there."

They got into the truck and Emily turned to Kay. "You were amazing. From the moment I saw you I thought that you looked like you could be good at softball, but I had no idea how good."

"You thought I looked like I could be good at softball when you met me?"

"Yes. It was one of the first things that came into my mind."

"That sounds a little strange," Kay said with a smile. "What exactly does that mean?"

"I don't know. I thought you looked athletic."

"Is that a positive feature in your mind?"

"Are you kidding me?" Emily stared at Kay. "I have never been as attracted to anyone in my life as I am to you. Watching you at practice today, I could hardly catch my breath."

Kay looked at Emily with a startled expression. "Oh really?"

"In fact, it's probably a good thing that we're going to meet up with the team. I might not be able to handle being alone with you right now."

Kay gave Emily a playful smile. "What will you do if I hit a home run for you at our first game?"

"I'd probably do anything you want."

"It's a deal."

* * *

They were the last ones to arrive at the Riverside Restaurant. The other players had secured a few tables with windows overlooking the river. Kay and Emily sat down at one of the tables and joined in the conversation.

The third baseman, Tony, raised his beer glass to Kay. "You're a good shortstop. What are you doing joining our team?"

The other players laughed and Kay answered, "Emily asked me if I wanted to be on the team and I thought it sounded like fun. I used to play for a team in Portland when I was working down there."

"How do you like working out of Augusta?" one of the other players asked her.

Kay glanced at Emily and said, "I like it a lot."

Kay and Emily relaxed into comfortable conversation with the group. Kay enjoyed meeting Emily's coworkers and getting to know them. She watched Emily turn to speak to Sam who had joined the group and was sitting nearby.

"Hey, Sam. You did pretty well out there today."

Sam nodded and stared into his beer. Emily turned back to Kay with a shrug just as the waitress came by and asked them if they wanted anything to drink.

Kay leaned toward Emily. "Do you want to get a beer and share a pizza?"

"I'd love to," answered Emily. "I haven't eaten since breakfast."

Kay was hoping that after they had a bite to eat they would get a chance to spend a little time alone together. It was nice to get to know everyone, but they never seemed to be able to have a chance to talk without having other people nearby.

Emily moved closer and spoke softly in her ear, "Maybe we can have a bite to eat with everyone and then go do something, just you and I."

"You read my mind."

The waitress quickly returned with their drinks. Alex was sitting at the table next to them. He turned around to Kay. "How is the search for Troy Pomerleau going?"

Kay didn't want to discuss the case. It wasn't the appropriate time and place, and she didn't know Alex well enough to feel comfortable giving him any details.

She replied with generic information, revealing nothing more than what had been reported by the media. "There is an APB out for him. The state police are searching and I'm sure he'll be found soon."

Alex nodded and turned back around to his table. Emily spoke to her quietly, "I was hoping we could forget all that for a little while, but I'm sure it's on your mind."

"I haven't heard any news this afternoon. Pete will call me if anything happens."

"Speaking of Pete," Emily said, "does he play softball?"

Kay laughed. "I told him I was playing and he didn't seem to have a very high opinion of the SBI team."

"Well, that's insulting but understandable. This season is going to be different, though. Our prospects are greatly improved."

Kay nudged Emily's arm. "You're just being nice to me so I'll be on your team."

Emily laughed. "You caught me."

Kay spoke softly to Emily so no one could hear. "I also told Pete about you and me."

Emily choked on her beer. "What? I thought you didn't want anyone at the office to know?"

"I wasn't planning to say anything, but he asked me. He said that he could tell and he was very cool about it. Does it bother you?"

"Of course not. I think it's great. I'm glad you don't feel like you have to hide anything from your partner."

"I'm still not sure about having Hixon know."

The waitress brought their pizza and they started eating. They joined in the conversation around the table. As the evening went on and people finished their meals, Kay was hoping that Emily would soon let her know when they had stayed long enough to be polite.

"I'm getting kind of chilly, do you mind if we get going?" Emily bumped Kay's leg with her knee to get her attention.

"Yeah, I'm a little chilly, too. I guess we should be going."

They said good-bye to everyone and headed out the door.

CHAPTER TWENTY-ONE

"You didn't want to stay longer, did you?" Emily asked, hoping that she hadn't made Kay leave too soon. "Sometimes our practices and games are so bad that our get-togethers can be awkward, but tonight was fun. Especially because you were there."

"I had fun too, but I didn't mind leaving. I want us to spend a little time by ourselves," Kay said. "Do you want to go watch a movie or something at my place?"

"Yes, that sounds good."

Emily drove them back to Kay's apartment. They got out of the car and Kay held her hand as they walked inside together.

"I'm sorry I acted so crazy earlier," Emily said.

"There's nothing to worry about and you don't need to be nervous. We're just going to relax and watch a movie or listen to some music okay?"

"Okay." Emily shivered as they sat down on the couch.

"Are you actually chilly? Do you want a sweatshirt?" Kay turned on her stereo and soft music filled the room.

"Maybe you should sit a little closer and warm me up." Emily turned and faced Kay, drawing her legs up onto the couch beneath her. "You know, I'm not nervous about having you touch me. I really want you to. I'm just worried that I don't know what I'm doing and I'll do the wrong thing."

Kay put her arms around her and looked into her eyes. "You won't do the wrong thing. It's just us, and there's no one judging."

Emily leaned into her and their lips met. The kiss started slowly and grew in intensity. Emily tasted Kay's mouth with her tongue while Kay sucked on her lips gently and slid her hand softly along her back. Emily gasped as goose bumps rose up and down her spine.

Emily broke away for a moment. "Can we lie here on the couch together?"

"Let's take our time. We can go at whatever pace feels right to you."

Kay stretched out and lay back along the cushions. Emily slid up alongside her. Their eyes met and Kay placed a kiss on Emily's lips then slid her mouth over to tease Emily's earlobe. Kay whispered softly into her ear, "See, we won't get this wrong. We just need to tell each other what we want."

"God, you feel good," Emily whispered. "I really want to touch you."

"Go ahead, it's all right." Kay continued to place kisses on Emily's ear and worked her way down to her neck, gently tasting and kissing her soft skin. Kay slid over and on top of Emily, turning her so that she was on her back facing up at her.

Emily looked up at Kay. "Your eyes are so beautiful. I actually noticed that just before I noticed that you looked like you'd be good at softball."

"I thought that you were beautiful the first time I saw you." Kay kissed Emily's lips again, lowering her weight down onto her.

Emily liked the feel of Kay's weight against her body. She raised her hips up and she couldn't stop herself from pressing against her. She slid her hands under Kay's shirt and felt the soft, smooth skin of her back. Her hands brushed over the fabric of her sports bra. She wanted to slide it off her, but wasn't sure how to best do it.

Kay shifted her weight to her left arm and reached inside Emily's shirt, stroking her stomach and sliding up toward her breasts. Her hand traced along her bra and caressed her breasts.

Emily gasped at the sensation. Her hips pressed against Kay's again. She stared into her eyes. "Don't stop."

Kay squeezed her gently. "Can I take your shirt off?"

Emily nodded and they sat up, Kay straddling Emily's lap. Kay lifted Emily's shirt up and tossed it aside. She put her hands under Emily's bra and slid it up and over her head. Kay smiled at Emily. "You're gorgeous."

Emily fought off her self-consciousness. "I want to take yours off now."

She lifted Kay's shirt while Kay raised her arms. She fumbled with Kay's bra and Kay helped her slide it off. She leaned back and let her eyes linger on Kay, sitting astride her lap with no shirt on. She could feel her heart racing. She wanted to reach for her but she started to panic.

Kay looked at Emily. "Are you getting nervous? Remember what I said before, we just need to tell each other what we want. No one is going to judge you."

Emily nodded and took a deep breath. "I really want to touch you. I don't know what I'm afraid of all of a sudden."

"It's all right, babe. I want you to touch me."

Emily reached her hands out and caressed both of Kay's breasts. Her palms rubbed across her nipples and she squeezed her soft flesh. It felt incredible. She couldn't believe that this was actually happening. She had spent most of her life suppressing her desires and now she was here where she belonged, with Kay.

"God, that feels good," Kay said. "I don't think I can hold out for much longer without touching you."

Kay leaned over and pressed her lips to Emily's in an urgent kiss. Emily responded, probing Kay's mouth with her tongue. Kay pressed her back down onto the couch and she began to lick and taste her way down Emily's body. Emily gasped in pleasure beneath her as Kay kissed her breasts reverently. Emily wrapped her fingers in Kay's hair and closed her eyes as Kay began sliding down further along her body. Emily froze when she heard her cell phone ring.

Kay lifted her head and looked at her. "Do you need to get that?"

"I probably should. It could be one of the boys and something may be wrong."

Kay rolled off her and helped her to her feet. She held onto Emily's hand for a moment and looked into her eyes. "I don't want to stop touching you."

Emily's body was pulsing with desire. She took a deep breath and tried to regain her self-control. Her phone had stopped ringing by the time she picked it up. Kay came up behind her holding her T-shirt. She helped Emily slide it back over her arms and kissed her.

"You want me to cover up?" Emily teased.

"Yes, you're too distracting that way."

"I see what you mean." Emily looked down at Kay's body. She pressed herself against her and rubbed their breasts together.

Kay's arms locked around her and then she stepped back and pointed to the phone. "Did you check your phone?"

"Oh, right. I was just about to." Emily looked at the screen. "It was Ethan. I'd better call him back."

Kay walked back over to the couch and sat down, trying to give her a little privacy.

"Hi, Ethan, what's going on?" Emily said when he answered.

"Hi, Mom. I talked to Ben and he said that you wanted us to come over tomorrow. I was planning to drive up in the morning and pick Ben up on my way. We should be there by lunch time."

"That will be good. We can have lunch and then go over the accident report together."

"What are you doing tonight? Is anything going on?" Ethan asked.

"I'm over at my friend Kay's house. We had dinner together."

"That's good. I'm glad you aren't home alone."

"Have a nice night, sweetheart, and I'll see you tomorrow," Emily said. "I love you."

"Love you, too," Ethan said and hung up.

Emily walked over and sat down next to Kay. Kay had put her shirt back on, which Emily was a little disappointed to see.

"My sons are coming over around noon tomorrow. We're going to have lunch and go over the accident report. Do you think you might want to come over?"

Kay gave her a startled look. "I don't want to intrude on your family time."

Emily didn't want to pressure Kay to come over, so she tried to cover up her disappointment. "If you have other plans, I certainly understand. I don't expect you to spend all your free time with me. I know you're a busy person. You probably have to catch up on work or hang out with friends from Portland, or something like that—"

"Emily." Kay interrupted Emily's nervous dialog.

"Yes?"

"I'd love to come."

Emily smiled happily. "Thanks."

Emily tried to keep her eyes away from Kay's lips. She wanted to kiss her mouth and taste her skin again."

Kay caught her looking and smiled. "You surprised me once you let go and loosened up."

Emily leaned against Kay's shoulder. "We could pick up where we left off."

"I don't want to take things too fast." Kay leaned forward to kiss her gently. "I want you to be relaxed and comfortable when we're together."

"You're right. I guess I probably shouldn't stay too late."

Emily sat up and reached for Kay's hand. "I was thinking that I wanted to tell the boys about us tomorrow."

"Are you sure about the timing? It might be hard for them to handle at the same time that you're talking about Tom's crash."

"I know. I'm sure that they would both be upset if I kept anything from them. On the other hand, I don't want them to think that I'm forgetting about Tom. It's hard to tell what would be best, but I don't want any secrets."

Kay raised Emily's hand to her lips. "It means everything to me that you aren't ashamed of our relationship. I don't want you to say anything to your sons if you aren't ready, though."

Emily looked fiercely at her. "Why would I ever be ashamed to be with you? It makes me angry to even think that you would ever believe anything like that."

"I know plenty of people who wouldn't want anyone to know. It happens all the time. I respect and appreciate the fact that you aren't trying to hide anything. I'm lucky that I met someone like you."

Emily softened. "We're lucky that we met each other."

She stood up. "I probably should get going. You're welcome to come over any time you want tomorrow. Like I said, the boys should be there some time around noon."

Kay got up from the couch and walked to the door with Emily. "I was hoping that we would get a chance to go over the phone records. I meant to tell you that they came back yesterday. Why don't I come a little early and bring the report? We can look it over before your sons get there."

Emily retrieved her bra from the corner where it had been tossed.

"Don't want to forget this," she said with a grin.

"I had a great time with you today," Kay said. "I don't know if I'm going to be able to sleep much. I'll be thinking about you."

Emily's breathing quickened. An image of Kay straddling her lap and kissing her came into her mind. "Yeah, me too," she said, staring mesmerized at Kay's lips.

Kay pulled her close and kissed her. Emily closed her eyes and savored the sensations passing through her body as she kissed her back. They were both braless and it felt exquisite to be pressed together.

Kay pulled her lips away and stepped back with a satisfied smile. "Good night."

Emily collected herself and stepped outside. "Good night."

CHAPTER TWENTY-TWO

Sunday morning Emily got up early and made a quick trip to the grocery store. She wanted to cook regular cheeseburgers for the boys and veggie burgers for her and Kay, since Kay had said she liked them last time. She made it back with plenty of time to spare before Kay was due to arrive. She decided to look through some of Tom's records in their office and see if she could find anything unusual.

Tom's files didn't appear to contain anything helpful. The paperwork for all of his jobs was stored in a large file cabinet. Each job was filed in a divided section containing folders for estimates and invoices. There was a folder containing pages of notes for most of the jobs. Tom also kept notes in a datebook that he stored in his desk and wrote in most days.

Emily looked in the datebook at the entries for the weeks leading up to the accident. She was looking for any references to the Bartlett job. The entries she found were details of hours and pricing, and showed nothing that looked out of the ordinary.

She pulled open the file drawer and found the files for the Bartlett job. She flipped through the pages of estimates and bills for materials. Nothing stood out. The pricing all looked the same as the other jobs. It was possible that someone had tried to steal something from the job site. Could that be what he had seen? It didn't make sense that anyone would want to kill him for something like that, but she supposed that they should consider it.

Emily looked through the rest of the Bartlett notes. Tom had mainly referenced Paul Bartlett. There were notes on the meetings that they had, which appeared to take place on a weekly basis. There was a mention of Sherry, his wife, at one of the meetings. Tom had noted that she had gone to one of their meetings and complained about the cost of some of the light fixtures that she had picked out. Interestingly enough, Sherry's friend Chris Brooks had been with her. That was definitely something to ask Julian about.

* * *

Kay showed up about an hour before the boys were due. She knocked on Emily's door and tried to wait patiently for her to answer. Considering that they had just seen each other the night before it was ridiculous how much she wanted to see her again. It was hard to explain, she was just so happy being with Emily that she was starting to crave being around her.

Kay wasn't used to feeling like this. She was used to being on her own and staying composed at all times. She'd never felt as out of control in a relationship as she did with Emily. She usually had been the one in charge in her past relationships and when things didn't go the way she wanted them to, she moved on. With Emily, she was more concerned with making sure that she was happy, and she didn't want to make Emily do anything that she wasn't ready for.

Emily opened the door with smile. "Come on in. I missed you."

Emily led her into the kitchen and they stood next to the counter. Kay's resolve to play it cool evaporated.

"Hi, babe," she said, leaning forward and kissing Emily. She sucked on her lower lip and started kissing her down her neck and behind her ear. "You smell good."

Emily reached up and ran her fingers through Kay's hair. "I love your hair. It's so soft. I can't seem to keep my hands off you."

Before they got too carried away, Kay stepped back with a smile and held up the folder with the phone records that she had brought with her. "You're very distracting, but we have work to do. Are you ready to go over these with me?"

"Yes, and I also wanted to show you some of Tom's notes that I found in the office."

Kay remembered the meeting she had scheduled with Paul Bartlett. "I meant to tell you yesterday that I got in touch with Paul Bartlett. I set up a meeting for us tomorrow afternoon at four. I hope that's okay?"

"That's perfect. I feel like we're finally going to start finding out what happened."

They went into the office and Emily showed Kay the notes that Tom had kept on the Bartlett job.

"There's really nothing out of place. I didn't see any odd figures or any indication that Tom might have caught someone stealing from the job site. The only thing that caught my attention was that Mrs. Bartlett only came to one of the meetings and she brought a friend. The friend is a salon owner from Orleans who is pretty well known around town."

Emily described Chris to Kay. "He tries to come across as a nice guy, but he's not. I've heard things from my friend Julian about how nasty he can be to people. Tom did some work for him and he didn't care for him. He has a reputation around town for being into drugs."

"Well, we can look at him a little closer. I'll call the MDEA detectives who I know and see if they're keeping an eye on him."

"I meant to tell you, Julian has been keeping his ears open for any rumors. He says that stylists are the first to know any gossip around town. I want you to meet him, by the way. Maybe we can go to trivia this week."

"I hope Julian's careful. Most dealers are violent people and they wouldn't want to hear that people were talking about them at all."

They started looking over the phone records, focusing on the calls and texts made the day of the accident. The report showed the name associated with each number that was dialed out or received for texts and calls. The plan was for Emily to look through Tom's notes and try to confirm each of the names.

Emily saw the call to 911 that Tom had made the day of the accident. Her heart ached at the thought of Tom trying to call for help, only to have the call get dropped. There was another dropped call that was made to Emily's phone that morning. She hadn't received it and had been unaware of the trouble he was in.

On the day of the accident there was one call to Paul Bartlett's cell phone and one call to Tom's phone from Paul Bartlett. If Tom had been able to reach Bartlett, then cell reception must have worked at the job site. He had probably been driving away from the project when he tried to make the calls that didn't stay connected. The North Road, where the accident occurred, was an area known for unreliable service.

There were numerous calls to suppliers and vendors.

"We can probably eliminate those calls," Emily said. "It seems doubtful that Tom would have called a supply company and they would have sent someone out to run him off the road."

There was one call left, which was made to a company that Emily said she didn't recognize. It was called Orleans Design Associates. The call had been placed a few minutes before Tom had tried to call Emily.

"I've never heard of it," Emily said. "Should we try calling it and see who answers?"

"We can look up the owners tomorrow and see if we recognize the names. I don't think that you should call from your phone. If it does end up being the person who stole Tom's phone, they would realize you have their number."

"Good point. It doesn't look like there's much else we can do. I wish we knew whose number that is. We could always look up the company records and see what names are listed, although that will probably just give us a lawyer's name. "

They went back into the kitchen and sat at the table. The boys were due to arrive at any time.

"Are you still thinking of saying anything to your sons about us?" Kay asked.

"Yes, I was planning to."

"I'm not sure that I should be here when you do. I think it might make it harder for them to talk to you."

Their conversation was cut short by the arrival of Ben and Ethan. They pulled into the driveway in Ethan's car. Emily went out to greet them and Kay followed.

"Hi, guys. I'm so happy to have you both home for a visit." Emily gave each of her sons a hug and turned to Kay. "I'm sure you both remember my friend Kay."

"Hi, Ben. Hi, Ethan." Kay nodded to them. They seemed like nice young men but she really didn't know them and was hoping that she wouldn't have to be here when Emily told them about their relationship. It was a potential confrontation that she wanted to avoid.

"Nice to see you again," Ben said.

"Thanks for helping us find out what happened to our father," Ethan said. "Do you think we'll be able to find out who did it?"

"I know that we won't stop looking until we have some answers," Kay said. "Your mother and I have been going over some of the information that we have and we have some ideas about how to find out more details about that day."

They went into the house and sat down at the kitchen table.

Kay watched Emily tap her fingers nervously. She knew that Emily was anxious about showing the report to Ben and Ethan and probably wanted to delay going over it.

"Are you hungry?" Emily asked. "I can start the grill and we could have some burgers before we go over the report."

"I'd rather see the report first, Mom," Ben said.

Emily went to the office to get the report while Kay waited with Ben and Ethan. Returning to the kitchen a few minutes later, Emily sat down between her sons and laid the report on the table. Kay sat across the table and observed quietly while they looked over the pages that Trooper Johnson had given to Emily.

Ben spoke first. "So basically, Dad was at a house that he was working on in Winchester when he left for some reason. Someone in another pickup truck deliberately ran into him and forced him off the road."

"Do you have any ideas about why he left the job site?" Ethan asked.

"We haven't figured that out. Kay and I think that he might have seen something. I don't know what it might have been, but I know your father wouldn't have stood by if something illegal was going on."

Ben nodded. "It must have been something like that."

"You said you had some ideas," Ethan said to Kay. "What did you mean?"

"The first thing that came to mind was the cell phone that was stolen during the break-in here at your mother's house. We've been checking on the numbers that were called on the day of the accident to see if your father made any unusual calls."

"We did come across a number that was listed on the phone records that we need to identify," Emily added. "Kay is planning to look into it."

"Did you check his pictures?" Ben asked.

"What do you mean?" Emily asked. "Did I check before the phone was stolen? I didn't get the chance."

"No, I mean on Google Photos. I had Dad's phone set up to sync his photos with his Google account."

Emily looked at Ben. "I had no idea."

"Can you get in and show us?" Kay asked.

"Sure. Where's your laptop, Mom?"

Emily ran into the office and retrieved the laptop. She opened it up and put it in front of Ben. They waited anxiously while he logged in to Tom's account and clicked on the Photos symbol. They all watched as the browser loaded the images. The photos with the most recent date were displayed first. Several images were present for the date of the crash. The first two pictures were clearly job related and showed the electrical panel at the Bartlett's house. There was a photo of Sally standing next to Tom's truck in the snowy driveway.

The next photo showed a black pickup truck parked on the other side of the house, visible through one of the windows. There was a second picture of the same truck taken from a slightly different angle. Two people were visible sitting in the truck, but the image was slightly blurry. There was a final picture of the truck and again the two people sitting in it were visible, but the picture was still not clear enough to identify them. There was a second vehicle behind the truck in the third photo. It appeared to be an SUV of some sort.

"You really can't tell who those people are," Ben said. "We still don't know anything."

"Ben, this is going to be very helpful," Kay said. "These photos confirm that your father encountered someone in a black pickup truck at the job site. That's our theory and this gives us actual evidence. This is excellent."

"Kay, do you think the photos can be enhanced so that we could see more details?" asked Ethan.

"I do," she answered. "Emily, we can bring these to the crime lab tomorrow and have them get to work on it."

"This is great guys, it feels like we're getting some real leads," Emily said. "Kay and I are planning to go meet with the owner of the house that your father was working on tomorrow. I'll let you know what we find out from that.

"I was also thinking that it might be helpful to run a data report to check all the car registrations in the area for black Ford pickups. There are bound to be a lot of them, but it might come in useful as we get more information."

"I'm really glad we came up," Ben said. "Ethan and I want to do whatever we can to help."

Ethan nodded in agreement.

CHAPTER TWENTY-THREE

Emily put the laptop away and started setting the kitchen table.

"Ethan, could you please go light the grill?" she asked. "Ben, can you help cook? You know I never cook your burgers the way you like them."

Ethan went outside and Ben followed with the two plates of burgers. They both enjoyed cooking on the grill and Emily was glad to have the help. She turned quickly to go toward the sink and bumped into Kay.

"Oh, sorry, I didn't see you coming," Emily said.

"I was kind of sneaking to the door. Don't you think I should leave you and your sons alone to have some family time?"

"Are you scared to be here when I tell them about us?"

"Yes, of course I am. I don't want them to hate me for coming along and taking advantage of their mother right after their father dies."

"I'm going to explain it to them. I think they would find it strange if you weren't here. They've already started to see what a good person you are."

"I don't know. I'm not used to getting involved in family matters. My family avoided conflicts, and we really didn't have any confrontations that I can remember."

"I think it's better to have things out in the open and have a confrontation than it is to try and keep secrets. That's why I don't want to hide this from the boys."

"Well, I might not be much help, but I'll stay if you want me to."

Emily poured glasses of lemonade for everyone and sat down at the table with Kay. She was feeling anxious about saying anything to her sons, but she knew them both well enough to know that it would be better to tell them now than later. It was the first time that she had seen Kay act nervous. She was usually very confident and assertive. This was an interesting new side to her.

Ben and Ethan came into the kitchen carrying the plates. They sat down across from Kay and Emily. Ben passed the plate with the veggie burgers to Kay. She took one and passed the plate to Emily. Ethan served himself some salad and set the bowl down.

Emily realized she hadn't asked Ethan about his girlfriend. "Ethan, how is Stacy?"

"She's good. She was going to come today, but I wasn't sure how late I'd be back and she has to work early tomorrow."

"I hope she comes up with you for a visit soon," Emily said. "I haven't seen her in a while. Maybe you can come up some weekend."

"I was thinking that we might come up soon. Boston is getting hot."

"How is work going, Ben?" Emily asked.

"Good," he answered. "Are those cameras that I installed working okay?"

"Yes, I think so. Did you check out the new alarm system? I'll have to give you guys the code."

Emily glanced at Kay and they exchanged a smile. The four of them had a relaxed, comfortable conversation as they ate lunch and she caught up on the latest news in her sons' lives. Emily hoped that their enjoyable visit wouldn't come to an excruciating end when she told the boys about her relationship with Kay.

"Is your burger all right, Kay?" Ben asked. "It was hard to tell if it was done."

"Delicious," she said. "Thank you."

"Do you like to cook?" Ben asked her.

"Yes, I enjoy it. I don't often get the chance to make very elaborate meals because it's usually just me."

"Do you live by yourself?" he asked.

"Yes, I do," answered Kay.

Emily decided that was a good way to lead into the conversation that she wanted to have.

"Ben, Ethan, there's something that I want to talk to you about," Emily said.

"What?" Ben asked. He exchanged a worried look with Ethan.

Emily was finding it difficult to come up with the right words. She looked at Kay who nodded supportively.

"You know that I loved your father and I always will."

"Of course," Ben said.

"Um, I've been spending a lot of time with someone that I've come to care for and I wanted you to know about it. It doesn't mean that I've forgotten your father or that I love him any less."

"You've found someone else?" Ethan said. "Is that what you mean?"

"I wanted you to know that I've started seeing someone."

Ben slapped the table in disgust. "Are you serious? It hasn't even been a year and you've already gotten over Dad."

"It's not like that," Emily said. "Just because I'm seeing someone doesn't mean that it takes away from your father."

"Yes, it does," argued Ben.

"Who?" Ethan asked quietly.

Emily glanced over at Kay. She reached over and grasped her hand. "Kay and I have been seeing each other."

Ethan closed his eyes and shook his head.

"No way," Ben said. "There is no way that you're serious."

Emily glanced over at Kay watching silently, probably wishing fervently that she had been able to slip out the door earlier. She didn't want Kay to get too upset by this confrontation or to have the boys say anything that would make her feel responsible for causing a family scene, but she needed to discuss this with Ben and Ethan.

Emily tried to rein in her immediate reaction to argue back with the boys. She was aware that they had all been through a lot and she didn't want her sons to be hurt any further.

"This has nothing to do with your father or either of you," she tried to explain. "I don't want to hurt you, but I wanted you to know. I don't want to hide anything from you."

"Well, maybe you should have hidden this," Ben said angrily. "You're our mother. Why would you just decide that you want to start running around with women? What would Dad think?"

"Ben, that's not fair. You boys have always been the most important thing in the world to me. I was hoping that you could try to be a little more understanding."

"How can I understand? It doesn't make sense," Ben said.

"I found someone who makes me happy. That makes sense to me," Emily said. "I'm sorry if it upsets you, I really didn't mean to do anything to hurt you."

"It's just a shock," Ethan said.

"It feels like you're betraying Dad," Ben said.

"I'm sorry you feel that way. I never would have betrayed your father and it hurts me to hear you say that."

"I need some time to process this," Ben said. He stood up and walked to the door. "I'm going to go out to the car. I'll talk to you later."

Emily stood and watched him leave, fighting back tears. She picked up some dishes and started clearing off the table. Kay looked at Ethan, who was staring at the table.

"I know you probably don't want to hear anything from me," Kay said. "I just want you to know that it took a lot of courage for your mother to tell you about our relationship. It would have been easier not to say anything. She loves you too much to try to keep anything from you. I don't have to tell you what a good person she is."

Kay stood up and walked over to the sink next to Emily. She put a hand on Emily's shoulder in silent support.

Ethan stood up from the table and walked over to his mother. Emily was facing the sink with tears running down her face. Ethan put his hand on her other shoulder.

"I'm sorry Mom," Ethan said. "It's going to be okay."

Emily turned to face him. She tried to wipe the tears from her cheeks. "I hope you don't feel like this is a betrayal of your father. I wasn't planning to have another relationship, but Kay has become very special to me."

"Mom, I want you to be happy. I know you would be there for me no matter what, and I'm here for you, too. I think Ben and I were just really surprised."

"I know. This is hard to take in on top of the news about your father's accident. I need you to know how much I love you," Emily said.

"I love you too," Ethan said. "I'd better go talk to Ben. You know how he gets. I'm sure he'll calm down and want to talk to you later."

"I hope so," Emily said. She and Ethan hugged each other tightly. Ethan let go of Emily and turned to Kay. He reached out and put his arms around her next.

"Kay, I'm glad you're here for my mom. I hope you guys are happy together," he said. "Thank you for helping us figure things out about Dad's crash."

He walked out the door and got into the car with Ben. Ethan waved as they drove away. Ben stared toward the road.

Emily watched their car leave and said quietly, "I guess you were right, I should have waited to say anything."

"Babe, I'm sorry Ben was so upset." Kay wrapped her arms around Emily and held her. "I don't think it would have been any easier or hurt any less if you had waited."

Emily leaned her head against Kay's shoulder. "I wonder if I'll ever stop feeling guilty. I felt guilty about my feelings while Tom was alive. Then I felt guilty after he died and I started caring about you."

She looked at Kay. "I don't want to feel like we're doing something wrong. That's why I wanted to tell the boys."

"I know," Kay said. "I hope you know how much I care about you. I think you're really special, too. I wish I could do something to make you feel better. I'm sorry that I'm causing this pain for you."

"You aren't causing any pain, just the opposite. Being with you brings happiness into my life. I hope Ben will understand that."

CHAPTER TWENTY-FOUR

The next day Emily skipped the gym and went to work early. She wanted to be sure that she would have plenty of time to run reports on black Ford pickup truck registrations in the area. She also wanted to think of some way to make things better with Ben. She still hadn't heard anything from him, and she wanted to give him a chance to calm down and think things over before she tried calling him.

Emily sat down at her desk and logged onto her computer. She set up the parameters for the search carefully, making sure she included all the local towns and other points of data that she was interested in. She ran a few different versions and saved the results into spreadsheets. Her next step was going to be transferring the spreadsheets from the SBI server over to her local machine so that she could have her own copies. She had just started to open one of the files when her office phone rang. She looked at the caller ID and saw that it was her boss.

"Hello, Alex."

"Good morning Emily. Can you stop by my office for a moment?" Alex normally spent most of the day in his office.

He allowed Emily and the rest of the developers to work independently the majority of the time. He would check in occasionally and get an overview of what she was working on.

Alex was very intelligent and his moods could be unpredictable. He could be caring and jovial one day and insultingly condescending the next. Emily tried to stay on his good side and avoid any possible conflicts. She would have liked to replace him on first base on the softball team, but that would make things too uncomfortable at work.

Emily hung up and went down the hall to find out what Alex wanted. She entered his office and he gestured to a chair. "Sit down, please."

"What's up?" she asked, taking a seat as requested.

"I wanted to check in and find out what you're working on. I haven't had a status report from you for a little while."

"I was just finishing up some vehicle registration reports for Detective DeLorme's investigation into Tom's accident."

Alex gave her a surprised look. "I didn't know there was an investigation. Why is MCU looking into it?"

"The crash reconstruction unit determined that the crash was caused by another truck running Tom's pickup off the road."

"Have they found anything out about the other truck?"

Not wanting to reveal many details, Emily worded her reply carefully. "No. They're looking for a pickup truck, so I was running some reports on trucks in the area."

"I see. Well, be sure not to fall behind on your other projects."

Emily tried to contain her anger. She never fell behind in her work and it was insulting for Alex to imply that she would. The case was related to her husband's death. Of course she was going to work on whatever reports were needed. It was surprising that Alex wasn't more concerned with the fact that Tom's crash had not been an accident, but he seemed to be in one of his bad moods.

"Anything else?" Emily asked.

"No. Has your friend heard anything about Troy Pomerleau?"

"Not that I know of," Emily said. Alex was definitely in a strange mood.

"It's been on the news so much that I was just curious."

"Let me know if there's anything you need me to do." Emily left Alex's office and returned to her own. She answered an email that had come in and then turned her attention back to the registration reports. She logged back into the server she was working on and retrieved the report spreadsheets.

Once she was done, she called Kay. "Good morning, honey."

"Hi. Are you sure that you're crabby in the morning? You sound as sweet as can be."

"It's just a front," Emily said. "Have you heard from Pete?"

"I talked to him this morning. Still no sign of Troy Pomerleau. I'm sure it's going to be a busy week trying to track him down."

"I ran the truck registration reports. I know you're busy with the Pomerleau case right now, but do you think you'll have a chance to go over the reports with me sometime today?"

"I'll always have time for you," Kay answered. "I also want to look up that phone number we found from the cell phone report. I was planning to bring copies of the photos from the phone over to the crime lab a little later this morning. Can I stop by your office after so that we can go over things?"

"Sure, I'll be here. I'd love to go over things with you."

"Okay, see you later."

Emily hung up and got back to work.

* * *

Kay opened up the file with Tom's cell phone report on her laptop. Scanning through the pages, she located the number that they were interested in for Orleans Design Associates.

Pete walked around the corner and over to her desk. "We just had a sighting for Troy Pomerleau. He was at a convenience store in Augusta."

"Do we know where he went?"

Pete shook his head. "Not yet, but now we know he's still in the area and must have found a place to hide out. Apparently, he stopped at a convenience store to get gas early this morning. He beat up a clerk pretty badly. I'm heading over to the hospital to see if we can talk to him. Want to come?"

"I'm right behind you. I'm going to take my own vehicle and follow. I need to stop at the crime lab on my way back."

Kay jumped up and grabbed her bag. She wanted to bring the photos from Tom's cell phone over to the crime lab in person, so she had downloaded them to a flash drive. Pete filled her in on Troy Pomerleau as they walked toward the entrance.

"Troy went into the store to get some cigarettes and junk food. We think that the clerk recognized him from all the news coverage. We haven't spoken to him yet. He's just a kid and he ended up with some serious injuries. There was a security camera that captured the whole thing."

"How did you find out it was Pomerleau?" Kay asked.

"The clerk was able to tell the paramedics on his way to the hospital."

"Why did Pomerleau go after him?"

"When the clerk recognized Troy, he said something that tipped him off. Troy didn't want to be identified. He's a big guy, and he grabbed the kid by the shirt and yanked him over the counter. He knocked the kid down and started pounding on him. Once the kid stopped fighting back, Troy stood up and started kicking him. It's a good thing some other customers drove in or he would have kept on going. It was vicious. The guy's an animal."

"Did the other customers see him?" Kay asked.

"No, they weren't paying attention. They pumped some gas and went in for something. That's when they saw the clerk on the floor and called 911."

"Was there a camera outside?"

"Yes. There was some decent footage, so we have the license plate. We're trying to track down the car Troy was driving." They had reached Pete's car. He opened up the door and got in. "I'll meet you at the hospital."

Kay got into her car and followed Pete. The hospital was only a few miles away, so it didn't take long to get there. They walked in together and stopped at the front desk. The volunteer working the information desk gave them instructions on how to find the injured clerk's room in the critical care unit where he was being treated. An officer was standing guard outside in the corridor when they reached the room. Kay and Pete greeted the officer and showed him their badges before stepping inside.

The clerk was lying motionless in the bed. He was hooked up to an array of monitors and IV lines. Kay couldn't tell if he was asleep or unconscious. Kay and Pete introduced themselves to a woman sitting in the chair next to the bed.

"Hello, I'm Detective DeLorme and this is Detective Harris. We're with the Maine State Police."

"My name is Helen," the woman answered. "I'm Danny's mother."

"How is he doing?" Pete asked.

"The doctor was just here. He said that they are going to need to operate on his eye socket, so they're getting the surgical team ready."

Bandages covered most of Danny's face. What little that showed was swollen and bloody. Kay sat in the chair next to Danny's mother.

"Have you been able to talk to him at all?" she asked.

"No. He's been unconscious since I got here. I got a call at work this morning telling me what happened and I couldn't believe it. Danny's a good kid, and he doesn't have an enemy in the world."

"I'm sure he is a good kid. We're trying to find the man who did this to him," Kay said. "We were hoping he might be able to tell us something."

"This was just his part-time job. He graduated from high school this past spring and he's supposed to be going to the University of Maine this fall."

Pete looked through the notes in the medical chart next to the bed.

Kay passed one of her business cards to Danny's mother. "Here's my number. We'll be back later today or tomorrow to check on Danny. I'm very sorry that this happened to him."

Kay and Pete stepped out of the room and walked down the hallway. Pete shook his head. "Pomerleau really did a number on the kid. His chart listed broken ribs, broken teeth and nose and a probable concussion. Not to mention his eye. We've got to find this guy, he's out of control."

"Any thoughts on where to look for him?"

"We'll start by finding the car he was driving," Pete said. "I'm going to find out what's going on with that now. How about you, what're your plans?"

"I've got some photos that I'm taking to the crime lab to see if they can be enhanced. They came from Tom Stratton's stolen cell phone. We're hoping they can help us to identify the driver of the truck."

"Good luck. I know those techs can do some impressive things. How was the softball team?"

"Um, I'm not sure if I should say too much because I want you to join the team, too. Some of the players aren't bad, including Emily. It's just that there are a few that must not have played any organized sports before in their lives."

Pete laughed. "So your girlfriend is not bad. I bet she'd love to hear that."

"That didn't come out right. She's awesome actually." Kay stopped. She hadn't meant to say that much.

Pete raised his eyebrows. "Oh, really? It sounds like I need to come to one of your games and see for myself."

Kay decided it was time to change the subject. "I'm waiting to hear back from the MDEA. They've been working with the New York police who are keeping Martin under surveillance. I want to make sure they keep us updated. We need to be ready if Martin decides to come up and try to get revenge for MacNamara and Jackson's deaths."

The walked into the parking lot and reached their cars. Kay turned to Pete. "Keep me posted on Pomerleau's car. I'll be sure to check back on Danny."

"Sounds good." Pete got in his car and drove back toward the office.

Kay opened her car door and tossed her bag onto the passenger seat before getting in. She started the engine and drove out of the parking lot, organizing her thoughts as she headed to the crime lab. She hadn't had time to check out the phone number for Orleans Design Associates yet. She also had to go meet Emily and go over the vehicle registrations. She didn't want to fall behind on anything in the Pomerleau investigation, but she felt like they could be close to finding some information on Tom Stratton's accident and she didn't want to put if off.

She pulled into the parking lot of the crime lab and went inside. Kay approached the receptionist's counter and said, "Hi, I was wondering if I could speak with Jennifer Adams?"

"May I tell her who is asking for her?" the receptionist asked.

"I'm Detective DeLorme and she helped me with a case last week."

"Please have a seat and I'll let her know you're here."

Kay sat in the waiting area with the flash drive in her hand. She could have emailed the images over, but she would get faster results if she brought them over and made contact with one of the technicians.

A short time later, Jennifer came out to greet Kay. "Hello, what can I do for you?"

"You were so helpful with the lab work you did on the van last week that I thought of you for another case I'm working on. I was wondering if you could help me with some photos that are part of a vehicular homicide investigation?"

Jennifer smiled at her. "I wish I could, but I work in the labs. I know someone that can help you though. Wait here and I'll send her out to you."

"Thank you. That would be great."

"It was nice seeing you. Stop by anytime." Jennifer gave her a flirtatious smile.

Kay was taken aback. Jennifer was good-looking and very nice, but Kay hadn't intended for her to think that she was interested. She was flattered, but Emily was the only one she was interested in. She nodded. "Thanks."

Jennifer left and Kay settled back in her chair to wait. The door opened a few minutes later and an older woman walked into the reception area. She approached Kay and extended her hand. "Detective DeLorme?"

Kay shook the woman's hand. "Yes."

"Hi, I'm Lori. I work with images. Jennifer said you had some photos?"

"I have them right here." Kay held up the drive.

"Come to my office and we'll fill out the request form and make sure that I can get them off your flash drive."

Kay followed Lori down a side corridor into her small office. Kay handed her the drive and Lori stuck it into the USB port on one of the computers sitting on her desk. When she was satisfied that she would be able to open the images, she ejected the drive and turned to Kay.

"Okay, I'm sure I can work with the images. I have some software that I'll use to clean them up and enhance them. I've got a big backlog right now, so it will probably take me a few days to get a chance to get these processed. Let me just get some information from you for this form."

Kay gave Lori the details she needed and thanked her as she walked back with her to the reception area.

CHAPTER TWENTY-FIVE

It was later than she had planned by the time Kay got to Emily's office. She recognized some of the faces from softball practice as she walked down the hallway. Tony, the third baseman, was sitting with Sam in the break room when she passed by.

Kay stopped for a moment. "Hi, guys. How are you?"

"Hi, Kay," Sam said.

"Are you ready for the first game this weekend?" Tony asked.

"Can't wait," she answered. "See you there."

Kay continued down the hall until she got to Emily's office. She paused and knocked on the doorway. Emily was sitting at her desk working on her computer and looked up.

"Hi there," Emily said with a smile, standing and walking over to her.

Kay entered the office and shut the door softly. She didn't wait for Emily to say anything more. She pulled her close and kissed her, pressing Emily back against the door. She leaned back and looked at Emily. "Hi. We're blocking the door so Sam doesn't come barging in. I want you all to myself for a minute."

"I've been thinking of this all day. I couldn't wait to see you." Emily smiled and leaned in for another kiss. "I'm getting really comfortable with this."

"I meant to get here earlier, but I got busy. Troy Pomerleau beat up a clerk at a convenience store early this morning."

"Is the clerk all right?"

"His injuries aren't life-threatening, but they're pretty bad."

"Did they catch Pomerleau?"

"Not yet."

They went over to Emily's desk and sat down. Emily opened up the file with the truck registration spreadsheets on her computer. "Ready to look at these?"

The reports listed over three hundred black Ford pickup trucks in the area. Emily had them sorted by town. They looked through the lists, but nothing in particular caught their attention. Kay watched as Emily looked through the data again for names of any people that Tom might have worked with or any clients that he might have had.

"Nothing." Emily sat back with a sigh. "I figured it would be a long shot to find anything good."

"Don't worry, this is going to be helpful," Kay said. "It's going to take some work, but we'll find more clues and maybe we can tie someone to one of the trucks on this list."

"Did you have any luck with the phone number? I checked the company records and all I could find was the name of the lawyer who files their paperwork."

"I got pulled away before I could look into it. Why don't I head back to my office and do that now. I can check in with Pete, too. Then I'll come back and pick you up so that we can go out to the Bartletts' together. Would that be good?"

"Yes, but I don't want you to go." Emily squeezed Kay's leg.

Kay stood up. "The sooner I go, the sooner I can get back."

Kay called the officer on duty at the hospital to check on Danny when she got back to her desk. The officer told her that Danny was out of surgery and was under observation in the surgical care unit. He wasn't expected to be awake for questioning until at least the next day.

Since there wasn't anything she could do about talking to Danny, she called Pete to check on the search for Troy Pomerleau. Pete answered from his car. He was headed to Rome again to look for Troy at his brother Kevin's house.

"We really don't think he's there. The house has been watched around the clock. We're going to check, just in case. There are plenty of places to hide around the property, so he could have snuck in somehow for all we know. Plus, I want to keep hassling Kevin Pomerleau."

"Who owned the car that Troy was driving at the convenience store?"

"It was registered to his cousin. We located the cousin, who claimed to have no idea how Troy got his car. We brought him in and he's being charged as an accessory. He's sticking with his story that he hasn't seen Troy."

"Let me know how it goes at Kevin Pomerleau's. I have to go talk to someone about the Stratton case, but I'll be back later."

"All right, I'll catch up with you later."

She looked up the number for Orleans Design Associates in her file. It was time to find out whose number this was. She didn't want to let the person whose number it was know that they were part of an investigation, so she was going to have to try to find out their name without mentioning Tom Stratton. She picked up her office phone and dialed the number.

A man's voice answered. "Hello."

"Hello, this is Detective DeLorme, with the Maine State Police. We are looking into a report of telephone fraud. This number was on a list of calls that was made by a company that may have tried to solicit personal information from you, such as your social security number or bank account number."

"Oh, um, no. I haven't received any calls like that."

"Could you please confirm your name, sir?"

"My name is Chris Brooks."

"We have this number listed as being owned by Orleans Design Associates," Kay said, hoping for more information.

"That's the holding company that I have set up for some property that I own, but this is my cell phone number."

"All right, sir. Please contact me immediately if you receive a call from anyone asking you for information. My number is 207-555-5100."

"Thank you. I will."

Kay hung up and sat back in her chair, thinking about the implications of this new information. Why would Tom have made one of his last calls to Chris Brooks? She needed to talk to Emily.

Kay drove over to pick Emily up at her office. She pulled in front of the building where Emily was waiting and greeted her as she got into the car. "Hi, there."

"Hello." Emily gave Kay's knee a quick squeeze.

Kay filled Emily in on the phone call she'd just made as they headed toward the Bartlett's. "The number for Orleans Design Associates is actually Chris Brooks's personal cell phone number."

"That is really strange," Emily said. "I wonder why Tom would have called Chris Brooks that morning while he was at the Bartlett's."

"You said that Tom's notes mentioned that Sherry Bartlett is friends with Brooks. That could be the connection. We can ask Paul about it when we talk to him. Maybe Sherry will be there too, but she didn't seem very cooperative on the phone."

They drove in silence for a few minutes, and then Kay turned on the radio. A Neil Young song came on and Kay started singing along. Emily looked at her. "You have a beautiful voice. I like listening to you talk, but this is even better."

Kay shook her head. "I just like to sing along with the radio."

"Seriously, you sing really well. Do you remember when I told you that there were two things that I always wished I was really good at?"

"Yes, I do. You said you wanted to be an awesome softball player and a great singer."

"Well as you know, I'm an average softball player, which is fine. The thing is, I am a really, really bad singer. The only song that I sing in front of anyone is the birthday song."

"You can't be that bad."

"When I was in high school, I tried out for chorus and didn't make it because the teacher said that I had a serious pitch problem. It was not pretty."

Kay laughed. "Not just a pitch problem, it's serious, huh?"

"Yes," Emily said. "Which is why I appreciate it when I hear a good voice."

They reached Winchester and drove though the center of the small town toward the Bartletts' house. They passed the turn where the road they were on branched off to the North Road, where Tom's accident had taken place. The Bartletts' road was the next turn. They pulled into the driveway and looked at the house where Tom had been on his last job. The two-story shingled cape had an attached garage and overlooked Long Pond. Trees bordered both sides of the home and the lake stretched across the back. The neighboring houses were far enough apart that they weren't visible, giving the home plenty of privacy.

Kay and Emily walked up to the house and knocked on the door. A middle-aged man answered.

"Hello, I'm Detective DeLorme and this is Emily Stratton."

"Nice to meet you, I'm Paul Bartlett. Come on in."

They stepped into the house and Paul led them into the living room, a large room with windows offering expansive views of the lake.

"Please, have a seat," Paul said.

Kay and Emily sat down on the couch and Paul sat in the chair beside them.

"Can I get you something to drink?" he asked.

"No thank you," Kay said. "We were hoping to go over some questions about Tom Stratton."

"Of course. I'm happy to help in any way I can. I have talked with some other officers before, as you probably know."

Emily spoke up. "Tom was my husband. We recently found out that Tom's accident was caused by someone running his truck off the road."

Paul looked at her in surprise. "I had no idea. I thought that he was just driving too fast. I'm very sorry to hear that. He was a nice guy and I enjoyed working with him."

"Thank you," Emily said.

"We're trying to find out what might have caused him to leave the job site that morning. We know he talked to you earlier. Was there any indication that something was wrong?" Kay asked.

"No. We went over some of the lighting details and I was planning to meet him here that day. When I got here at the time we had planned, no one was here."

"Did you see anything unusual when you got here?"

"No, no one was around. There were tire tracks in the snow. I do remember thinking that it looked like there may have been more than one vehicle here, but we had contractors coming in and out so that wasn't unusual."

"Do you know if any of the other contractors drove black pickup trucks?" Kay asked.

Paul thought for a moment. "I stopped by almost every day to see how things were going, so I was pretty familiar with the guys who were working here. A lot of them did drive trucks, but I don't remember if there was a black one."

"We'd like to get a list of the people who worked here. We're going to want to check in with them as well, and see if we can find out more information about what happened that morning."

"Sure, we have all the contractors' names and contact info. I can get that for you now, if you like?"

"Yes, please," Kay answered.

"Hold on, I'll see if my wife can help me get those files. I'll be right back."

Emily turned to Kay after Paul left the room. "Are you going to ask him about Chris Brooks?"

"I'm hoping his wife comes out. I'd like to ask her. We need to do it discreetly though. I don't want to raise any suspicions. I also wanted to look around outside a little bit and see if we can get an idea of the angles that those pictures were taken from."

When Paul returned to the room, Sherry was with him. She was wearing a heavy layer of makeup and dangerously high heels.

"This is my wife, Sherry," Paul said.

"Hello," Sherry said. "I'm quite busy, so I really can only spare a few minutes."

"Nice to meet you," Emily said.

Sherry sat down in a chair next to Paul. Paul handed them a piece of paper with a list of names and numbers.

"Here are the contractors who worked on the house. They also had people who worked for them, but you'll have to get that information from the contractors themselves because I don't have it."

"Thank you," Kay said.

"Sherry, do you by any chance get your hair done by Chris Brooks? I think I may have seen you in his salon," Emily said.

"Why yes, I do," Sherry answered. "He's a dear friend of mine."

"Your house is lovely. Has Chris ever been out here?" Emily asked. "I can just imagine how much he would love it."

Sherry clearly enjoyed the flattery. "I have had Chris out several times, and he adores our new home."

Kay asked, "What's the name of his salon?"

Sherry gave Kay a disdainful look. "It's called Hair By Brooks, but I don't think that you would really care for it."

Kay raised an eyebrow at Emily.

Paul spoke up. "Is there anything else we can help you with?"

"I'd like to take a quick look around outside, if you don't mind," Kay said.

"Sure, I'd be happy to show you around."

Paul took Kay and Emily out through the kitchen into the garage and they walked out the garage door to the driveway. There were windows on the side of the house that had a line of vision through to the other side of the house.

"This must have been where Tom was parked that day. It looks like the right angle," Emily said.

Paul agreed. "This is where Tom usually parked. There were tire tracks in the snow here that day. I saw some tracks from your dog, too."

"Did you notice tire tracks on the other side of the house?" Kay asked.

"Yes, I did. Like I said though, that wasn't unusual. I looked around when Tom wasn't here for our meeting that day. I saw some tire tracks and cigarette butts over on the other side and that was about it."

"Thank you for taking the time to meet with us," Emily said.

"Sorry that I couldn't be of more help. I hope you find the person that caused Tom's accident," Paul said.

"Here's my card. Please call if you think of anything else," Kay said.

They got into Kay's car and drove back toward Augusta. They took the route that Tom would have taken toward Orleans. The crash site was about eight miles from the Bartlett's house. Emily watched her phone as they drove along.

"Pretty much what we thought," Emily said. "There hasn't been any cell phone service since a little while after we left the Bartletts'. Tom wouldn't have been able to call for help if someone was following him."

"I noticed when were outside looking around that the way the house was angled, Tom could have parked on the side and not been visible to someone else who drove in," Kay said.

"That's true. He may have been parked there and the person in the truck drove in and didn't know he was there."

"Right. Tom may have seen or heard something and taken those pictures with his phone. When he tried to leave, they followed him and ran him off the road."

"My God, that must have been what happened." Emily gazed out the window.

"It would be good to figure out why he was calling Chris Brooks," Kay said. "It may not even be related, but it was awfully close to the time that he left the job site. Sherry Bartlett wasn't very helpful, but at least we know now that Chris Brooks has been out to their house."

Kay arrived back at Emily's office and pulled up next to her truck. "I wish we could go get a bite to eat or something but I have to go back to the office."

"Thanks for letting me help with this." Emily put her hand on Kay's and squeezed it gently. "I know you didn't have to bring me with you and I really want to help find out who did this to Tom."

Kay smiled at her. "You're welcome, and you're very helpful. I think we work well together actually."

"We do."

"Have you heard from Ben?" Kay asked.

"No." Emily sighed. "If I don't hear from him tonight, I think I'll go down after work tomorrow and try to talk to him."

"Do you want me to go with you?"

"Thanks, but you're busy and it's probably better if it's just me."

Kay was relieved. She would have gone if Emily wanted her to, but she really didn't want to be there if Ben and Emily started arguing about her.

Emily brushed a kiss against her lips. "Bye."

CHAPTER TWENTY-SIX

The next afternoon Emily set her bag down on the chair next to the table when she walked into the house. The weather had turned hot. She had stopped at home for a moment to change into cooler clothes before heading down to try and talk with Ben. It had been two days since she'd heard from him and she didn't want to let it go any longer.

Emily hadn't had much of a chance to talk to Kay that day. She had tried to catch up with her but Kay had been busy with Pete, tracking down Troy Pomerleau. Emily ran upstairs and changed into some shorts, then headed out to her truck for the drive down to Portland. Once she was on the highway, she decided to check in with Julian and give him an update on things. She placed the call on her Bluetooth headset.

"Hello, little tickle," he answered.

"Hi. Don't ever call me that again."

"What're you up to?"

"I'm headed down to Portland, hoping to catch up with Ben. I told him and Ethan about my relationship with Kay this past weekend and he didn't react very well."

"Oh, my. You jumped right into that, darling."

"You know Ben, if he had found out before I had a chance to tell him, he would have been even more upset."

"Is he upset that it's another woman or because you are starting a relationship?"

"I'm not sure, probably both. That's what I want to talk to him about."

"Good luck."

"Thanks. I also wanted to tell you that we've been making some progress on Tom's accident. We were out to the house where Tom was working that day. Do you know the Bartletts?"

"Isn't the wife a good friend of Chris Brooks?"

"Yes, she and her husband had a new house built, which is why Tom was there."

"If she's a friend of his, I wouldn't trust her for a minute."

"She was pretty obnoxious, but the husband seems nice."

"I'll see if anyone knows anything about her. I'm still looking for clues on that nasty Chris Brooks."

"Try to be careful and discreet."

"Discreet is my middle name," Julian said.

"I thought it was margarita."

"I'll see you at trivia tomorrow, right?"

"Yes," Emily said. "I'm hoping that Kay can come so you can meet her."

"She sounds enchanting. I can't wait."

Emily pulled into the parking lot at Ben's apartment in Portland. It was in a nice location, near the shops and restaurants of the Old Port section of the city. She was in luck; his car was in the lot. She walked up the steps and pushed the buzzer.

Ben answered on the intercom, "Hello, who is it?"

"It's Mom," she replied.

The door buzzed and she opened it and walked in. She went up the stairs to his apartment where Ben was waiting in the doorway.

"Come on in," he said.

"I thought maybe we could talk?"

"All right."

She looked around. She was glad to see that his apartment was fairly neat and tidy. She had never dropped in on him without calling first. She sat down on the couch and he sat next to her.

"I was hoping that I would hear from you," Emily said. "I'm sorry you're so upset."

He nodded. "It just seems like it's all too much. First Dad dies, and everyone blames him for the accident. Then we find out it wasn't an accident. Now you've moved on and you've decided you like women. It's like our family is gone."

"Ben, that's not how I see things at all. Our family is not gone. You know that you and Ethan and our family are the most important things in the world to me. I have met someone that I care about, but it doesn't take away from you guys. It doesn't take away from your father, either."

"I don't know. It seems like it does to me."

"Your father and I were together for twenty-five years. We had our ups and downs but we loved each other and stayed together. There was never anyone else in my life. Since he's been gone, I've come to care about Kay. Is it the fact that she's a woman that bothers you?"

"I think it's the fact that it makes me wonder if you ever really loved Dad."

"Of course I did."

"Then how could you decide you want to be with a woman now?"

"I don't know. I can't explain it, but I can tell you that it doesn't change how much I love you and your brother. I would hope that it doesn't change how you feel about me."

Ben thought silently for a moment.

"I'm trying to understand, but I feel like you betrayed us," Ben said.

"Ben, I don't want to hurt you, but I don't think that I am doing anything wrong by being with someone I care about."

Ben bowed his head. "I'm sorry, Mom. I just need some time to think about all of this."

"I guess all I can do at this point is give you some time then. If you want to talk about anything, please call me, okay?"

Emily called Kay on her way back home. "Hi."

"Hi, babe. How did it go?" .

"Not very well. Ben is a lot like me. He gets upset and overreacts. I was hoping that once he had time to think about everything he would be more understanding."

"I'm sorry. I know how much you love your sons."

"He sees our relationship as a betrayal of him and his father."

"I wish that I hadn't caused this. I never would have wanted to come between you and your sons."

"It wasn't your fault at all. This is something that I don't want to hide from and I need to deal with it. I just hope that Ben can accept me for who I am."

"I hope he realizes how lucky he is to have a mother like you."

"Thanks, but I think he's wishing he didn't have a mother like me," Emily said. "I talked to Ethan earlier. I'm glad that at least one of the boys understands that whatever is going on between the two of us really doesn't have anything to do with how I feel about them."

"Speaking of the two of us, I want to plan to do something special this weekend."

"We have our first game on Saturday, that will be special."

"I meant just the two of us, Coach."

"Oh. What would you like to do?"

"I'd like us to plan to go out together after the game. We could still have a beer with the team after, but I want to do something with just the two of us on Saturday night."

"That sounds nice, Kay. I would love to."

"You're not going to get all nervous on me, are you?"

"I can't promise anything like that. Hey, do you want to come to trivia tomorrow night? I want you to meet Julian."

"Sure, that sounds fun. As long as nothing comes up with the Pomerleau case, I'll be there."

"Just be aware, Julian loves to try to shock people. He's actually very sweet once you get to know him. He'll probably say something arrogant and obnoxious just to see what you do. I love him, but I know he can be hard to take if you don't know him."

"I'll keep that in mind and try not to be offended. If he's a good friend of yours, there must be a reason."

CHAPTER TWENTY-SEVEN

Kay was working late, so she made plans to meet Emily at the pub for trivia instead of riding there together. It had been another busy day working the Pomerleau case with very little to show for it. They had been chasing down leads all week, but were still not able to locate Troy Pomerleau.

The convenience store clerk's condition was improving. She and Pete had been able to speak to him that afternoon. Unfortunately, he wasn't able to tell them anything that might help them find Troy. As they had suspected, Danny had recognized Troy when he came into the convenience store. Danny had made the mistake of telling Troy that he knew who he was, which had resulted in Troy attacking him. He had come close to losing the vision in one of his eyes, but he was lucky to be alive.

The progress on Tom Stratton's case had slowed down. Kay had worked her way down the list of contractors that Paul Bartlett had given them, but none of them was able to provide any new information. None of them drove a black pickup truck, either. She was hoping that the photos from Tom's cell phone would be ready soon and that they might give them a fresh lead.

Kay's thoughts turned to Emily, as they often had lately. They hadn't been able to spend much time together this week and she was missing her. That was kind of funny, considering that in the past her exes had always complained that she never wanted to spend enough time with them. She couldn't wait for their date on Saturday night. She kept telling herself to be careful and go slow, but she couldn't stop herself from falling for Emily.

Kay pulled into the parking lot next to Emily's truck. She walked in and saw Emily and her friend sitting at a corner table across the room, laughing with their waitress. Julian was a good-looking man and Emily had already warned her that he was a little vain. That didn't sound very pleasant, so this should be interesting. Emily spotted her and waved her over.

Emily stood up and gave her a hug when she got to the table. "Hi, Kay."

"Hi," she answered. "Hello, Julian, nice to meet you."

"Nice to meet you, too," he said, standing up to greet her.

They all sat back down at the table.

"Well, I can see what you see in her. She has a very sexy look about her," Julian said.

"Julian, be quiet," Emily said.

"What? She does. Very androgynously pretty, with a confident, relaxed air about her."

"I'm sitting right here," Kay said.

"Julian, if you don't behave, I'm going to tell Debbie to shut you off," Emily said.

"Okay, no need to be dramatic."

The waitress came over and took Kay's drink order. She ordered the same type of beer that Emily was having.

"What are you going to have for dinner?" she asked Emily.

"I usually get a salad. Almost all of the dishes have meat."

"Don't tell me she's a vegetarian too?" Julian said. "What is the world coming to?"

"Let's talk about something that we can all agree on," Emily said. "Kay, what did you think of Sherry Bartlett?"

Kay tapped her finger on the table in irritation at the memory of their meeting. "I don't know her very well of course, but she sure didn't want to be helpful."

"That woman is a good friend of Chris Brooks, who I cannot stand," Julian chimed in. "He is a sleazy, backstabbing, pathetic excuse for a stylist. If she's anything like him, I wouldn't want to know her."

"What was up with that comment about me not being one to care for his salon?" Kay asked. "That was a direct slam against my hair, wasn't it?"

"Are you kidding me?" Julian gasped. "Your hair is gorgeous. A bit of a utilitarian cut, but how dare she!"

Kay saw Emily smile as she glanced between the two of them.

"I know," Emily said. "She was really rude to Kay."

"She was probably just jealous," Julian said. "Kay, you must come to my salon and I'll take care of you. A slight shape up of that wonderful hair of yours and she'll be eating her words."

"Thank you, that would be really nice."

"My pleasure. Notice how good Emily's hair looks? That's all thanks to me. Isn't she lovely?"

"Yes, she is," answered Kay. She looked at Emily and smiled.

Emily smiled back at Kay clasped her hand under the table.

"Julian, Emily told me that you hear a lot of interesting things as a stylist," Kay said.

"You would not believe what people tell me. I hear all the dirt on everyone in town. Did Emily tell you that I've been listening for any talk about Tom's accident?"

"Yes, she did. Have you heard anything?"

"No, total silence. I'm on the case with Chris Brooks and Sherry Bartlett, too. I'll let you ladies know if I hear anything juicy."

"Just be careful. I wouldn't want you to get into trouble with anyone," Emily said.

Kay agreed. "It would be great to have your help if you hear anything, but please don't put yourself at risk."

Julian looked pleased to hear that Kay wanted his help. "I am enjoying my role as an undercover detective. The main thing that I hear about Chris Brooks is that he's into drugs. The word is that you can get more than a style and a manicure at his salon."

"Emily mentioned that you told her something like that," Kay said. "I asked around at the MDEA and they hadn't heard anything about him. They did say that they'll be keeping an eye out now that I mentioned it to them."

"I meant to tell you that that one of the last calls Tom made was to Chris Brooks," Emily told Julian.

"That's odd," Julian said. "Do you suppose Chris wanted him to do some work?"

"He didn't make any notes about it and he usually wrote everything like that down in his date book."

Debbie brought over Kay's drink and took their orders. The next round of trivia began and they focused on the questions.

"What is the largest lake that is completely in the Unites States?" repeated Emily.

"I think that's Lake Michigan," Kay said.

Julian nudged Emily's foot. She glanced up at him and he gave her an inconspicuous nod of approval when Kay wasn't looking.

"I think it's sweet how you two are getting along, by the way," Julian said.

Kay looked at Emily in alarm, hoping that he wouldn't continue with a public analysis of their relationship.

"Julian," Emily warned, "I'm glad you think that, but let's talk about something else."

"There's nothing to be self-conscious about. It's adorable that you're holding hands under the table so that no one sees."

Kay and Emily dropped their hands quickly. Emily was saved from responding by the arrival of Debbie with their meals. They finished the round of trivia while they ate dinner, then Kay had to get going. She had a few things she still needed to check on for work.

"It was nice meeting you, Julian."

"Yes, you too. I have heard a lot about you and it was nice to finally meet you. I like to tease, but I really am glad to see Emily happy."

Emily patted his arm. "Aw, thanks. I'll be right back, I want to walk Kay out to her car."

The warm summer air hit them as Emily and Kay walked outside to the parking lot. Emily stood with Kay at her car and hugged her good-bye. "Thanks for coming. I know you're busy."

"I enjoyed it, and I want to get to know your friends."

"I was really happy to see you and Julian get along so well."

"It looks like I'm going to have a new stylist."

"Maybe we could have lunch together tomorrow?"

"That sounds good. I'll give you a call and let you know if I can." Kay looked around to be sure that they were alone. "Right now though, I'd like a little more than a hug."

She pulled Emily close to her and leaned her back against the car. Kay rested her hands on the car on either side of Emily and pressed their hips together. Their lips met in a kiss and Kay probed Emily's mouth with her tongue, enjoying the taste of her. Emily pulled Kay's hips closer and joined Kay's tongue with her own, kissing her back with growing desire.

"Mm, that's nice," Kay said. "I'd better get going while I still can."

They stood still together for a moment as they caught their breath.

"How do you do that to me?" Emily said softly. "It's going to be really hard to concentrate on trivia now."

Kay got into her car with a wave. She watched Emily go back inside to join Julian and then she drove off.

CHAPTER TWENTY-EIGHT

Emily's day was not going well. Alex had given her two new projects to start working on and was expecting her to have already completed the one she was currently working on, even though that one was not supposed to be due until next week. On top of that, Sam had decided to ask for her help with the web form he was working on and she didn't want to say no.

Even though she probably shouldn't take the time, she was hoping that she could get away for lunch with Kay. She would have to stay late and make up for it. When Emily still hadn't heard from her and it was getting close to noon, she decided to give Kay a call.

"Hi, Kay. I hope I'm not bothering you."

"Hi. No, I've been meaning to call you, but it's been a hectic day. I was in a meeting with Sergeant Hixon for half the morning and I didn't realize it was so late."

"It sounds like you're too busy for lunch today. It's not a big deal, I just wanted to check in with you," Emily said.

"I'd like to go. Why don't we meet at the crime lab and go to the restaurant across the street? That way we can check on Tom's photos."

"Okay, what time should I meet you?"

"How about in a half hour?"

Emily wrapped up the report she was working on and headed over to the crime lab. She was hoping that getting out of the office for a little while would improve her mood. It was hot outside in the parking lot, so she locked her truck and went in to the lobby.

The receptionist greeted her. "Can I help you?"

"I'm waiting to meet someone, thanks." Emily took a seat in one of the chairs across the room. She watched out the window for Kay. A few minutes later she saw her car pull in.

The main door to the lab offices opened and a young woman came into the reception area. She walked toward the exit just as Kay opened the door.

* * *

"Well, hello, Kay. How are you? I was hoping you would stop back by. Can I help you with something?"

"Hi, Jennifer. I'm here to check on the photo enhancements that Lori is working on for me," Kay said. "Thanks again for your help with those fingerprints."

Jennifer put her hand on Kay's arm and looked at her with a smile. "If there's anything at all that I can do for you, please call me. I'd love to hear from you again."

Kay looked across the room and saw Emily. She was not sure of how to best let Jennifer know that she wasn't interested without offending her. She decided that ignoring her would be the most diplomatic option.

"Thanks. I'm going to see if Lori is in," Kay said to Jennifer as she stepped toward the receptionist.

"Is Lori in? I'm Detective DeLorme and I wanted to check on some photos she was working on for me," Kay said to the lady behind the counter.

"Hold on, I'll check."

Kay looked over at Emily and saw the expressionless look on her face as she stood up and walked over.

"Hi, how are you?" Kay asked.

"I'm fine. I just realized, I have to get back to the office. Something came up." Emily walked quickly past Kay and Jennifer toward the door.

"Wait, Emily."

"Sorry, I'm really late." Emily opened the door and walked to her truck.

Kay watched her get in her truck and drive off. She wasn't sure if she should follow her or if she would be making a scene by running after her at the crime lab. Here was a good example of why it wasn't smart to get work mixed up with personal life.

"Who was that?" Jennifer asked.

"That was a friend that I was supposed to be meeting here."

"I guess she didn't feel like waiting. Well, have a nice day, hope I talk to you again soon." Jennifer stepped out the door.

Kay clenched her teeth in frustration. She hadn't done anything to respond to Jennifer's flirtations, so why was she feeling guilty? Emily had jumped to conclusions without even giving her a chance to explain. She didn't know if she should go find her and talk to her or give her time to calm down.

Lori opened the lab door and came out to the reception area. "Hello, Detective DeLorme."

"Please, call me Kay. I wanted to see if you'd had a chance to look at the photos for the Stratton case."

"I'm afraid that I haven't had time to work on your photos yet, Kay. I had a couple other things come up. I expect to be able to process them either tomorrow or Monday, at the latest. I'll let you know as soon as I have anything."

"Thank you. I'm sure you're busy, I was just checking in."

Kay left the lab and headed back to her office. So much for lunch.

* * *

Emily tried not to get too upset as she drove back to her office. She replayed the scene at the lab in her mind. Kay obviously knew the young woman who had said she wanted to hear from Kay again. Did that mean that Kay knew her professionally or had they dated in the past? Emily had never talked to Kay about people she had been with in the past. It hadn't seemed to matter. They had never talked about seeing each other exclusively either, now that she thought about it. In her mind she hadn't even considered wanting to see someone else, but that didn't mean that Kay felt the same.

Emily knew she was going to have to talk to Kay about it but for now she just wanted to put it out of her mind and go back to work. She got back to her desk and sat down. She opened up some files and tried to concentrate on her work. Thoughts of Kay kept creeping in. Maybe she was overreacting, or maybe she just wasn't ready to be in a relationship. Who knows if she would ever be, she certainly didn't feel like she knew what she was doing. So far, all she had done was upset her sons and get in over her head.

Emily's phone rang. She looked at the number and saw that it was Kay. She knew she was being childish not to answer, but she didn't want to get into a discussion here at the office. She texted back a message, "*Sorry, busy, I'll call you later.*"

Emily struggled to stay focused on the project she was working on. She wanted to accomplish something productive out of this miserable day. The afternoon finally came to a close and she left for home.

When Emily got home she went upstairs to change into something cooler and decided it was time to call Kay. She sat down in a chair on the back deck and collected her thoughts. It would probably be better for everyone all around if they took some time off from this relationship. She needed to explain it to Kay so that she would understand that she had her best interests in mind, too. She didn't want to hurt Kay, but she didn't think she could handle this whole thing, either.

Emily dialed Kay's number.

"Hello, Emily. What's going on?"

"Hi, Kay. Listen, I think we need to talk."

"I'm listening."

"You know how much I care about you," Emily started. This was going to be harder than she thought. "I think that it might be best for both of us if we took a little time off to think things through."

"What?" Kay whispered.

"I feel like I can't compete with the women that you're used to. I have no idea what I'm doing most of the time. You don't have a problem with your self-confidence, but I just can't handle worrying about being too old or not enough for someone. I'm happy with myself and I don't want that to change."

"But I don't want you to compete with anyone. I don't understand what happened. You have nothing to be jealous about with anyone, especially that woman you saw today. I don't even know her."

"Let's just take a little time and think things over."

"You're breaking up with me," Kay said.

"I just want us to be sure before this goes any further."

* * *

Kay hung up from Emily's call in a daze. She was still in her office, working late again. How had they gone from being perfectly happy together to Emily needing to break up with her so quickly? She hadn't done anything. Jennifer had hit on her, but Kay hadn't reciprocated. Kay sat back in her chair. She couldn't believe what just happened.

Pete appeared from around the corner. "Kay, what's happening?" He took a look at her face and sat in the chair next to her. "What's wrong?"

Kay let out a deep breath. "I don't really know. I went to meet Emily and this woman hit on me. Emily got upset and broke up with me."

This was the first time that Kay had confided in Pete about anything personal. She was just so shocked by what had happened that she needed someone to talk to.

"Maybe she just needs some time to calm down," he said.

"It didn't sound like that," Kay replied. "I don't understand. I didn't do anything."

Pete shook his head. "It's funny how two people can read the same situation completely differently. You may not have done anything, but who knows what she was thinking. It's hard to predict how people in love are going to react when they get jealous."

"I don't think she was jealous and I never said that we were in love."

"You're both having pretty strong reactions for people that aren't."

Kay glared at him. "I wouldn't say that."

"All right, all right. I take it back." Pete held up his hands. "Let's go get a beer and relax. Get your mind off things."

Kay stood up. "That sounds like a good idea."

"You know, she may have just overreacted and she'll see things differently in a day or two."

"It really didn't sound like that," Kay replied.

"A pretty lady like that is bound to have a temper. She's probably just very passionate."

"Okay, don't even go there."

CHAPTER TWENTY-NINE

Emily awoke the next day and didn't want to get out of bed. The alarm had gone off and it was time to go to the gym, but she was too unhappy and tired to move. Hoping that exercise would help her feel better, she dragged herself out of bed and got ready to go.

She brushed her teeth and looked at herself in the mirror. Not bad, but not great, either. Kay was definitely going to be better off finding someone a little younger with a lot more experience. She wouldn't be surprised if Kay never wanted to talk to her again, but she'd had to call a stop to things. She didn't want to have her self-confidence undermined by having to second-guess if the person she was with was going to be attracted to other people.

Sitting at her desk later that morning, she still didn't feel any better. Emily thought about what Kay had said. Of course she wasn't responding out of jealousy. She had never been jealous in her life. Had she? Was she reacting out of jealousy or self-preservation? The more she thought about it, the more confusing it became. She wished she could talk to Kay again and let her know that she didn't mean to hurt her. She was surely the last person that Kay would want to talk to.

How were they going to continue to work together on Tom's case? She assumed that Kay would have let her know if the cell phone photos had been ready. They were definitely going to need to talk about the case at some point. Kay might decide that she wanted someone else to handle it. She might have it assigned to another detective. Emily truly hoped that wouldn't happen. Kay was the best detective she knew. No one else would work as hard to try and find out what happened to Tom.

* * *

Kay decided to call in sick. She really didn't feel well at all. When she woke up her body felt like it was weighted down. Her head hurt from all the beer she had with Pete the night before. Her heart hurt when she thought about Emily. She didn't realize that a heart could actually hurt from missing another person, but hers did.

Why did Emily feel like she had to compete with anyone or that she couldn't be happy with her? She hadn't done anything to make her feel that way. She wished that she could talk to her again and explain to her how she felt. Maybe she hadn't let Emily see how important she had become to her.

She would be the first to admit that she had tried to live so that she didn't need anyone else. She didn't want to depend on another person for her happiness. When she met Emily, she had tried to be careful and keep her distance. She hadn't been able to listen to her own advice and she'd let Emily into her heart. Now she was going to face the consequences of letting that happen. Just like Emily had talked about that night at her house.

Kay got up and found her phone. She left a message for Sergeant Hixon, letting him know she wasn't going to be coming in that day. She'd call Pete later and check in. Hopefully she wouldn't be needed. If anything important came up, Pete would know how to reach her. She got back into bed and pulled the covers over her head.

* * *

Emily checked her phone again when she got home. Still no calls, not that she expected any. She had been the one to tell Kay that she needed time. This whole mess was her fault. Now that she had calmed down and had time to think, she wasn't so sure that she had done the right thing. It had seemed like it at the time.

She had wanted to protect herself and she didn't want to have to compete with other women if Kay wasn't committed. That was what she wasn't sure of. Did Kay feel as strongly about her as she did about Kay? She would never know. She could have given her a chance, but it was too late now.

Emily sat on the couch and contemplated the long evening ahead. She could probably go visit Julian and Mark if she really wanted company, but she didn't feel like talking to anyone right now. She would watch television and go to bed early. She just needed to stop thinking about Kay.

The first softball game was tomorrow. Since Kay wouldn't be there, they were definitely going to lose. She remembered how fantastic Kay had been at practice. So much for not thinking about her. Emily turned on the television and tried to find something good to watch to kill the time before she could go to bed.

* * *

Kay was glad to see the day come to an end. She would have been better off working instead of sitting around thinking about Emily all day. She wished she had never gone to the crime lab in the first place. If only she had just met Emily somewhere for lunch. That wouldn't have changed the fact that Emily was so unsure about her though. She should have made sure that Emily understood how much she cared about her. She'd told her that she cared, but Emily must not have realized how much she meant it.

The softball game was tomorrow. She really wanted to go, but Emily probably didn't want her there. She didn't want to put her on the spot by showing up. On the other hand, maybe if she did show up, Emily would see that she could depend on her. Kay was tired of thinking about this whole mess, and she just wanted to go to sleep.

Kay's phone rang. She grabbed it, hoping that Emily had decided to call. She saw Pete's number come up.

"Hi, Pete," she answered.

"How are you doing, partner?"

"I'm okay. I just wasn't feeling very good today. I probably should have come in."

"No, you needed a break, that's cool," Pete said. "Get some rest this weekend. You can come back swinging on Monday."

"Thanks, Pete. And thanks for hanging out with me last night."

"Listen, the reason that I'm calling is that I heard from the MDEA today. They got word from New York that Martin has gone missing. They've had him under surveillance, as you know, and they lost track of him some time since last night."

"Do they think he's headed this way to see the Pomerleaus?"

"It's possible. No one knows if he'll show up here, but we have an alert out for him and hopefully someone will spot him if he does."

Kay stretched back on the couch. "Thanks for letting me know. Give me a call if you hear anything else."

"Will do. I'll talk to you later."

Kay hung up and let the phone slip to the floor. She was sick of lying around. She needed to do something about this mess she was in with Emily. She was going to try to talk to her tomorrow. Now she was going to have to decide how to do it.

* * *

The next morning Emily got up early so that she could get a run in before it got hot. She was hoping that it would help her to shake off some of the sadness she was feeling. What she really wanted to do was stay in bed, but if she did that then she'd only feel worse. She put on some shorts and a T-shirt and laced up her running shoes. She grabbed her iPod and headed out the door. The trails were quiet and peaceful. Running in the cool morning air with the music from her headphones gave her a chance to get some perspective on things.

She had made a mistake in not giving Kay more of a chance. She had reacted the way she did partly because of her own insecurity, because she was scared of getting hurt. She was at a point in her life where she knew herself well enough to understand that it was time to decide what she wanted and not let her fears hold her back anymore. It would hurt if Kay didn't feel as strongly about her, but she wasn't going to hide from her feelings anymore. She had done that for too many years.

She got back to the house and headed straight for the shower. Time to get ready for the day. The cool water felt great. She took her time and let the shower spray ease the tension out of her muscles. She stepped out and dried off with one of her favorite towels. There was something to be said for living alone and taking as long as you wanted to get ready. The game wasn't until this afternoon, so she had plenty of time to get dressed and relax.

The morning passed quickly. She caught up on housework and debated organizing the office before deciding to put it off a little longer. After making herself a sandwich for lunch, Emily sat on the deck in the backyard with a big glass of Diet Coke, which she knew was bad for her but she didn't care. She needed to appreciate the beauty of this day. There were plenty of people much worse off than her, and she was going to stop feeling sorry for herself. She closed her eyes and leaned back in her chair, letting the sun warm her face. The heat began to lull her to sleep.

* * *

Kay woke up at sunrise and couldn't get back to sleep. It was too early to go anywhere, so she decided to sit on the deck and have a bowl of cereal. She finished eating and checked her email. No messages about Martin or anything related to the Pomerleau case. She stood up and stretched and headed back inside to take a shower and get ready for the day.

Kay had been thinking about last night's decision to talk with Emily. Although she still wasn't quite sure what she would say, she wanted to have a chance to catch up with Emily and speak to her before the game. She was planning to go by later today. Emily may not want to talk to her, but it was worth a try. Kay needed to let her know how she felt about her. If Emily still thought that they shouldn't be together, at least Kay would know that she gave it her best shot.

After her shower, she picked up the kitchen and then sat on the deck for a while. Sitting outside in the warm sun gave her more time to think about what she wanted to say. She figured she'd head over a little later since she didn't want to go too early. Maybe she would stop and get Emily some flowers on the way over. That should give her plenty of time to be up and about.

Kay spent the rest of the morning running around doing errands, trying to keep herself occupied. After making a quick stop back at her apartment to drop off some groceries, she finally decided it was as good a time as any to go to Emily's house. The short drive over only took a few minutes. She pulled into the driveway and parked next to Emily's car before getting out and walking up to the house. Stopping at the door, she took a deep breath and got ready to knock, reminding herself that the worst that could happen was that Emily would refuse to talk to her.

Kay glanced out back and caught sight of Emily reclining in a chair on the deck. The sun was shining down on her and the sight of her took Kay's breath away. Her hair was glowing in the sun and her bare legs looked lean and muscular stretched out on the chair. She was wearing a tank top that showed her toned shoulders and soft, smooth skin. She had sunglasses on, so Kay couldn't see her eyes, but it looked like she might be sleeping.

Kay swallowed and squared her shoulders. She was carrying the bouquet of flowers that she had picked up, which was a new experience because she had never bought flowers for anyone before. She walked around the house and up the steps onto the deck. She sat down on the lounge chair next to the one Emily was lying on and cleared her throat. "Hello, Emily."

* * *

Emily's eyes snapped open. She had been thinking about Kay and had drifted off to sleep. When she opened her eyes, there was Kay, sitting next to her and holding flowers. Could she be dreaming? Kay looked gorgeous. Those beautiful eyes were looking into hers. Her dark, silky hair was combed back and Emily wanted to reach over and touch it. She shook her head and tried to clear her thoughts. She sat up.

"Hi, Kay."

"Are you ready to talk to me yet?"

"Kay, I..." Emily wasn't sure how to begin. She wanted to tell Kay how sorry she was and that she had made a mistake.

Kay started to stand up. "I understand. I was just hoping that I could explain things to you. I know you don't want to talk to me."

"No, Kay, wait." Emily swung her legs around and faced Kay. "I do want to talk to you, I just don't know where to begin."

"I'd like to say something to you first." Kay sat back down. "I still don't understand exactly what happened, but I think it happened because you didn't trust that I was committed enough to our relationship. I want you to know how much you mean to me. I've always held myself back when I've been in relationships and not let my heart go to anyone.

"It's different with you, Emily. You're always on my mind and I want you in my life. You have nothing to worry about with me wanting anyone else. All I see is you, and you don't have to compete with anyone."

Emily took off her sunglasses so that Kay could see her eyes. "What I want to begin with is to tell you how sorry I am. I let my insecurity get the best of me. I think I was afraid that I was going to get hurt and I ended up hurting you instead and I'm so sorry. I promise, if you give me the chance, I won't let my fears hold me back again."

Tears began to stream down Kay's face. "I was afraid that I'd lost you before I had even gotten a chance to tell you how I felt. I think I'm really falling for you and this has never happened to me before."

Emily moved across the space between their chairs to kneel over Kay and slid onto her lap, straddling Kay and looking into her eyes. She held Kay's face in her hands and kissed her tears away gently. Kay pulled her close and kissed her, sliding her tongue into Emily's mouth and tasting her hungrily. Emily slid her hands through Kay's hair and felt it's silky softness.

"I missed you so much," Emily whispered into her ear. "I promise I won't chicken out on you again."

Kay kissed Emily's neck and sucked on her earlobe. "I called in sick yesterday because I could barely get out of bed. Please don't ever do that to me again."

Emily gently pushed Kay back until they were lying down together on the chair. "I didn't mean to hurt you. I overreacted and I thought that we would both be better off if you were with someone else."

Kay slid her hands down Emily's back to her waist, pulling her closer between her legs. "I don't want anyone else. Just you."

"You've got me. I am completely yours."

Kay smiled at her and drew her in for another kiss. "This is supposed to be our date night after the game tonight."

"I was afraid you wouldn't want to go to the game."

"I wasn't sure if you would want me there."

"Oh, I want you there." Emily kissed her mouth and ran her hand down Kay's neck and over her breast, tracing her nipple with her fingers. Wanting more, she slipped her hand under Kay's shirt and into her bra. She squeezed her nipple and caressed her breast, needing to feel Kay's skin. She wanted to slide down and taste her breast with her tongue.

Kay moaned, grinding her hips into Emily's. "I don't think that I can stop if you keep touching me like that."

"Why do we have to stop?"

Kay gave another moan as she rolled them both over to their sides. "I want our first time together to be special and I don't want to rush. We have to get ready for the game soon."

Emily kissed her and ran her fingers through her hair again. She pressed up against Kay and breathed in her scent, trying to calm her racing heart. "I can wait. I just want to be near you."

"Emily, will you spend the night with me tonight? We don't have to do anything, I just want us to be together."

Emily stared into Kay's eyes. "I would love to."

CHAPTER THIRTY

Emily rode with Kay to her apartment so that she could change into jeans and her game shirt. They were going to drive to the game together. She waited downstairs while Kay ran up to her bedroom. Emily looked around at the pictures of Kay with her parents and friends that she had displayed. She wanted to be a part of Kay's life and have a picture of the two of them in her living room.

Kay jogged down the stairs. "I'm ready."

Emily turned to the door to go.

"Hold on a sec," Kay said, dropping her gym bag to the floor and pulling Emily into her arms. "Do you remember what I told you at practice last week?"

Emily had a feeling that she knew exactly what Kay was talking about. She smiled. "Remind me."

"I'm going to hit a home run for you," Kay said confidently.

"How about we have a little bet. If you hit a home run, I'll do anything you want. If you don't, you have to do whatever I want."

"That's very motivating, Coach."

Emily laughed. "I know. It's kind of a win-win situation for me."

They went out to Kay's car and drove over to the field where they pulled into the parking lot and started unloading the equipment. Soon the other players began arriving and warming up. The day had turned out sunny and hot. Emily was forced to put her hat on to keep the sun out of her eyes.

Kay looked at her and chuckled. "You know, you do look kind of funny in a hat. Still really cute, but there's something not quite right."

"I tried to warn you."

Emily called the team together and went over the lineup. Their team was up first so the other team went out onto the field and took their positions. Alex was the first one up. Emily suppressed a groan as she watched him hit a weak grounder that the pitcher fielded easily and threw to first.

Emily stood close to Kay in the dugout and filled her in on the other players. "The pitcher and catcher are really good. They're a couple and their names are Dawn and Jo. The outfielder is a really good hitter. Actually, they're all really good. This team usually slaughters us."

"They do look like they'll be a tough team for us to beat," Kay said. "But we have some players with a lot of enthusiasm."

"That's a very diplomatic way of putting it."

The SBI center fielder came up to bat and hit a grounder that the shortstop caught and threw to first base for another out. Emily was up next. She hit a line drive over the second baseman's head and made it to first.

Kay stepped up to the plate. Emily watched from first base as Kay stared at the pitcher with focused concentration. Kay stepped into the ball and connected solidly. The ball arced out toward the outfield where the center fielder made a spectacular leaping catch. Kay carried her bat back to the bench and grabbed her glove. She passed close to Emily on her way out to the field and whispered in her ear, "Don't worry, I'll get one for you next time."

Emily tried to hide her smile as she retrieved her glove and jogged out to second base. Her eyes were drawn to Kay and she watched as Kay passed a ball back and forth around the infield. Watching her in motion was enough to make Emily's heart pound. She ran with such natural grace that it was hard not to stare.

"All right, team. Let's get these guys out," Emily yelled, hoping to motivate the team.

The innings passed quickly. The other team had scored three runs while the SBI team was still scoreless. Sam had gotten a good hit but no one else had been able to get on base. Kay had made some sensational catches that had kept them in the game. Alex had managed to miss or drop most of the passes to first base that were thrown his way. Emily was hoping that he would twist an ankle or something and have to be replaced.

The last inning arrived. Emily was the first one up and she hit a sharp grounder between first and second and made it to first base. She caught her breath and looked over at Kay who was walking toward home plate. Kay saw her looking and pointed to the outfield and smiled at her.

Emily called out, "Come on Kay, get us on the scoreboard."

She watched as the pitcher wound up and threw the ball. Kay made it look effortless as she stepped toward the ball and crushed it. The ball went soaring into the outfield and over the fence. It was the first home run that Emily could remember the SBI team ever getting. She ran around the bases and jumped on home plate. She waited there for Kay to finish running in from third base and gave her a high five along with the other players that had run out to greet her.

If ever Emily had any doubts about how much she wanted Kay, they were gone. She was ready for whatever Kay wanted her to do. At least, she hoped so.

None of their next three hitters made it to base, so the game was over. They were all hot and sweaty, but the game had ended on a positive note. They went out onto the field to congratulate the other team.

"Nice game," the opposing pitcher said to Emily.

"Thanks, Dawn," Emily replied. "I think we're going to do better this year."

"Your shortstop is pretty good," said the catcher, looking over appreciatively at Kay, who was picking up equipment.

"Yeah," Emily said. "She's awesome."

Dawn looked at her catcher with annoyance. "She's not bad looking, either. Jo couldn't take her eyes off her."

After their talk this morning, Emily now realized that she had nothing to worry about from other people's interest in Kay. She felt secure and confident about Kay's feelings for her. She watched as Kay approached. Kay looked in her eyes and grinned. Emily started feeling a little dizzy as she smiled back.

Emily introduced her. "Kay, this is Dawn and this is Jo."

"Nice to meet you." Kay extended her hand to each of them. "Good game."

"Good game," Dawn replied.

"If you ever get tired of playing on the SBI team, let us know," Jo said.

"Thanks, but I don't think so. I'm very happy with Emily and her team." Kay placed her hand lightly on Emily's lower back.

Emily was surprised, she looked around but no one seemed to be paying any attention. She hadn't been expecting any public displays of affection, but she found that she liked it. Kay was making a clear statement that they were together. Jo and Dawn exchanged a startled glance.

"Emily, I didn't realize," said Dawn.

Emily shrugged and smiled.

They finished gathering up the equipment and walked back to the parking lot with the other players. Emily spoke to the group. "We had a really good game today. I think that our team is going to have a chance to win some games this year. Great job, everyone. Our next game is the same time next weekend, so I hope I'll see you all here."

"We're headed over to the Riverside," Tony announced loudly. "Anyone who feels like getting together for a cold drink can join us there."

Emily and Kay stood by Kay's car and watched everyone drive off. Another game had started up and they were alone in the parking lot. The sun was hot, so they got in the car and Kay started the air conditioner.

"Are you ready to go get a drink?" Kay asked.

Emily turned to her. "I have not been able to keep my eyes off you. You have no idea how much I love to watch you play softball. You are extraordinary."

She leaned over and kissed Kay's mouth, slipping her hand up to Kay's chest and squeezing her breast.

Kay let out a startled breath. "Oh. I didn't realize how much you liked softball players."

"Just one player." Emily continued to press her palm into Kay's breast, feeling her nipple harden. She ran her tongue along Kay's lips and sucked on her lower lip.

Kay began to kiss her and Emily felt her body's immediate reaction. Her heart was pounding as Kay reached over and started stroking her thigh, sliding her hand up along the inseam of her jeans. When she placed her hand between Emily's legs and pressed down, Emily let out a moan and clenched her legs together as sensations shot through her body.

Kay sat back abruptly and gasped. "I think we should probably go for that drink. If we don't stop now, we might go a little further than I want to in a parking lot."

Emily was panting. "God, I don't know what came over me. I didn't mean to get carried away in a public place."

Kay smiled mischievously. "You liked the home run I hit for you, huh?"

"I certainly did."

They pulled into a parking spot at the Riverside Restaurant. The team had saved them a couple seats at one of the tables. Emily sat down next to Sam.

"Nice game, Sam," she said. "Did you play baseball as a kid?"

"Yes," he answered.

Trying to think of something else to say, she asked, "Where did you grow up?"

"In Augusta."

"Well, I'm glad you're on the team."

"Kay's good," he said.

"Yes, she is." Emily wondered how long she could keep this painful conversation going.

"Are you and her, uh, together?" Sam asked.

Not sure how to answer such a personal question, Emily paused. Kay might not appreciate it if she broadcast their relationship to her coworkers but she had basically announced it to the ladies on the other team when she put her arm around Emily. She decided this was part of not chickening out even though it wasn't any of Sam's business.

"Yes, Kay and I are together."

Sam's attention turned back to his drink.

Emily glanced at Kay beside her. She was deep in conversation with Kelly, their pitcher, on the strategy for next week. Emily leaned on her elbow and sat quietly watching for a minute, enjoying listening to her talk.

Alex was seated across the table from Kay and Kelly. Emily watched him lean over and wave to get Kay's attention, interrupting their conversation.

"Nice hit today," he said.

"Thanks," replied Kay.

"How are things over at MCU?"

"Fine."

Emily knew that Kay was not interested in getting into a conversation about work. Since this was Emily's boss, she was obviously making an effort to be polite.

"The SBI seems like an interesting place to work," Kay said.

"Oh yes. We provide an integral service for the state police. People don't realize how important the management of data is today," Alex said with a self-important smile.

"I know Emily has been a big help on some of our cases with the data she's provided."

"Speaking of which, what's going on with the Pomerleau case these days? I haven't heard of any progress on the search for Troy Pomerleau."

Kay gave a noninformative answer. "We have some leads that we're following up on. We will find him."

"What about Mike Martin? What's going on with him?"

Kay gave another noncommittal answer. "I couldn't really tell you."

The waitress arrived to take orders for another round of drinks. Some people were ordering food. Emily leaned over to Kay. "Are you hungry?"

Kay looked at her. "Starving. But I don't want to eat here. I want to get something with just the two of us."

Emily dragged her eyes away from Kay's lips. She didn't want to wait any longer to be alone with her. She nudged Kay's foot and nodded her head toward the door.

Kay nodded and they stood up.

"It looks like we need to get going. See you all next week and have a good rest of the weekend," Emily said.

After finally saying good-bye to everyone, they made it to the door.

CHAPTER THIRTY-ONE

Kay started the car and pulled out of the parking lot. "I was thinking that we could go back to my place to take showers and get changed before we go out. I still feel all sweaty and disgusting."

"That's what I was hoping. I brought a change of clothes."

"Where would you like to go for dinner?" Kay asked as they approached her apartment.

"You know what I'd really like?"

"What?"

"I'd like to get some takeout and sit out on your deck with some cold drinks. We could listen to some music and spend some time together."

"That sounds perfect. Do you like Thai food?"

"Sure."

They pulled into Kay's driveway and walked into her place.

"Why don't you make yourself at home and take a shower. I'll order some Thai food and go pick it up. I'll take a shower when I get back," Kay said. "The bathroom is right at the top of the stairs and the towels are in the closet."

Emily went upstairs to get ready. She took a long, cool shower and felt clean and refreshed when she got out. She dried off and got dressed and peeked into the bedrooms while she towel dried her hair. Kay's bedroom was the larger room. She had a beautiful shaker style bed with a cream-colored bed spread. The room was done in tones of cream and green, which gave it a very peaceful air. Emily finished getting ready just as she heard the door open downstairs as Kay returned.

She walked downstairs and Kay greeted her with a kiss.

"You look and smell beautiful. I need to get in the shower before I contaminate you."

Emily laughed. "I'll hang out down here till you're ready."

"Okay babe, I'll be back shortly. Help yourself to a beer or whatever you want."

Emily sat on the couch and thumbed through one of the books in the bookcase. Apparently Kay liked reading mysteries. Emily tried to keep her mind occupied because she was starting to get nervous. She didn't want to have a panic attack again like the first time that she came over here. She'd had plenty of time to think things through and she wanted to be with Kay more than anything. It was just her fear of the unknown and doing the wrong thing that kept worrying her. She went into the kitchen and got a beer, hoping to calm her nerves.

Emily sat back on the couch and jiggled her leg as she watched Kay jog down the stairs. She looked really good. Her face was flushed and her hair was still damp. Emily resisted the urge to jump up and tried to sit still.

"You look great," Emily said.

"Thanks." Kay sat down beside her.

"So I see that you like to read." Emily gestured toward the bookcase. "I like to read in the evening. In fact I prefer reading to watching television. Have you noticed that there's usually nothing very interesting on television?"

Emily couldn't stop talking. "I like mysteries, too. It's kind of funny that you're a detective and you like mysteries. Who is your favorite author?"

"I'm not sure who my favorite is," Kay said in a calm voice. "Emily, you don't need to get all nervous on me. Everything is going to be fine."

"Why would you think I'm nervous? I'm really happy to be here and I'm sure we'll have a nice evening. There's nothing to be nervous about." Emily felt her panic building.

"All right." Kay looked at Emily intently. "So let's relax and talk about the game. I thought it went pretty well today, but I kind of wish you could put someone else on first base. Too bad Alex is your boss. We might have won if someone else had been covering first."

"I know. It's also weird how he keeps asking you about your cases."

"Yeah. I really don't want to be rude to your boss, but I also don't want to discuss cases with him." Kay reached over and held Emily's hand. "Are you ready to have something to eat?"

"Sure."

"Let me put on some music and we can go sit out on the deck." Kay stood up and switched on the stereo. She turned around and almost bumped into Emily who was standing right behind her.

Emily took a deep breath and hugged Kay. Emily's heart was pounding like she was running a race. She felt like she was going to hit the ceiling if she didn't calm down. "I'm sorry that I'm so bad at this. It's what I keep worrying about."

"Don't worry. Everything is fine. Let's just go have something to eat. If that's all we end up doing, that's all right."

Kay headed toward the kitchen.

Emily sighed. She didn't want that to be all they ended up doing. At this rate, she was going to ruin the evening. It was time to stop acting like this. There was nothing to be afraid of.

"Hold on. I just had a momentary panic attack. I'm so happy to be here with you that I wasn't thinking straight. I was overthinking and I know everything is fine, like you said."

Kay stopped and turned to her with a smile. "I'm so happy that you're here that I can barely think straight, too. The last couple days when I thought that I'd lost you, I was so miserable I could barely move."

"I'm really glad you came over to talk to me today."

"Me too."

They put some food from the takeout containers on their plates and carried them out with their drinks. The warm summer night was quiet and peaceful. The only sound was the music coming from the speakers on the deck. Emily slid her chair next to Kay's so that their legs were touching.

"This is delicious, and the beer is really good, too," Emily said.

"Good food and good company. Here's to us." Kay raised her bottle.

"Okay, there's one thing that I do need to talk about."

"What?" Kay took a sip of beer.

"That home run was awesome. I can't even tell you how attracted I was to you at that moment. I seriously wanted to leave the game and get naked."

Kay almost choked on her drink. "Oh, uh, okay. Do home runs always affect you like that?"

"They never have before. There's only one person that's ever affected me like this." Emily looked into Kay's eyes.

Kay set down her beer and leaned toward Emily. Their lips met in a kiss and Emily opened her mouth, reaching for Kay's tongue with her own. Emily felt Kay's fingers tracing their way under the hem of her shorts and touching the soft skin of her inner thigh.

A wave of desire washed over Emily's body as she reached for Kay. The chairs were in the way and she couldn't get close enough. Emily stood and pulled Kay up with her. Kay looked at her with questioning eyes.

"Do you want to go inside?" Kay asked.

"I feel like I'm on fire. I want to touch you and the chairs are in the way."

"Let's go in." Kay grabbed her hand and led her into the living room. Kay closed the blinds and turned back to Emily.

"Remember, there's nothing to get wrong as long as we tell each other what we want. It's just you and me," Kay said.

"I really want to touch you," Emily said.

"Remember our bet?"

"Yes." Emily smiled.

"You know what I want?"

"I think I have an idea. I told you that I would do anything you want, and I meant it. I trust you."

"What I want is for you to let me touch you and I want you to touch me. Can I take your shirt off?"

Emily nodded and Kay began to unbutton her shirt, pausing to kiss the bare skin that she was revealing. Kay tossed Emily's shirt aside and touched the button on her shorts and looked at her questioningly. Emily nodded and Kay unbuttoned her shorts and slipped them off. Emily stood smiling at her in her bra and underwear. Kay looked at her and kissed her softly.

"You look incredible," Kay said. "Your turn."

Emily slid Kay's soft cotton shirt up and over her head, tossing it toward the corner. She crouched down onto her heels and kissed Kay's stomach, then she opened up the clasp on her shorts and slid them down. Kay stepped out of them and Emily stood up slowly, sliding her tongue up her body.

"You taste good," Emily whispered into her ear. She unclasped Kay's bra and stared at her, wanting to touch. She reached toward her and hesitated, looking at Kay.

Kay drew a deep breath. "It's all right to touch me if you want to."

Emily placed her palms on Kay's breasts. She felt her nipples harden as she squeezed and caressed her. Kay moaned and pulled Emily closer.

"Can I finish undressing you?" Kay asked.

Emily nodded.

Kay slid off her own panties and then kissed Emily as she carefully unhooked her bra. She let it drop to the floor and knelt down. Hooking her fingers into Emily's panties, she slid them down her legs and tossed them aside. She traced her hands up Emily's legs to her waist and looked up at her. "You're stunning, babe."

Kay began to kiss Emily's stomach and worked her way up toward her breasts. She ran her tongue lightly across her nipple and Emily felt her stomach tremble. Kay took Emily's breast into her mouth and Emily's legs almost gave out. She was throbbing with desire.

"I don't think I can stand up much longer," Emily gasped.

"Let's go upstairs." Kay took Emily's hand in hers and walked with her up the stairs.

Emily looked down at Kay. "I had no idea you would look so good without your clothes on. You're the sexiest thing I've ever seen."

Kay laughed. "Have you been thinking about me without my clothes on?"

Emily blushed. "I don't know, it may have crossed my mind once or twice."

"I'll admit that I've been thinking about what you would look like. A lot."

Kay covered Emily's mouth with hers and guided her toward the bed. She pulled back the sheets and they got in and lay side by side. The light from the summer evening shone in through the windows.

"This is where you need to tell me what you want," Kay said. "I want to make you feel good."

She rolled over and slid on top of Emily, supporting her weight with her arms. Emily spread her legs apart and their hips met. The feel of Kay's body pressed against hers was pushing her to the edge. Kay bent her head down and began kissing Emily gently. She ran her tongue along Emily's mouth and sucked on her lower lip.

"Does this feel good?" Kay asked, grinding their hips together.

"Yes, don't stop," Emily gasped, thrusting her hips up to meet Kay's.

"Don't worry babe, I won't stop." Kay continued to press her hips into Emily's, matching her thrusts. She lowered her head to Emily's breast and began to lick it.

Kay reached between them and slid her finger into Emily. "Do you like this?"

Emily was blind with arousal. "Yes, yes, don't stop."

Kay slid another finger into Emily and began to stroke her while sucking her nipple into her mouth and running her teeth across it gently.

Emily moaned as her body shook. She couldn't stop herself as she bit her lip and arched her back from an intense wave of pleasure. She felt wave after wave of gratification that left her speechless and limp. She finally caught her breath and opened her eyes to see Kay smiling at her with a pleased look on her face.

"Oh my God, I had no idea that it could feel like that." Emily reached up and held Kay's face in her hands and kissed her gently.

Kay rolled off her and onto her side, facing Emily. "There's a lot more that I want to show you, but there's no rush. We have all night."

"Now I want you to tell me what you want. It's only fair."

"Come here." Kay pulled Emily on top of her. "I want to feel your body, it's nice and soft but strong and I like having you pressed against me like this."

Emily slid down the length of Kay's body. "Can we try this?"

She shifted up onto her knees between Kay's legs. She slid two fingers into Kay's wet center and looked into her eyes. "Do you want me to do this?"

Kay gasped with pleasure. "Yes, I definitely want you to do that."

Emily smiled. She began to stroke Kay with her fingers and squeezed her with her thumb. "Am I doing this right?" she asked.

Kay wrapped her legs around Emily and moaned. "Yes, yes, you're doing it right."

Emily slid down on top of Kay and kept her hand in place, using her hips to help her reach deeper while she stroked Kay in the exact spot she knew she would like. She let go of her inhibitions and gave herself over to pleasing Kay. She could tell what she liked and she knew that she wasn't getting it wrong.

* * *

Kay had almost come watching Emily earlier. Her body was aching with desire. Now Emily's touch pushed her over the edge quickly. Kay closed her eyes and moaned as she felt waves of pleasure shudder through her. She had been holding back her arousal for so long that it crashed over her with a surge of intensity that left her struggling to recover.

Kay opened her eyes and looked at Emily. She started kissing her mouth and didn't want to stop. She pulled her close and felt a wave of love for this woman that she had never felt for anyone. "That was amazing. I don't know why you were worried. You knew exactly what to do."

Emily smiled at her. "Once I knew that we could tell each other want we wanted, I realized that I could relax. I knew you would tell me what felt good. Then I could see in your face what you liked. I've never shared this much pleasure with anyone before."

"There's still a lot that we're going to share and I'm going to kiss every inch of you. I just need to catch my breath."

Emily slid off her and propped herself up on one elbow. She ran her hand gently along Kay's body. "Your skin is so soft."

"Does our bet count for just this week or can we extend it for the whole season?" Kay asked.

"I think it should definitely be extended."

CHAPTER THIRTY-TWO

Kay woke up with Emily snuggled up against her side, her leg draped across Kay's. She was too comfortable to move. Emily had amazed her the night before. She hadn't been expecting her to be so uninhibited. They had spent hours discovering each other.

Kay lay still, contentedly watching Emily sleep. She had opened her heart up to Emily in a way that she had never done before. She had realized last night that she had fallen in love with her and she was waiting until they had some quiet time today to tell her. Kay didn't want Emily to think that she had to say it back to her if she wasn't ready, and she hadn't wanted to pressure her last night.

Kay watched Emily open her eyes and look around as she awoke. The warm summer sun was shining in on them. Kay took a moment to appreciate the tranquil morning before moving closer to Emily and gently pulling her in for a quick kiss.

"Good morning." Emily smiled.

Kay gave her another soft kiss. "Good morning. I didn't mean to wake you."

"You didn't. I really hate to move. I want to stay here in your bed all day, but I'd better brush my teeth."

"I would like nothing better than to keep you here all day, but I guess I'll let you out." Kay pulled back the sheets and stood up. She walked to her closet and took out two shirts, handing one of them to Emily and slipping her arms into the other one, leaving it unbuttoned.

Emily got up and slowly ran her eyes up along Kay's body until their eyes met. "How am I supposed to walk past you looking like that?"

Kay saw the look in Emily's eyes and knew she needed to get back into bed as soon as possible. She held up her hand. "I'll be right back. I'm going to run downstairs to the other bathroom and brush my teeth. You can use the bathroom up here."

Kay hustled out of the room, leaving Emily with some privacy. She went down the stairs to the other bathroom and started getting ready. She didn't want to leave Emily's side today, which was definitely not how she usually felt after spending the night with someone. After washing up and brushing her teeth she jogged back up the stairs and knocked softly on the bathroom door.

Emily opened the door. "Hi, there. I don't want to take my eyes off you again."

"Want to share a shower?" Kay asked, sliding her shirt off.

Emily nodded.

Kay stepped past her and started the water. She held out her hand to Emily and they stepped in together. Kay poured some body wash into her hand and started rubbing it onto Emily's skin, starting at her shoulders and working her way down. She savored the taste of Emily's breasts, kissing them and licking the water from her nipples.

Emily braced herself with her hands against the sides of the shower as Kay's fingers entered her. She pushed herself against Kay's hand, and Kay felt the waves of her climax shudder through her body as the water pulsed down on them. She pressed her body against Emily's and kissed her, running her tongue along her lips.

Emily tilted her head back and opened her eyes. "Now it's my turn. I want to taste you again this morning."

Kay brushed her wet hair back from her eyes as she watched Emily take some body wash and begin caressing her. Emily slid down to her knees and spread Kay's legs apart, lifting one of Kay's knees. Kay braced her leg against the shower as Emily began to lick and probe her with her tongue.

"Is this right?" Emily looked up and asked.

Kay could barely speak. "Yes," she gasped.

Emily leaned back on one hand while she slid her finger in and began to suck on her. Kay lost control quickly, closing her eyes and crying out. Water sprayed into her face as she arched her back. Waves of pleasure crashed over her until she was limp and panting. She pulled Emily up to her and held her close.

"God, that was amazing," Kay murmured into her ear.

"I had a good teacher." Emily gave her a satisfied smile. "I also think that yoga classes have been very helpful with my balance and flexibility."

* * *

Curled up on the couch, Emily watched Kay making breakfast in the kitchen. "I do love to watch you, but isn't there something I can do to help?"

"You can set the table if you like," Kay answered as she scrambled eggs for the omelettes she was making. "Or you can chop up some vegetables. But you can just relax if you want. I like making breakfast for you."

Kay started singing softly along with the music that was playing. She peeked in the oven at the muffins that were baking. Emily watched with fascination. She usually regarded cooking as a chore to be finished as soon as possible. Kay clearly enjoyed prepping her ingredients and cooking different dishes. Emily finished setting the table and started chopping some tomatoes. She wasn't all that interested in the cooking, but she wanted to be closer to Kay.

Every time she looked at her, Emily thought of different things they had done the night before. A vision of Kay in the

shower that morning passed through her mind. A wave of arousal passed through her body again.

"I love listening to you sing," Emily said.

"Put on whatever music you like."

"This is perfect. It's not just the music, but being able to spend time together with you. What else do you have to do today?"

Kay smiled at her. "I'm all yours. The only plan I have is to be with you."

"How did I get so lucky?" Emily reached over and kissed Kay. "I do need to call Julian and tell him that we aren't going to meet him for brunch. He and Mark go every Sunday."

"We could invite them over here."

"I want you all to myself today." Emily returned to the couch and picked up her phone, dialing Julian's number.

"Hello, Emily, did you behave last night?" asked Julian. "I know you had plans with Kay. Let's hear it."

She laughed. "I'm over at Kay's right now actually."

"Well, well. Did you spend the night?"

"Maybe," Emily teased. "I'm calling to say that we can't meet you for brunch today, sorry."

"I understand, darling. You're probably exhausted."

"Watch it."

"Just teasing. I'm glad to hear you sounding so happy."

"Thanks. Listen, tell Mark that I said hello and that I'll definitely catch up with you guys another time. I'll call you tomorrow."

Emily hung up and walked over to the table where Kay was placing their plates. She sat down and looked at the omelette, toast and fruit that Kay had served her. A basket of fresh blueberry muffins sat on the table.

"This looks great. Thank you, Kay. I can't remember the last time that anyone cooked breakfast for me."

"My pleasure, babe. I don't know about you, but I'm hungry. We didn't get a chance to eat much last night."

Emily took a bite of her omelette. "Wow, this is fantastic."

She took another bite and then tried a piece of a muffin. "This is the best muffin, seriously. How did I not realize what a good cook you are? This is the most delicious breakfast I've ever had."

Kay chuckled. "Thanks, but you don't have to get too carried away."

"I can't help it, this is so good." Emily took another bite and looked at Kay. "Who taught you to cook?"

"I enjoy it, so I've picked things up over the years."

They finished their breakfast and cleaned up the kitchen. Kay turned to Emily. "Is there anything that you want to do today?"

"I was thinking about that. We've both been so busy at work that it would be nice to just relax. We could go for a walk or go for a drive to the beach?"

"Maybe we should go upstairs and discuss it?" Kay asked.

"I was kind of hoping you would say that. It could be a good day to stay in, don't you think?"

Kay grabbed her waist and pulled her close. "I think that sounds good," she whispered in Emily's ear as she ran her tongue behind her earlobe and kissed her.

Emily shivered. "I do have to go home by this evening so that I can get ready for the week."

Kay kept kissing her. "What do you have to do to get ready?"

"I just have to get laundry done and stuff like that. I want to call the boys. I'm hoping that Ben might be more willing to talk to me."

Kay leaned back and looked at her. "I hope he is. I'm sorry about all of that. I never wanted to be the cause of any problems between you and your kids."

"Like I keep telling you, it's not your fault at all. It's really nothing to do with you personally. I think it's just going to take time. I hope that we can find out more about Tom's accident this week. It might help if Ben realizes how much we're both trying to find out what happened."

Emily took Kay's hand and started walking toward the stairs. Kay followed her and stopped her when they got to her room.

"Emily, I want to tell you how much you mean to me."

Emily kissed her. "I've been wanting to tell you that, too. This past day has been incredible. I didn't realize that I could feel this way about anyone."

She slipped her hands up under Kay's shirt and slid it up over her head. Reaching for her own shirt, she pulled it off quickly and tossed it aside. Both braless, Kay leaned into Emily with an open mouthed kiss. Kay swiftly stripped off her shorts and reached for Emily as they stumbled back onto the bed.

"We can talk some more later," Kay said.

CHAPTER THIRTY-THREE

Kay spent the morning sitting with Pete at his desk and going over case notes. The MDEA had been working with the New York police to find Mike Martin, but still hadn't been able to locate him. Pete and Kay were growing frustrated at the lack of progress in the Pomerleau case. There had been no sightings of Troy Pomerleau since the convenience store clerk's beating.

"Troy may have headed out of state," Kay said.

"I don't think he's bright enough," Pete said. "I think he's hiding out somewhere and his brother is helping him."

"The surveillance on Kevin Pomerleau's place hasn't turned up anything. He must have some other location where he's hiding Troy."

Pete nodded. "Right, and if Martin is here he's probably looking for Troy too. He can't lose face by letting Troy get away with killing two of his men, even if he and Kevin are partners."

"Hixon wants a report. Do we have any new information to tell him?"

"Not really. I know we've already checked on all the property owned by Pomerleau and his family, but let's check again. We can send troopers to check on all the addresses and maybe something will come up. Do you want to call someone at the SBI and have them run some data for us again?"

"I can call and get that going. By the way, I wanted to tell you that Emily and I got back together."

"I thought you seemed pretty happy this morning." Pete smiled. "I hate to say I told you so, but I can't resist. She overreacted and it took her a little while to calm down right? I know a lot about passionate women like that."

"What do you know about passionate women like that? Wait, I don't want to know. Anyway, things are good. Now we need to get some leads on Tom Stratton's case. Maybe we can get some information from those photos I was telling you about."

"You'd better be careful going to the crime lab," Pete teased.

After the past weekend, Kay didn't think that Emily would have any worries. She hadn't found the right time to tell her that she was in love with her, but Kay had shown her in every way she knew. She hadn't wanted Emily to leave the night before. She was missing her, and she was hoping she would get a chance to stop by the SBI office and see her later.

"We have a little time before we're supposed to go meet with Hixon. I think I'll go and check on those photos now, actually. They should be ready. I'll meet you back here."

Kay went back to her desk and grabbed her keys. She headed out to her car and decided to give Emily a call.

"Hi, honey," Emily said. "I was just thinking about you."

"Hi. I missed you last night."

"I still can't believe how incredible this past weekend was. I didn't realize it was possible to do some of those things and I never thought that I could feel this way. You were very sweet to make me breakfast, too."

"I'll make you breakfast any time you want, babe."

"Maybe we can get together tonight after work and have dinner?"

"You read my mind. I really want to see you tonight. I'm calling because I thought I'd check in and tell you that I'm headed over to the crime lab to see if the photos are ready. I know they could email them, but they seem to process things a lot quicker if you stop by in person."

"That's good. Let me know if you get them, I can't wait to see if we can tell who's in that truck. I have a meeting in a few minutes, but it shouldn't last too long."

"I'll call you and let you know either way."

Emily paused. "I hope you didn't worry that I'd get upset if you went over to the crime lab without telling me. I don't have any doubts in my mind about us."

Kay was relieved. "I didn't think so, but I just wanted to be upfront about everything with you. You're the only one I care about."

"I didn't realize that before and I acted foolishly. I promise that I won't do that again. I don't want you to worry about it anymore, okay?"

"All right, good. I'll let you know what I find out." Kay hung up.

When she reached the lab, the receptionist recognized her. "Hello, Detective DeLorme."

"Good morning. Please call me Kay. I'm here to check with Lori on some photos she was working on for me."

"I'll see if she's in."

Kay had just taken a seat in the waiting area when Lori appeared at the door.

"Good morning," Lori said. "I was planning to send you the updated pictures today. They are finally ready. We were able to clean up the three images so that you can see the details quite well. I have them saved here in a new folder on your flash drive, along with the originals."

"That's fantastic, thank you so much. This could be a really big help for the case."

"I was happy to help. Sorry it took so long."

Kay thanked her again and headed for her car, anxious to get a look at the photos. She still had a little time before she and Pete were supposed to meet with Hixon, so she called Emily to see if she had time to look at them with her. The phone went to voice mail and Kay hung up, knowing that Emily would see that she had called.

* * *

Emily was debugging a script that she was working on when her phone rang. She had just gotten out of her meeting with Alex and was trying to get a problem fixed for him. She glanced at the number on her screen. It was Mark, which was unusual.

"Hi, Mark," she answered.

"Hi, Emily. Sorry to bother you at work, but I'm worried about Julian. Have you heard from him?"

"Not since yesterday morning. What's going on?"

"We went to brunch like we usually do. We took separate cars because I was planning to stop by and visit my mother afterward and he had other things he needed to do. We were getting ready to leave and he went to the men's room. When he came back he was acting really strange, all nervous and jumpy and he couldn't wait to get out of there. I asked him what was going on and he said something about *Charlie's Angels* and I got irritated. Next thing you know, we had a fight and we both left. I haven't heard from him since."

"He didn't come home last night?"

"No. We have little quarrels all the time, you know that, but he's never stayed away all night before and I'm really worried. Our fight yesterday wasn't a big deal, so I don't know where he could be. I was hoping that he might have called you."

"I haven't heard from him. Now I'm worried, too. I'll try calling."

"He's not answering me when I try," Mark said.

"I'll see if I can find anything out. I'll call you if I reach him."

"Thanks, I'll let you know if I hear anything."

Emily hung up and noticed that she had missed a call from Kay while she had been in the meeting with Alex. Hoping that the photos were ready, she started to call her back when her phone rang again. It was Julian.

"Julian, where are you?" she answered.

Silence greeted her. She looked at her phone and it looked like the call was connected, but she didn't hear anything. "Julian, are you there?"

She looked at the screen again and the call had disconnected. She tried calling back and he didn't pick up. He must be somewhere with bad service. Other than driving down to Portland, Julian didn't usually go too far from Augusta. She was surprised that he had gone anywhere where cell service was unreliable.

Her phone buzzed with a text. It was from Julian. "*Help! I followed Brooks and a brutish man caught me in the parking lot at his salon. They brought me to a cabin in the wilderness. Got away but have no idea where I am. Looks like hiking trails, sign said Round Top Trail. Am desperate for a cigarette. I hate nature. Phone won't work, hope you get this.*"

Emily read the message and sprang into action. She had to let Mark and Kay know what was going on and she had to get to Julian before Brooks and the other man caught up with him. How on earth had he managed to escape? She tried calling him again, but still had no luck. She sent him a reply to his text telling him to stay put and out of sight, hoping that he would get it.

Emily raced out of her office and called Mark as she headed to the parking lot. His phone went to voice mail and she left him a message. Next, she called Kay, whose phone also went to voice mail. Didn't anyone answer their phones? She left a message for Kay as she got into her car.

She was pretty sure that she remembered the Round Top Trail in the Kennebec Highlands, a large conservation area in Rome. There were miles of trail systems in the rocky, wooded acres of the Highlands. There were a few different parking lots. She would have to find the sign for Round Top Trail in one of them and go look for Julian. Hopefully he would be looking for her and see her if she went by wherever he was on the trail. She knew it wasn't the best plan, but once Kay got her message, she was sure that she would head over and help her find him. She couldn't wait for Kay if Julian was in trouble.

CHAPTER THIRTY-FOUR

Kay put the flash drive into the USB slot on her laptop. Clicking on the folder, thumbnail versions of the three photos opened up. Kay clicked on the first one to enlarge it. It showed the front of the black pickup truck much more clearly. The first half of the license plate was visible and she could read the first four numbers.

She enlarged the second photo and could now clearly see the two people sitting in the truck. The driver's face was turned toward the camera while the passenger's head was turned away and only the back of his head was visible. She wished that Emily were here, she might be able to identify the driver. Her meeting must have taken longer than she thought it would, because she hadn't called her back yet.

She clicked on the third photo. It showed the people in the truck at a slightly different angle. In this one, the passenger's head was turned more toward the camera. The red Jeep in the background was clearly visible.

"Oh my God," Kay picked up her phone and dialed Pete's number.

Pete picked up. "Hey, what's up?"

"Get over here to my desk quick," she said.

Pete appeared at her desk seconds later.

"You won't believe this," Kay said. "I finally got the pictures back that we were hoping would show who was driving the truck that ran Tom Stratton off the road."

"And?"

"Look at this picture and tell me who you think it is." Kay pointed to the third photo.

Pete blinked in surprise and looked closer. "That's Troy Pomerleau."

"I think that Tom saw a drug deal going down and they caught him."

"Any idea who the other driver is?"

"No. I want to ask Emily, but I haven't had a chance to talk to her yet. I have half of the plate in the first photo, so I'm going to see if I can find any matching registrations."

Kay opened up a screen and ran a search through one of the apps that the SBI maintained. She looked up black Ford pickup trucks with licenses starting with the numbers that they were looking for and a short list of results came up. She scanned through the list and saw the name Orleans Design Associates.

"Why didn't we see this before?" she said to herself.

"You've heard of that name?"

"Yes. We had some other evidence linking the name to Tom Stratton's cell phone. It's a company owned by a man from Orleans that Emily knows of. His name is Chris Brooks and the MDEA has their eye on him. This registration wasn't on the list that Emily had earlier for local registrations."

She opened up the file that Emily had sent with all of the black Ford truck registrations in the area. Nothing was there for Orleans Design Associates and there were no registrations listed for the city of Orleans. She knew that Emily had Orleans in her list because she had showed Kay all of the search criteria that she used. Had someone altered the list somehow?

"We need to bring Chris Brooks in," Pete said.

"It's time for us to meet with Sergeant Hixon. We can fill him in on this while we get an arrest warrant ready."

They headed to Hixon's office and Kay knocked on his door. "Come on in."

Kay and Pete walked in and sat in the two seats in front of the desk.

"I'd like to hear a report on the Pomerleau case. It seems to have lost momentum and we need to start making some progress," Hixon said.

"Sir, Kay has come across some information linking another case with the Pomerleau case. We are hoping to bring in a suspect for questioning who could possibly give us more information about Troy Pomerleau," Pete said.

"What case is that?" asked Hixon.

"The Stratton case," Kay said. "We were able to obtain some cell phone photos and we had them enhanced by the crime lab. They just came back today. The photos show a local man named Chris Brooks meeting with Troy Pomerleau. This was the meeting that led to Tom Stratton's truck being run off the road."

"That could help us build even more of a case against Troy Pomerleau, but it doesn't help us find him," Hixon said.

"True, but if we can bring Brooks in for questioning he may be able to tell us some locations to look for Troy," Pete said. "He may possibly implicate Kevin Pomerleau as well."

"All right. Let's bring Chris Brooks in," Hixon said. "Let me know when you have him."

Pete and Kay nodded in agreement.

"Let's get going," Pete said. "I have Brooks's address, we can start there."

"I'll meet you out front." Kay headed to her desk and picked up her keys. She checked her phone and saw that there was a message from Emily that had come in while she was in Hixon's office.

She listened to the message. "*Hi, Kay, sorry I missed you. I just got a text from Julian, who has been missing since yesterday. He gave me a few sketchy details and his phone isn't getting much service. He must have overheard something from Chris Brooks at brunch yesterday and followed him. Someone caught him and has taken him out to Rome. He got away and I think he's lost near the Round Top*

Trail at the Kennebec Highlands. I'm really worried that Brooks or one of his friends will be out looking for him, so I'm going to go out and try to find him. When you get this message, please call me and send someone to help me find him."

Kay dialed Emily's number and got no answer. She must be out of the service area. Cursing the cell phone service out by the lake, Kay ran toward the front of the building. Pete was standing there waiting for her. She pushed open the door and headed for her car.

"Change of plans," she said to Pete, trying to control her panic. "I had a message from Emily. She's on her way to find her friend Julian. Apparently Julian was following Brooks and someone caught him. He got away and now he's lost somewhere in Rome near the Kennebec Highlands."

"That's next to Pomerleau's place."

"Right. I don't think Emily knows that and I haven't had a chance to tell her about Troy Pomerleau and Brooks. We need to get out there and find them before someone else does."

"Do you want me to drive?"

"No, I'm driving." Kay was angry that Emily had gone looking for Julian without waiting for her. What was she thinking that she was going to do if Brooks was there? She didn't even have a weapon. Kay could only hope that Troy Pomerleau was still hiding out and wasn't anywhere around Julian or Emily.

Kay sped down the road toward Rome while Pete called for backup to meet them at the Highlands.

"We definitely have enough for a warrant on Chris Brooks," Pete said. "I'm sending people over to see if he's there and to search his place."

"He runs a hair salon and I think he owns the whole building and lives upstairs," Kay said. "Make sure they search the whole place."

"I'll let the MDEA know what's going on. They'll want to be in on this."

Kay kept a tight grip on the steering wheel. She wished she could have warned Emily about the Pomerleau connection. If they had seen Chris Brooks's truck registration when Emily looked up the registrations, they would have known what was going on last week. Had someone tampered with the registration list? It would have to have been someone at the SBI but how would anyone have known Emily had the list?

Someone had also known that Emily had gotten Tom's belongings back around the time that her house was broken into and the phone was stolen. Kay was definitely going to follow up on both of these things. Right now, though, she needed to turn her focus onto finding Emily as quickly as possible and making sure that nothing happened to her.

CHAPTER THIRTY-FIVE

Emily reached one of the parking lots at the Kennebec Highlands and jumped out to look at the map near the trailhead. It looked like Round Top Trail was accessible this way but might be closer if she went to a different parking area. She drove a few miles down the road to the lot she was looking for and parked. Like the previous lot, it was empty. She was hoping that some other people might have been around in case they needed help. Unfortunately, there weren't too many people using the trails during a weekday.

She tried calling Kay again, but the call didn't go through. She decided to make her way cautiously down the trail and hope that Julian would see her. She didn't want to risk calling out to him and alerting anyone that might be searching for him.

Emily had been here a few times over the years. There were over six thousand acres of protected conservation land that was accessible though a network of trails. She had come hiking here with friends and with Tom a couple times. Sally had loved it here. It was a large area and she hadn't come often enough to be all that familiar with the trails. She headed in what she hoped would be the right direction.

She walked along the trail, stepping over rocks and branches. There were some blue blazes intermittently painted on trees that marked the trail. The trail began to incline gradually as she made her way through the woods. She tried to walk quietly, listening for any footsteps or voices around her. There was nothing except the sound of birds calling and the wind blowing through the trees.

The trail grew steeper and she climbed around several large boulders. She eventually reached a clearing where the trail left the trees and went upwards through outcroppings of granite. The view was beautiful, overlooking the chain of Belgrade Lakes. She would have to bring Kay here to go for a hike some time.

There had been a few trail signs along the way, but she had yet to see anything that said Round Top Trail, so she wasn't sure where Julian might have been when he saw the sign he had mentioned. Her plan was to keep walking the loop, coming back through as many times as necessary until Julian spotted her or she found some trace of him.

She saw a blue blaze up ahead near a higher spot on the trail. It looked like another trail intersected with the one she was on. She got closer and saw that there was finally a sign marking Round Top Trail. She supposed that it could have been the same sign that Julian saw, but it was hard to tell. She stood still for a moment and didn't hear anything. Julian must not be here. There were probably other trail signs. She would just have to keep walking and see if she came across some of them.

She walked along the top of the trail to Round Top Mountain, which was actually a rocky hill. She saw the point in the trail up ahead where it started to descend the hill and walked in that direction. Suddenly pounding footsteps came rushing up behind her. She felt like she was in a bad dream where the attack from all those years ago was happening again. Like before, time seemed to slow down. She didn't have a chance to turn around when she felt something hard strike the back of her head, knocking her forward onto the rocky ground. The world went black.

* * *

Julian watched in horror from his hiding place a few yards away in a large crack between two slabs of granite. He had seen Emily approaching and had been about to call out to her when he saw a man come running up behind her. It was the same huge, beastly man that had grabbed him from his car the day before. Poor Emily, she had dropped like a rag doll when the man hit her with what looked like a rock.

The man stood over Emily. He looked around and started reaching down to touch her. Julian couldn't tell what the man was going to do. Was he going to hit her again or was he going to rape her? He might even try to throw her over the rocky overhang on the side of the trail next to them. Julian decided that enough was enough. He wasn't going to stand by and let this happen to his friend. She was the only one besides Mark who put up with him.

Julian picked up a small rock and threw it in the direction of the trail where Emily had come from. It clattered down the side of the hill. The man stopped what he was doing and looked back down the path. Julian threw another rock. The man took a step away from Emily toward the area where the sound came from. Julian hoped that the wind would cover any noise that he might make as he slipped out of his hiding place and leaped over to Emily. He pushed the man with all his strength. The man turned his head to Julian in surprise, but Julian had caught him off balance. He toppled over and went crashing down the overhang onto the rocky ground below.

Julian peered over the edge. The man lay motionless below, his leg turned at an odd angle. Julian gave him a smug nod. "How do you like that?"

He turned his attention to Emily. She was lying on her stomach with her hands near her head. He could see her head bleeding where the man had struck her but it didn't look like it was bleeding too badly. Her face looked like it had gotten a little scraped up but luckily she had landed on a mossy area on the rocks.

"Emily wake up. It's me, Julian," he said. "Did you bring me any cigarettes?"

Emily didn't respond and Julian wasn't sure what to do next. He had always heard that you weren't supposed to move someone who was injured, but what if she was bleeding internally? Who knew when someone might come along to help him and the next person to come could be another friend of Chris Brooks. Julian wished he could push Chris Brooks over a cliff.

He decided to give Emily another minute or two to wake up and then he was going to have to either carry her or leave her here and go for help.

* * *

Kay and Pete had stopped at two parking lots before spotting Emily's truck at the third. Emily's was the only vehicle in the lot and their backup hadn't arrived yet. Pete called Sergeant Hixon and filled him in on what was going on. The units that had been keeping the Pomerleau residence under surveillance had been told to make sure no one left the property and to stop anyone from entering. So far, Chris Brooks had not been located.

"I'm not waiting," Kay said. "I'm going to head down the trail."

"We should probably secure the area first, but I'll radio the troopers that are on their way and tell them we have reason to believe that we can't wait," Pete said.

"Have you ever been here before?"

"No, but there's Round Top Trail." Pete pointed at the sign. "It looks like you could go in a couple different directions."

"Let's head this way," Kay said, picking the closest section and hoping that was where Emily had gone. She was growing increasingly worried that something bad had happened to her. She promised herself that she wouldn't be angry with her if they could just find her safely.

They started down the trail cautiously, keeping an eye out for any movement in the trees around them. There was no sign of anyone as they hiked through the woods and up toward the rocky hill. They had gone a few miles in silence when Kay thought she heard a branch cracking up ahead in the thick underbrush on that section of the trail.

She put up a hand and made a motion for Pete to stop. He nodded and stepped behind a tree on the side of the trail. Kay slipped behind a tree on the other side. They listened for a few minutes and didn't hear anything.

Kay looked at Pete and pointed to the trail. He nodded and they stepped back out. They walked silently around the stretch of undergrowth and approached an opening to the rocky base of the hill. Pete touched her arm and pointed.

Up ahead, a small man with a slim build was walking stealthily along the side of the trail. Taking cover behind trees and granite outcroppings, he was making his way up the steep hill. Kay tried to get a good look at him, but could only get a glimpse of his dark hair. He turned his head and she got a good view of his face.

Kay tapped Pete's arm and whispered, "Martin?"

Pete looked closely at the man for a moment then nodded.

They both took out their weapons and continued up the trail, trying to stay as hidden as possible so that they wouldn't alert Mike Martin that they were behind him.

Kay's mind was racing. If Martin was here, he must be after Troy Pomerleau. Troy must be looking for Julian. They still didn't know where Brooks was, and he could be somewhere out here, too. Where was Emily? If Troy had found her and Julian they were in huge danger. They already knew that he was a vicious sociopath and wouldn't think anything of killing them. She had to find Emily.

If they tried to stop Martin, they might alert Troy and make things worse for Emily and Julian. If they didn't stop him, he might find Emily and Julian before they did.

Kay signaled to Pete. They paused for a moment and she whispered, "Do you think we should try to stop him while we have him in our sights?"

"Yes," Pete agreed. "How about if I outflank him on the right and you come up behind him? The terrain on the left is too steep for him to get away."

Kay nodded. "Give me a signal when you're ready and I'll give him the order to stop. Be ready. He probably won't surrender peacefully."

Pete took off silently up the right side of the trail, skirting around Martin until he had effectively blocked off his escape route on that side.

Kay took up a protected position behind Martin where she could track his movements. She got her gun ready and watched Pete. He gave her the thumbs-up signal.

Kay shouted to Martin, "This is the Maine State Police. Stop where you are and put your hands up."

Martin's head snapped around. He dove behind a nearby rock. Kay looked at Pete and saw him point to the spot where he could see Martin was hiding.

Pete repeated Kay's command, "This is the Maine State Police. Come out and put your hands up."

Martin fired a shot at Kay. It missed widely. She didn't have a clear shot back so she looked for another tree close by that might give her a better angle. Pete returned the shot at Martin and it ricocheted off the rock he was hiding behind. Kay took the opportunity to move to the better location.

Martin fired a shot at Pete and she heard Pete give a soft grunt of pain. She slipped from behind the tree she was at to another one with a better angle. She had a clear shot at Martin and she took it without hesitation, knowing that his next shot could hit Pete again.

She saw Martin slump over behind the rock. She wasn't sure how badly he was hurt, so she made her way carefully over to where he was hiding. She eased around the side and listened. There were no sounds coming from him, but she couldn't be sure until she actually looked. She quickly pointed her gun and looked behind the rock, where she saw that Martin was lying on his side, clearly dead. She took the gun he was holding from his hand and hurried over to Pete.

Pete was holding his side. He saw her coming and gave her a weak smile. "You got him?"

"I did," she answered. "How are you? Let me help."

She made him lie back on the ground. She took off her shirt and folded it up, pressing it against the bullet hole to stop the bleeding. Satisfied that Pete was stable for the moment, she picked up her radio and called for help. "We have an officer down on Round Top Trail near the lower part of the hill. We need to get him airlifted as soon as possible. We also have a suspect down."

The backup officers responded and help was on the way. Kay looked around, wishing she knew where Emily was and hoping that she hadn't made things worse for her.

CHAPTER THIRTY-SIX

Julian was not sure what he should do next. Emily was still unconscious. He finally decided that he would pick Emily up and carry her with him to find help. Hopefully it wouldn't hurt her to be moved because he couldn't leave her lying there alone and defenseless. The sound of gunshots suddenly broke the silence.

"This is why I don't like hiking. Nothing good comes from getting too much fresh air." He picked Emily up gently and carried her quickly to the hiding place that he had found before. The gunshots stopped after a few minutes and he started to feel like a sitting duck.

"Emily, I wish you would wake up and tell me what to do. I don't think we should just sit here. Someone could come along at any minute. I'm going to try and get back down the trail, because we need to get you to a doctor."

He carried Emily back along the side of the path, hiding behind trees and rocks and trying to stay out of sight. If the gunshots had been the police, he had to go in that direction so they could be rescued. If not, they needed to try and get away.

"You're heavier than you look, missy," he said to Emily. "I would never tell you that if you were awake, of course. It's a good thing I am in such fine shape."

They started down the steep incline. Julian spotted movement down near the base of the hill and ducked behind a stand of trees. He peered down the hill and tried to see who it was. He was overjoyed to see that it was Kay. She was crouched next to someone who was lying on the ground. There also appeared to be a second person lying on the ground beside a nearby rock. He didn't see anyone else. It looked safe.

He stepped from behind the trees and called out, "Kay, it's Julian and Emily."

* * *

Kay stood up and looked up the hill. She saw Julian standing near some trees at the top and he appeared to be carrying Emily. She must have twisted her ankle or something. She wanted to cry with relief at the sight of them. She turned to Pete and pressed his hand against the shirt she had been holding.

"Pete, I'll be right back. I need to go help Julian and Emily get down the hill."

"I'll be fine." Pete nodded. "Go."

"Keep pressure on your side if you can. I'll be right back," she repeated.

Kay started running up the hill. As she got closer, she saw that Emily was hanging limply in Julian's arms. She ran harder to reach them as Julian climbed carefully down the hill. Gasping for breath, she finally got to them.

Emily's chin was scraped up and her arms hung down loosely by her sides. Her eyes were closed and her head was tipped back. She could see blood on Julian's arm where it had dripped from the back of her head. Kay couldn't stop her tears from falling as she put her hand on Emily's cheek and touched her gently. She put her hand on Emily's chest and felt her heart beating. She wanted to take her from Julian's arms and hold her.

Reaching for Emily's hand, she looked at Julian. "What happened?"

"She came looking for me and before she got to me this big, horrible man who had been looking for me came up behind her and hit her with a rock."

"Where is he?"

"I pushed him over the side of the rocks. The last time I saw him he wasn't moving, so he's still there as far as I know. Emily hasn't woken up since. I heard the shots and came to see if it was the police or if there were more people after us."

Kay looked at Julian with new respect. Who would have thought that he could get away from anyone and then save Emily?

"We need to get back down the hill. Medical help is on the way. My partner's been shot and I can't leave him alone," Kay said. "I can help carry Emily."

"I've got her, don't worry. Let's go."

They made their way carefully down to Pete. Julian laid Emily down gently near Pete and flopped down onto the ground.

"Pete, how are you doing?" Kay asked.

Pete opened his eyes. "I'm all right. Where's our backup?"

"They should be here soon. Julian and Emily are here, too."

"That's good." Pete closed his eyes.

Kay sat between Pete and Emily, holding the shirt in place against Pete's side with one hand and holding Emily's hand with the other. Pete seemed to be holding his own but she was sick with worry that Emily was still unconscious. All she was praying for was that Emily would be all right. She hadn't even gotten a chance to tell her how much she loved her yet.

Kay felt Emily's hand return a slight pressure on hers. She looked at her and saw her eyes start to flutter open. She let go of Emily's hand and started stroking her cheek.

"Emily, it's Kay. Wake up."

Emily opened her eyes and looked at Kay. "You found me. I knew you'd come."

Kay was so thankful to see Emily open her eyes that she couldn't speak for a moment. She picked up her hand again and squeezed it gently. "Julian saved you, but we can talk about all of that later. Help is on the way and we're going to get you out of here."

"Julian's all right?" Emily asked.

Julian sat up. "I'm right here and I never want to go hiking again."

"I'm so glad you're all right, I was afraid that you were lost in the wilderness."

"I can't wait to get back to civilization. Thank you for coming to get me." Julian flopped back down.

"How did you end up all the way out here anyway?" Kay asked Julian.

"I was at brunch and I overheard Brooks on his phone when I went to the men's room. He was talking to someone about a drop off, so I followed him."

"You should have called me or Kay," Emily said. "You could have been killed."

"It seemed so adventurous at the time. Believe me, I was regretting my Charlie's Angels membership by the time they brought me to that cabin in the middle of nowhere. Luckily, they underestimated me and I ran away when they weren't paying attention."

"That shows you what can happen when you assume people are going to act a certain way," Emily said, closing her eyes. "They probably thought you wouldn't dare to try and get away."

Kay brought Emily's hand to her lips. She wanted to try to keep her awake until medical help arrived. She started to tell her about what they found on the cell phone photos when they heard the sound of people approaching.

A group of state troopers came charging up the trail toward them. Several of the troopers spread out to search the area. An EMT came over and Kay relinquished her hold on Pete's side.

"A helicopter is on its way to bring the injured parties to the hospital," the EMT told Kay. "It should be here any minute."

"I'm going with them."

She was not going to leave Emily's side, so she gave instructions to the troopers from her spot between Emily and Pete.

"We need to locate a suspect that may be somewhere near the top of the trail. He was attacking this woman and was pushed over a rocky incline by this man." Kay pointed to Emily and Julian. "I want you to spread out and search the trails until you find him."

A group of troopers headed up the trail. Kay heard the sound of the helicopter approaching. She breathed a sigh of relief.

* * *

Kay sat in the atrium of the trauma care unit at the hospital in Augusta, waiting for word on Pete and Emily. There hadn't been enough room in the helicopter for Julian so she had promised him that she would call as soon as she heard from the doctors about Emily's condition. She also needed to call Ethan and Ben. Maybe she would ask Ethan to call Ben. It had been a very long day. Sergeant Hixon walked into the room and Kay stood up.

"Hello, sir," she said.

"Any word on Pete?" he asked.

"Not yet."

She sat back down while Hixon stood looking out the window. He turned and faced her with a nod. "Good work in the field today. Has anyone filled you in yet?"

"No, sir."

"The man that you shot was identified as Mike Martin. I understand that he was the one who shot Detective Harris and he was also attempting to shoot you."

"Yes, sir."

"You'll need to get some counseling for that, but obviously you did the right thing. Policy requires that you will have to take a few days of paid leave until you're cleared to come back."

"I'll check in with human resources first thing in the morning."

"I'm very pleased to say that Troy Pomerleau was apprehended. He was the man that attacked Emily Stratton and he was unconscious when we found him," Hixon said.

Kay had surmised that it was probably Troy who had been following Julian and Emily. "What's his condition?"

"He has a broken leg and a concussion. He's been taken into custody and everyone is very happy that he's off the streets."

"Were you able to locate Chris Brooks?"

"The gentleman that had been abducted by Brooks and Pomerleau directed officers to the cabin where he had been taken. It was near the Pomerleau place and apparently hadn't been under observation by the surveillance team because it was an unoccupied seasonal camp that was owned by some people from out of state. It turns out that the owners were relatives of Chris Brooks."

"Was he at the cabin?"

"Yes, he was there. He was also taken into custody and hasn't stopped talking since we brought him in. We've collected enough evidence and information that we were able to take Kevin Pomerleau into custody and shut down the whole operation. You and Harris have done an excellent job."

Kay looked out the window, thinking about how all the pieces had come together so quickly. There was one thing that was still bothering her.

"I think there's someone at the SBI office who might have been working with the Pomerleaus," she said.

Hixon looked at her. "What makes you think that?"

"A couple of strange coincidences. First, Tom Stratton's cell phone was stolen from Emily's house months after the accident but right after she got it back from the crash reconstruction unit. Second, a report that Emily ran for truck registrations was missing some crucial records that would have pointed us to Chris Brooks."

"I'll be sure to see that Chris Brooks is questioned about it. He hasn't held back any information from us, so perhaps he'll have some answers."

"Thank you, sir."

A doctor came into the waiting room and walked over to them. "Are you here waiting for news on Detective Harris and Emily Stratton?"

"Yes," Kay answered.

"My name is Dr. Rowe. I wanted to let you know that both patients are doing well. My colleague, Dr. Erikson, was able to remove the bullet from Detective Harris's abdomen with no complications. It did not hit any organs and he should have a complete recovery. We will want to keep him for a few days, but he should be feeling much better in a day or two."

Kay smiled at Sergeant Hixon with relief.

"Thank you doctor," Hixon said.

"I attended to Emily Stratton. There was no fracture to her skull and we didn't find any swelling of her brain, which was our main concern. We did a CT scan and everything looks good. She was unconscious for quite a while and she has a fairly serious concussion. We want to keep an eye on her overnight. She is going to have a pretty bad headache for a little while and we'll need to watch for any symptoms that might arise from the concussion, but she should be able to go home tomorrow. She's going to need plenty of rest."

"Thank you," Kay said. "Can we see them?"

"Yes. Detective Harris is still in the post-op recovery room, but he'll be brought up to his room in a little while. Ms. Stratton is a few doors down the hall. We brought her to her room a few minutes ago."

Kay and Sergeant Hixon thanked Dr. Rowe again and he left to return to his other patients. Kay turned to face Hixon. "I'm going to go check on Emily."

"I think I may wait here until Pete gets to his room. I want to make sure he's all right before I go," Hixon said. "I spoke with his parents and they're on their way here. I would like to meet them as well."

"Sir, I did want to mention something to you. I thought I should let you know that I'm in a relationship with Emily Stratton."

Hixon blinked. "I see. Your personal life is your own. As long as it doesn't interfere with your work, I really don't see that it's any of my business."

"Right. I just wanted to make sure that you were aware."

Kay hurried out of the room and down the hall to see Emily.

CHAPTER THIRTY-SEVEN

Kay walked into Emily's room and saw that the lights had been turned down low and a curtain had been pulled around the bed. She pulled back the side of the curtain and looked in to see Emily lying there.

"Come on in," Emily said.

"How are you feeling?" Kay asked.

"Kind of dizzy and a little sick. They gave me some medication, so my headache should get better. Be warned, the doctor said that a concussion may cause irritability."

Kay sat in the chair next to the bed. "I'm just so glad you're all right. You can be as grouchy as you want. I'll be right here if you need me tonight, and I'm not going anywhere."

"I want to hear all about everything, but I'm so tired that I don't know if I can stay awake."

"The doctor said that you need to rest. We can talk about everything tomorrow. I need to call your sons and let them know you're here. Can I get Ethan's number from you?"

"It's on my phone. I think my things are in that bag over there." Emily waved a hand toward the corner as she closed her eyes and fell asleep.

Kay stood up to get the bag and leaned over Emily, brushing a kiss across her lips. "I really want to get the chance to tell you I love you one of these days."

* * *

Emily opened her eyes the next morning to see Kay sleeping in the chair next to her bed with her head draped uncomfortably on her shoulder. She was still wearing the light tank top that she'd arrived in. The shirt she had been wearing over it had been discarded after Pete no longer needed it for a bandage. Her hair was tousled and her clothes were streaked with dirt from the trail. Emily's heart filled with love at the sight of her.

A nurse came into the room to check on Emily's vital signs.

"Is it all right if I go to the bathroom and brush my teeth?" Emily asked the nurse.

"Yes, just take your time getting out of bed. You may still be feeling lightheaded and a little unsteady."

Emily cautiously climbed out of bed and made her way to the bathroom. Her head was aching and she cringed at the sight of herself in the mirror. When she came back out to her room, she sat down on the hospital bed with a tired sigh. After making sure that Emily was safely seated on the bed, the nurse finished her notes and left.

Emily saw that Kay was starting to wake up and watched her stretch her neck and look around in a sleepy daze.

"Good morning," Emily said with a smile. "I look a little scary today."

"Morning," Kay mumbled. She rubbed her eyes and looked at Emily. "You're still beautiful, but you are a little banged up. You probably should be lying down."

Emily nodded and laid back down. "How is Pete?"

"I saw him last night and he's doing well. He's right down the hall."

"How did he get shot?"

"It's a long story. I'm going to go brush my teeth and then I'll be back to tell you all about it." Kay went to the bathroom to freshen up and returned a few minutes later.

Emily patted the spot next to her on the bed and Kay climbed on and slid up next to her.

Kay took Emily's hand in hers. "I didn't get a chance to tell you what we saw in Tom's cell phone pictures. They showed that the passenger in the truck was Troy Pomerleau and the driver was Chris Brooks. We were able to see a partial license plate in one of the pictures and identify the truck, which belongs to Chris Brooks. It looks like Tom saw them making some sort of drug deal and they must have caught him."

"It was Chris Brooks? That's who killed Tom? I can't believe that he acted so friendly whenever I saw him."

"He's been arrested and has confessed to everything."

"So Chris Brooks is mixed up with Troy Pomerleau. Why didn't his truck show up on our list?"

"That's a good question. I talked it over with Sergeant Hixon and he's planning to have Brooks questioned about how that could have happened. Hopefully we can find out some answers." Kay went on to bring Emily up-to-date with the events of the previous day. "Troy Pomerleau was the one who attacked you on the trail. He was looking for Julian. Troy had been hiding out at a camp owned by Brooks's family, which was where they brought Julian. I'm sure they were planning to kill him. Meanwhile, Mike Martin was looking for Troy Pomerleau. Martin had been planning to get revenge for Troy shooting Jackson and MacNamara up at Moosehead. We came across Martin while we were looking for you and Martin shot at us. He hit Pete and I shot Martin. He died at the scene."

"Are you all right?" Emily squeezed Kay's hand.

"I'm fine. I think it's all over now. Sergeant Hixon said that Brooks told them everything when they brought him in. Kevin and Troy Pomerleau have both been arrested, along with Brooks."

"I can't believe it's finally over. It's such a relief to know who killed Tom and Sally. I have to tell Ben and Ethan."

"I called Ethan last night and told him you were here. I think he's going to be coming up some time today. He said that he would let Ben know what was going on."

"Thank you for calling him."

"I also called Julian and told him how you were doing. I'm sure he'll call you today."

"I just want to go home," Emily said. "I want a nice, long shower."

"You have stitches on your scalp that can't get wet, so you'll have to be careful. I was thinking, I have a couple days off and I could stay at your place and help you if you need anything."

Emily smiled and closed her eyes. She had to admit that it would be nice to have Kay stay over and take care of her for a couple days.

* * *

Kay didn't see Emily smile and was worried when she didn't answer. "I'm sure that you'll want a little privacy. I can just check on you if you like. I don't have to stay over. I just don't think that you should be home alone all day in case you get more symptoms from your concussion."

Emily squeezed her hand again. "Of course I want you to stay. I was just thinking about how nice it would be to have you there with me when I get home."

Kay's phone rang. She glanced at it and saw that the call was from Sergeant Hixon.

"Hello, sir," Kay answered.

"Good morning. I wanted to give you an update. I passed along your concerns about a possible Pomerleau contact at the SBI. The team that has been questioning Brooks asked him about it and you were right."

Kay looked at Emily wondering which of her coworkers it could have been. "Who is it?"

"His name is Alex Andrews," Hixon said.

"Alex is Emily's boss."

"Yes. According to Brooks, Alex was a client at his salon. Alex discovered that Brooks could get prescription drugs for him. He's been a regular customer for a few years now. Brooks said that he and Pomerleau caught Tom Stratton taking pictures of one of their drug deals with his cell phone. After Brooks forced Tom's truck off the road, he was in a panic that he would get caught. He threatened Alex that he would cut him off if he didn't get him information on the investigation."

Kay was taken aback to hear that Alex had been on drugs. She hadn't known him very well, but she hadn't noticed anything out of the ordinary.

Hixon continued, "Alex was the one who let Brooks know when Tom Stratton's personal effects had been released. Brooks had Troy Pomerleau break into Emily's house and get his cell phone."

"I'm surprised that Brooks is telling us all of this," Kay said.

"He's hoping to make a deal. He also told us that after Trooper Williams was killed and the Pomerleau case escalated, the Pomerleaus put pressure on Brooks to force Alex to keep them informed. Alex found out about a report that Emily was using to look for vehicle registrations and he modified it to remove records that would implicate Brooks."

"I knew it," Kay said. "Have you brought Alex in for questioning?"

"That's the interesting thing," Hixon said. "Alex Andrews is nowhere to be found. We have an APB out on him but it looks like he's left town."

Kay thanked Sergeant Hixon for letting her know and hung up. She turned to Emily. "You aren't going to believe this."

"I could hear everything you and Hixon were saying," Emily said. "This is crazy. Alex was helping the Pomerleaus and he hid Tom's killer from us."

Emily pounded her fist into the bed. "I'd like to be the one to find him."

"Well, the good thing is that you don't have to have him on first base anymore. He was a terrible softball player."

CHAPTER THIRTY-EIGHT

The next evening, Kay and Emily said good-bye to Ethan and Stacy as they headed back to Boston. Emily gave Ethan a hug. "Call me when you get there so I know you've made it home safely."

"Bye, Mom. I'm glad you're feeling better," Ethan said. "Bye, Kay, and thanks for everything."

Ethan pulled his car out of the driveway and headed down the road.

Ben had stopped by the previous evening for a short visit after Emily was released from the hospital. Kay had offered to leave before he got there and Emily was glad that she'd convinced her to stay for a while. Ben had been friendly and appreciative toward Kay when he saw her, which Emily had been thrilled to see. Kay had gone home to her own apartment later that night since Ethan and Stacy were there to keep an eye on Emily.

Kay and Emily stepped out back onto the deck. This was the first chance that they had gotten to be alone since Kay had brought her home from the hospital.

"I think everyone is feeling a sense of relief now that we know what actually happened to Tom and the people responsible are being punished," Emily said. "I know the word closure is overused, but that describes how I'm feeling. I hope the boys can focus on all the good memories of their father now."

Emily leaned her head on Kay's shoulder.

"I'm going to cook dinner for you, babe," Kay said. "I brought over a bunch of vegetables that I'm going to cook on the grill and I picked up some fresh bread and cheese from the market downtown."

"That sounds delicious. What can I do to help?"

"Next time you can help, but I want you to relax tonight. You're supposed to be resting." Kay pulled her close for a kiss. "I want to take care of you and make you feel better."

"I'm feeling really good actually," Emily sat down and stretched out on a lounge chair. "My headache has gone away and it's nice to be sitting out here with no worries."

"Are you allowed to drink a beer? I brought some over."

"The doctor didn't say that I couldn't and I certainly came home with a long list of instructions."

Kay went into the house and brought back two cold bottles. Handing one to Emily, she sat down and stretched out beside her in the chair and took a sip. They lay next to each contentedly for a few minutes.

Kay turned to face Emily. "I've been wanting to tell you something for a while now."

"What is it, honey?"

Kay looked into Emily's eyes. "I've been wanting to tell you how much I love you."

Emily reached for Kay's hand. "I was waiting to say this until I was sure, but I've known in my heart for a while now that I love you, too. "

"I'm not always good at expressing myself," Kay said. "I've never given my heart to anyone before. I promise I won't run out on you if things get hard and I'll be here for you if you need me."

Emily was overwhelmed with happiness and she wanted to convey her true feelings to Kay. "You have already been here for me when I needed you, and I love you for that. I want you to know that I'm all in. I won't let anything hold me back and I'll always be here for you, too. I love how you never passed judgment on me. You must have had your doubts about caring for a woman who had been married for twenty-five years to a man. Somehow you understood that you were the one who I've been waiting for all my life."

Kay slid over and rested herself on top of Emily, pressing down on her lips with a deep kiss. "I've been waiting for you all my life, too. I think we have a lot of adventures ahead of us."

Bella Books, Inc.

Women. Books. Even Better Together.

P.O. Box 10543
Tallahassee, FL 32302

Phone: 800-729-4992
www.bellabooks.com